GW01326348

Blood Moon: Dark Vampire Romance

Silver Moon, Volume 1

Rose Knight

Published by Rose Knight, 2024.

BLOOD MOON: DARK VAMPIRE ROMANCE

First edition. October 7, 2024.

Copyright © 2024 Rose Knight.

ISBN: 979-8227186393

Written by Rose Knight.

Table of Contents

April

When my sister vanished, I knew I had to find her. But my search led me straight into the lair of the Leblanc vampire coven. Now I'm trapped in their opulent mansion, surrounded by a dangerously alluring family of immortals.

None intrigue me more than Cedric - the brooding, enigmatic heir to the Leblanc dynasty. His magnetism is as intoxicating as it is terrifying. I know I should fear him, yet I can't resist the pull between us. As I uncover the Leblanc's dark histories, I find myself at Cedric's mercy, spellbound by his manipulation.

I must navigate this treacherous game, where the line between predator and prey blurs. If I can't unravel the truth behind Cedric's tormented soul and my sister's disappearance, the shadows may claim us both.

Cedric

April is an intoxicating temptation I can't resist. Her racing pulse, the scent of her fear - it awakens a primal hunger within me. As the Leblanc heir, I should eliminate her. Yet there's something about her defiant spirit that draws me in.

I'll keep her close, manipulate her fascination, until she's at my mercy. Once she's mine, body and soul, I'll savor every last drop. I won't let April break down my barriers. I'll use every tool to bend her to my will. In the end, she'll be just another pawn in my family's game of power.

PROLOGUE

The moon was shining in the midst of that darkness. I watched it with the window open, even though the cold air was creeping into my room.

It was a full moon, but it was tinted with a reddish color, as rarely happened. I took my phone out of my jeans pocket and tried to take a photo that did justice to what I was seeing. However, as often happens, photos fail to capture what we are seeing, let alone what it feels like in the face of what we want to capture.

I sent the photo to my sister, hoping that she would come up to my room to look. I strained my ears, hoping to hear the beep of her phone, but it didn't ring. I closed the window and left my room. The bathroom was unoccupied, so I descended the narrow wooden stairs to reach the dining room.

The walls were filled with family photos from when my parents were alive, and we were a happy, complete family. However, a hundred crucifixes also hung from the walls, wrapped in sprigs of verbena.

"Is Aixa here?" I asked as I reached the living room and confirmed that it was empty. "Are you here?"

The only response I got was silence. A silence that became increasingly unsettling. I entered the kitchen and scanned it with my eyes until my gaze stopped at something.

There was a piece of paper torn and written messily with a black pen on the fridge. I approached and took it down. It was undoubtedly written by her, and it said: "April, for a few days, vampires have been chasing me. I've scared them away twice, but I don't know how much longer I'll succeed. I'll find a place to hide, and I'll let you know where I am. It's clear they're looking for me and know where I live. Please be careful, and never forget to carry Dad's verbena with you. I love you."

I swallowed hard as I thought quickly about what to do. I didn't know where she could have gone. Would she still be nearby? Maybe she had just left.

I rushed to the front door with my heart pounding in my chest. I grabbed the doorknob, but before leaving, I grabbed a handful of verbena sprigs and tucked them into my sock.

I opened the door wide and ran into the street, looking in all directions. It was a too quiet street, no cars, and very little light. I started moving towards the main street, where she had probably headed to avoid the vampires. I ran with all my strength, with my heart pounding in my ears, but when I was about to reach the main street, and I began to glimpse the lights of the avenue and the cars passing by at full speed, something suddenly blocked my way, appearing out of nowhere. I didn't have enough time to stop, and I collided forcefully with that something, or rather, someone.

I fell sitting on the ground, somewhat confused. The person, however, hadn't even stumbled. In the darkness, eyes between blue and violet looked at me coldly.

They extended a hand to help me up, but I ignored it and stood up on my own.

"Are you April Fontaine, right?" they asked with a confident and velvety voice.

"Do I know you?" I asked, while I looked at the palm of my hand, injured from the fall. I couldn't see well in that darkness, but I was sure that the person had lifted their face a bit and was openly sniffing the air.

Then I understood what they were... But it was too late.

"Yes, you're definitely her," they said as they lifted me with their arms in a second. They jumped onto a roof with incredible ease and ran, taking me with them..

CHAPTER 1

I kept my eyes tightly closed as everything moved around me at a speed I had never experienced before.

The vampire carried me slung over his shoulder like a sack of potatoes. One arm was wrapped around my legs to keep me from falling, and I could feel him squeezing them tightly, though not enough to harm me. The air around me, already cold, felt icy on my skin, seemingly hitting me like an invisible whip.

I could feel every time we jumped from one roof to another, my hair moving, and my hands tightly gripping some part of his jacket due to the terror of falling from up there. I also felt each time he landed after a jump, the elegance with which he did it and his lightness.

My father had been a vampire hunter, and my sister, following in his footsteps, had also become one. They had always told me horrible situations involving them, described their expressions when they thirsted for blood, and warned me about how difficult it was to be near one without wanting to submit to their will. But they had also told me the kind of monsters they were and the ways they made the victim go to them.

Vampires were beautiful but monstrous creatures. Elegant but wild. Similar to humans, but never the same.

When the vampire stopped for more than a minute, I dared to open my eyes. I still hung from his shoulder like a ragdoll, but he no longer held me. Instead, I continued clutching his jacket, unaware.

"Planning to get down? You're wrinkling my coat," I heard him say, with some skepticism.

"Where am I? Why did you kidnap me?" I said, moving away and clumsily standing up.

"Get in," he ordered.

I turned in the same direction he was looking. We stood before the door of a mansion I had never seen before. A rectangular structure that must have been at least a hundred meters wide. The walls were bone-colored granite, rising many meters to end in pointed roofs, like an ancient church.

There were huge windows covered by heavy dark red curtains, so the interior of the place couldn't be seen. The entrance consisted of marble stairs leading to a heavy dark wood door.

"No..." I swallowed hard and clenched my fists at the sides of my legs. "I refuse to go in!"

"I didn't ask," he said, furrowing his brow a bit, but I held his gaze, trying to seem less terrified than I was. "Humans are so annoying," he sighed and slung me over his shoulder again without warning.

"Put me down! Put me down right now!" I exclaimed, and as a response, I heard the noise of the main gates opening and his footsteps on the gravel path leading to the mansion.

A few seconds later, we were inside. The vampire let me go without warning, and I fell onto a cold floor, also made of darker marble. I didn't dare to ask anything else and slowly stood up. It was such a large place that I couldn't even imagine what lay behind each of the doors.

In the middle, there was a wide staircase that branched off in two directions, which in turn connected with corridors. Above my head hung a huge chandelier with crystals reflecting light, forming spots on the walls.

"Who is she?" I heard a voice behind me.

I turned and saw a child a few centimeters from me, watching me with a gloomy face and a black cat in his arms.

I almost had a heart attack; I hadn't even seen where he came from. I stepped back and bumped into someone else.

"She's bleeding..." I turned again. "Who is she?"

Behind me was a terribly perfect girl. Her skin was pale and seemed extremely smooth. She had black, straight hair, cut just below the chin, and a straight fringe covering her forehead.

I felt my heart about to explode. It wasn't just the vampire who had brought me there; there were many more of them in that place, and I was there alone, with my heart pounding so loudly that everyone could probably hear it, and with scratched hands.

"Gary, I told you to leave my cat alone," I heard the vampire who had dragged me to that place say.

"Let me borrow him for a bit," the child, despite being around nine years old, was terrifying. "It's funny to see him scared."

The cat, with its shiny fur and a golden bell hanging from its neck, seemed to be desperately looking for a way to get away from Gary, but the child had it firmly in his grasp and seemed to enjoy that little suffering.

"Let him go," the vampire told him.

"Sorry, Cedric," the child sighed and let go of the cat without further ado.

"As for your question," Cedric continued, "this girl is April Fontaine."

"So, it's you!" The girl stood in front of me, quick as lightning, and pushed me, throwing me against the stairs.

I fell backward, with the steps digging into my skin, and clenched my teeth, trying not to let anyone know how much it had hurt me.

"Stay, Destiny," Cedric's voice suddenly became icy. The vampire walked slowly toward me, but before reaching me, someone positioned themselves on the top step where my head was and bent down to look at me with a lecherous smile.

"How lucky... I was starting to get hungry," said the vampire who observed me from above.

I stood up as fast as I could. There were four vampires around me, and one of them had already tried to kill me.

"Listen to how her heart beats," the vampire continued, who bore a striking resemblance to the girl who had just pushed me. "She's scared," she laughed, "like a rat in a trap."

"Enough," Cedric's voice echoed through the mansion's walls as he stopped beside me and scrutinized everyone with a warning look. "She's the sister of the girl we're looking for. It's not her, and none of us will touch her until we decide what to do."–

CHAPTER 2

"Godric, take the human to the basement and come back. I'll go call my father," Cedric ordered the last vampire who had appeared.

As a response, Godric released a growl, something that sounded quite like a complaint. Without even looking at me, he firmly took my arm and began walking to the right. One of the doors on that floor covered the entrance to stairs leading down to a completely dark basement.

"Wait here," he told me with a tone so firm that even the most experienced vampire hunter would have obeyed. He let go of me, pulled a thin chain hanging from the ceiling, and a dim light flickered every five seconds. I turned to look at the vampire, hoping he would indicate for me to go down the stairs, but the door closed with force. He had already left.

I descended the steps slowly, brushing away cobwebs that had formed down there with the tips of my fingers. The place had a terrible smell of dampness, and it was very cold. The walls, which must have been white at some point, were now stained with a yellowish and old color, with peeling paint. There were some elegant pieces of furniture, covered in a layer of dust, and paintings with gold frames, intricately carved.

I approached one of them and observed. It seemed to be an oil painting, a portrait of a beautiful and wonderfully elegant woman. She wore a black dress with lace at the neckline and puffed sleeves. Her dark brown hair and her eyes... They looked terribly similar to the vampire who had kidnapped me. To tell the truth, everything about her resembled him.

Cedric had dark brown hair, carefully combed to one side. His eyes, a mix of blue and violet, like those of that woman, emitted a cold and stern gaze. He had pale skin, like all vampires, but the fine nose and thick eyebrows were just like hers.

I continued looking around for something that could serve as a defense. Obviously, there were no crucifixes, knives, or holy water. I opened the drawers of the abandoned furniture, but inside, there were only old papers.

Then I crouched down and took a sprig of verbena hidden in my sock. It wouldn't serve to defend myself against them or to prevent them from biting me. But if they tried to control my mind, at least I could prevent them from succeeding. I put it in my mouth and swallowed it with some effort. Despite the delicious scent, the taste was extremely bitter, like eating a strand of grass.

I looked around again. There was something else, covered by a thin white sheet, full of dust and dirt. I looked back, hoping no vampire was watching me while I rummaged through their things, but tiny eyes were fixed on me. The black cat that had been in the child's hands was watching me from the last step. Despite having a bell hanging from its neck, it had been so stealthy that I hadn't heard it.

"What are you doing here?" I asked as if it could answer me.

As a response, the cat meowed once and started climbing the stairs again. If it had come down there after me, maybe it meant the door wasn't locked. I followed it, trying to make as little noise as possible in case the vampires were nearby. Indeed, the door was slightly open. The cat calmly went into the living room, and I, imitating it, first peeked my head to make sure no one was there, and once I saw there was no one, I slipped out of the basement.

An unsettling silence prevailed, not even the slightest murmur could be heard. Only my steps, which despite going on tiptoes seemed to want to attract everyone's attention. The cat headed to the front door. Could it be possible? Was it telling me to escape?

There was a distance of ten meters from my position to the exit. I started moving very slowly in its direction, while the cat waited for me at the door. Still, nothing could be heard. I held my breath to be even quieter. I didn't know how far they could hear me, but I hoped it wouldn't give away how loudly my heart was beating. Eight meters, six meters... The door getting closer every time, my heart beating faster and faster... Four meters... Two meters. I reached the door and quickly grabbed the doorknob. I pulled it, but it didn't open. I struggled for a few seconds in a desperate attempt to get it to open. The cat watched me expectantly.

"Forget it, it's sealed," I heard a voice behind me, and my entire skin bristled. Cedric was looking at me with a sly smile, as if something had failed inside my head. "Let me out!" I exclaimed, frowning.

"Why would we do that?" he asked, raising his eyebrows.

"Are you going to kill me?"

"Not yet," he said, squinting his eyes, as if giving me even a minimal explanation was already annoying.

"So, I serve some purpose to you..." I concluded, crossing my arms over my chest.

"Instead of speculating further, come with me," he told me, turning his back and starting to walk.

"I'm not going anywhere," I declared. "Let me out!"

Before I even realized it, I had backed up until my back was against the wall, and his two arms were on either side of my body.

"Let's clarify something," he said, locking his eyes with mine. "That I don't kill you doesn't mean you're immune. You won't obey because I hypnotize you; you'll do it because I, being a vampire, and you, being a human, that's all."

"You are monsters," I said, almost spitting out the words and looking at him with hatred.

"And you are food," he stepped away from me and began walking again towards the stairs.

I bit my lip hard, and with all the anger I could feel in my body, I followed him. The answers I was looking for were where he was taking me, whether I liked it or not.

CHAPTER 3

We climbed the main staircase, hearing only the sound of our steps on the marble. As soon as we reached the top of the stairs, we turned left, and as I imagined, there was a corridor illuminated only by dim lights and a hundred doors.

"How many vampires live here?" I asked Cedric, swallowing my pride.

"For now, we are only five, but we usually have guests," he replied, continuing to lead me down the narrow hallway.

Finally, we stopped in front of an elegant dark wooden door. Cedric opened it and entered, leaving me behind.

"How uncourteous," I heard a deep voice say with a hint of coldness. "That's not how I taught you to behave."

"She's just a human," Cedric sighed, dropping onto a red velvet sofa.

I looked around. This room looked like an office. It was spacious, with a shiny wooden floor. There was a library that covered the entire left wall, filled with books that seemed extremely old. In the center of the room was a wooden desk, also shiny, and behind it sat a young man who looked about twenty years old.

He had brown hair, styled back with gel, a sharp face, a slightly aquiline nose, and a pair of blue eyes, so deep that, looking into them, it seemed like you were diving into them. The vampire wore an elegant black suit and observed me with a malicious smile from his seat.

Next to Cedric, on the other hand, were the other vampires I had already seen. They were also watching me, but without even pretending to smile.

"Excuse my son. He still has much to learn about manners," the vampire said, getting up and circling his desk to approach me. "My name is Cornelius Leblanc, and I am the head of the family."

"Is... Is he your father?" I asked, unable to believe it. I knew that vampires, born with that condition, stopped growing at the age of twenty, but it was very strange to see a father and a son who seemed to be the same age.

"Don't let appearances fool you," he preempted me. "I am exactly two hundred years old."

"May I ask now?" I said, trying to appear as polite as possible, not to change the fact that they were starting to talk to me.

"No," Cornelius denied. "Better sit and listen."

I clenched my teeth, a little irritated, and settled on the edge of the couch, as far away as possible from the other vampires.

"We are looking for your sister," Cornelius began. "So, since it seems she likes to play hide and seek, we decided to keep you as a hostage until she shows up. And this goes for all of you," he said, looking at each of the vampires surrounding me. "No one is going to touch her; you all have your own donors. We don't want more problems with the Council, so you will do things very well. Understood?"

"Of course," Cedric replied.

"I haven't heard the others," Cornelius repeated. "Understood?"

"Understood," the others said in unison, with an irritated tone.

"Miss Fontaine will be treated as a guest; the only thing she won't be able to do is leave this place," he said, looking at me as a warning. "And I hope you don't make us regret our hospitality because, in that case, I won't have any problem draining you to the last drop of blood. Do you understand?"

"Yes," I nodded, holding his gaze, despite how challenging that could be.

"Destiny, please, accompany April to her new room," Cornelius instructed.

Destiny narrowed her eyes but didn't object. She stood up and gestured with her head for me to follow her. We walked in silence until we reached the right hallway, and once there, she opened any door, and we entered.

"You can stay here," she said without looking at me, shrugging. "Don't even try to escape; we are faster, stronger, and we hate you. There's no way you'll come out on top."

"Why are you looking for my sister?" I said, crossing my arms.

"That's none of your business."

"Of course, it is," I retorted. "She's my sister, and you have me here as a hostage. I should know why."

"I'm sorry," she said with a cold smile. "Unfortunately, I can't decide what to do or what to tell. So, don't ask me these things."

"Fine," I said, sitting on the double bed in the middle of the room. "How long will I be here?"

"That depends on your sister," Destiny walked towards the door, her black dress waving with each step. "Try not to get too comfortable," she warned, turning towards me, and then left..

CHAPTER 4

My room wasn't a very welcoming place, and I didn't feel like a guest at all. I lay on a bed that wasn't mine, feeling cold, and there was no trace of warmth anywhere in that place.

Next to the bed, there was a small bedside table with a bedside lamp emitting a faint orange light. And then, all there was, was a heavy blood-red curtain covering an immense window.

My stomach growled; I had no sheets, no spare clothes other than the tight jeans and dark blue sweater I was wearing, and no way to get any of those.

I heard a couple of knocks on the door, and someone peeked into my room. Cedric cleared his throat and entered.

"Do you need anything?" he asked me, and my mouth was about to open wide in surprise.

"What are you doing here?" I said, frowning.

"Asking if you need anything," he said, forcing a strained smile.

"Am I not just food anymore?" I said, crossing my arms.

"You still are," he replied, raising his eyebrows, "but it seems my father has other plans for you, and he intends for me to be someone educated, even with humans."

"Well... I don't need anything," I said, looking at him harshly, but my stomach betrayed me, growling and reminding me that I hadn't eaten anything since lunch.

"I guess you're hungry," he said, reopening the door behind him, "come with me."

Cedric led me through that mansion that seemed like a labyrinth until we reached the most incredible kitchen I had ever seen in my life.

It was a spacious area, filled with cabinets, spacious countertops, and ebony furniture. There was also a silver refrigerator that looked new. In the center was a quite large island and some stools matching the furniture.

"Why do you have all this?" I asked, unable to stop looking at everything around me.

"We eat too," he replied, sitting on one of the stools.

There, sitting in the middle of a kitchen, dressed in a fine black shirt and a pair of jeans, he didn't look like a vampire at all, just someone extremely beautiful but human.

"Can I see?" I said, pointing to the refrigerator, somewhat uncomfortable.

"I would say no," he sighed, "but I suppose my father wouldn't agree. Go ahead."

My stomach growled again, and I opened the refrigerator, jumping back in fright.

The refrigerator was full of blood bags, like those used in hospitals for donations. I turned to him, and I noticed he was watching me with an amused smile.

"If you move the blood aside a bit, there's also food."

"It doesn't matter," I said, closing the refrigerator without even looking again.

"In the pantry, there's something," he said, pointing to one of the cabinets.

I looked at him with a displeased face, prepared to find more blood bags, but when I opened it, I saw he wasn't lying. There were some packages of noodles and instant sauces. I took them and searched through the cabinets until I found some pots because apparently, Cedric wasn't willing to help me at all.

"So... You not only drink blood?" I asked while stirring the noodles to prevent them from sticking.

"We like to eat human food. It's delicious, but it doesn't fill us. It's like entertainment," he explained, "now... Ask what you really want to know."

"Yes, well... What do you want with my sister?"

"Kill her, that's obvious," he said as he got off the stool and walked to one of the countertops, where there were many bottles of alcohol.

He poured himself a glass of whiskey and looked back at me while taking a sip.

"Your sister killed one of ours," he continued, "and now she has to pay."

"How do you know it was her?"

"We know, and that's it."

"Is it for revenge? Is that all?" I inquired, unable to believe it.

"You know... For your own good, it's better if you never bring up this topic with Destiny. She's angrier than anyone."

"You... Are you all a family?"

"Enough questions," he interrupted me, finishing his drink, "eat and do whatever you want. I advise you to sleep in the morning because during the night, you won't be able to do it."

"Wait! I would need... I don't know... Clothes... A bath."

"You're quite pretentious," he said, raising an eyebrow and rinsing the glass he had just used in the sink, "there's no clothing."

"That's not true," Cornelius's deep voice interrupted, entering the kitchen, "you have clothes to give her."

"I don't think it's a good idea," Cedric replied, while I looked at both of them as if it were a tennis match.

"It doesn't matter... I really don't need it," I started saying, scratching my forehead.

"I think you do," Cornelius cut me off sharply, "Cedric, give her those clothes."

"I'm sorry, but no. Let her ask Destiny or use something from the donors," he replied, leaving the kitchen.

"Look for her; she surely has something she no longer uses," Cornelius told me, "but hurry... I might go hunting." –

CHAPTER 5

Destiny was nowhere to be found, so I assumed I had arrived too late and that she had already left. However, I found someone who apparently didn't feel like killing humans that night.

"Hello, April," Godric greeted me from the living room sofa.

"You stayed?" I asked, pursing my lips slightly.

"I don't feel like going out tonight, and besides, the donors will come in an hour anyway."

"Who are the donors?" I asked, looking towards the entrance as if they were going to appear suddenly.

"Doesn't the name tell you anything?" he asked very seriously. "They are humans who come to us to be bitten... and entertain us."

"What does that mean? Why would they do that?" I asked, widening my eyes.

"They are our fans, humans who have discovered our existence and, unlike your little sister, have decided not to hunt us."

"So... Do they volunteer?" I asked, somewhat confused.

"That's right... They hope we decide to turn them, but that won't happen. All of us here are pureblood, and we're not interested in creating hybrids with humans."

"I don't think it's right..."

"No one asked for your opinion, April. It's better if you leave, unless you want to witness it."

"Why did the others go 'hunting' then?"

"Because we like to kill. Because we like humans running for their lives, with terrified faces, and..."

"I got it," I interrupted, raising my hands for him to stop. "You don't need to continue the description."

"Maybe... I prefer it too," he smiled, showing me his fangs openly.

Before I knew it, Godric had me by the neck and was looking at me with eyes suddenly tinged with red. He squeezed my throat so hard that I couldn't breathe, and I knew I was looking at him with terrified eyes, just as he had said he liked, but I couldn't help it.

"Tell me, April," he said, looking directly into my eyes, "where is your sister?"

I knew what he was doing; he was trying to hypnotize me. However, I had ingested vervain, and his attempts had no effect on me. That was my only secret weapon against him; if I wasted it, I would have no more ways to defend myself. So, while feeling the remaining air running out, I did my best acting.

"She's... She's in..." and then I closed my eyelids and let my body completely relax.

Godric let go of me, cursing. Even with my eyes closed, pretending to faint, I felt myself collapse to the floor, and my head hitting it, but I kept up my act as best as I could.

"It had to be a human," he sighed, as I heard his footsteps move away.

A few minutes later, I heard the doors opening and someone entering the mansion. I wanted to see what was happening, but I needed to appear unconscious for at least a few more minutes so that Godric wouldn't notice.

"What happened here?" I heard Cedric's voice echoing in the living room.

"Godric, why is the human on the floor?" I heard Destiny inquire.

"Someone had to do it..." he replied.

I felt fingers touching my neck for a few seconds. Would they realize I was awake?

"You didn't kill her, but she has a marked neck... Did you try to strangle her?" Cedric asked, sounding surprised.

"No, I didn't try to kill her... I wanted to interrogate her, find out where that damn hunter is."

"And for that, you needed to choke her?" Cedric responded, seeming to start raising his voice. "Are you an idiot?"

"I'm sorry, Cedric."

"I don't know where my father is, but I hope he didn't hear anything because he'll hate that you disobeyed," he replied. "Destiny, can you take care of Gary? Apparently, now I have to keep the human away from Godric."

"I'm sorry; it's just... she walks around the house while we waste time... The hunter could be anywhere."

"Leave it to me," Cedric replied.

I felt myself being lifted in his arms and starting to walk. My body was still limp, my head resting against his chest, and there was something. Something I didn't imagine I would hear. In his chest, a heart was beating. Was he alive?

A few minutes later, I felt him depositing me on a bed. I waited a few minutes and began to open my eyes slowly. With a surprised expression, I looked in all directions and understood that I was in my room. There was no need to pretend. Cedric wasn't there..

CHAPTER 6

I spent the whole morning of the next day sleeping. By the time I woke up, I saw through the huge window of my room that it was evening.

The sky had been dyed a beautiful pink color, with clouds that looked like liquid gold. With the clothes from the previous day, I left my room and decided to start looking for a bathroom in that huge maze of doors. I walked along one of the corridors and opened door after door, not caring much about who could be on the other side.

When I was reaching one of the last doors, I heard a meow coming from somewhere near me. I stopped in silence to listen to where it was coming from. The cat meowed again, and I heard it scratching a door with its claws.

Without further ado, I opened it. Cedric's cat shot out of the room before I could even pet him, and as soon as I looked up, I knew why.

Gary, the vampire kid, was pressed against a wall in the room, with his eyes wide open and fixed on his bed. I looked in the same direction. The sheets were stained with a large circle of dark blood, and there was someone, a girl, pale and unconscious on it.

"Gary... What happened?" I said in a low voice.

"Can you help me?" the kid said, fixing his violet eyes, like Cedric's, on me. "No... I didn't want to do this."

"I... I'll try... Better leave me with her," I said, entering the room and running to the bed where the girl lay with her eyes closed.

I brought my fingers to her neck to feel if there was still a pulse. It was soft but present. Her throat was stained with blood, but the wounds were closed; surely, as I already knew, vampire saliva healed them quickly. Only a small red mark, like a bruise, remained.

"There's... There's still a lot of blood smell," Gary said suddenly, while trying to walk towards the door of his room to leave.

"Gary, you have to leave her... You're going to kill her."

"I don't want that!" he said, wrinkling his face in suffering. "Her blood is so delicious."

Unable to stop him, Gary threw himself onto the bed again with fiery eyes. He opened his mouth, and I could see his fangs, his monstrous face, and his bloodlust. But he wasn't going to kill that girl. He wasn't going to kill anyone.

With all the strength I could muster, I pushed him out of bed. It was very strange to be hitting a nine-year-old, but after all, he wasn't human, and he was much stronger than me.

He looked at me with a face that didn't even show anger; he just seemed thirsty, and I seemed to be in his way. Gary got up and circled the bed to grab me, but before he could, I took the bedside lamp from his nightstand and smashed it against his head.

He fell to the floor again, his red eyes fixed on me, his breath was heavy. And then, strong and muscular arms took him forcefully. It was Cedric, with his dark hair somewhat disheveled, shirtless, and wearing loose black pants. He grabbed Gary tightly and pushed him against the opposite wall from where I was.

"Breathe, Gary, it's a little blood," he told him, trying to calm his brother, who was struggling futilely to get away. "Gary, calm down!" he repeated over and over.

I kept an eye on them while slowly advancing towards the bed to get closer to the girl.

"Cedric, she's very weak," I said, holding her head in my hands.

I didn't have the strength to lift her and take her away, but at least I could be with her and scare away anyone who wanted to touch her.

"Gary, you have to calm down so I can get her out of here," he told him.

"I want her blood! I want it!" the kid screamed desperately.

"I'm going to take him out of here; try to help her," he asked me. "Make sure no one else comes in."

"Sure... That will be easy with a puddle of blood and three more vampires," I said sarcastically, putting on a poker face.

Cedric ignored me and dragged Gary out of the room. I heard him screaming desperately for blood, even growling.

As soon as they disappeared from my sight, I ran to lock the door. As best I could, I pulled the bloodstained sheets and found a bathroom right behind a door. It was spacious, with a small bathtub. I put the sheets in it, turned on the water, and started washing them to remove as much blood as possible, so the smell would dissipate and not attract anyone else's attention.

Then I returned to the girl and touched her face. She didn't seem to have any intention of waking up, but her heart was still there, beating slowly. She was cold, with slightly bruised lips, and breathing very slowly. I opened Gary's closet and took a thick dark green blanket, which seemed of beautiful and very expensive quality. I wrapped the girl in it as best I could and decided that the best thing would be to go down to the kitchen to prepare something with a lot of sugar.

I left the room and locked it to prevent anyone from entering while I wasn't there. I quickly reached the kitchen and put water to heat for tea. Cedric appeared a second later, like a flash, and stood there looking at me as if something didn't add up.

"And the donor?" he asked, crossing his arms.

– Very well, she's gone – I said sarcastically – I locked her in Gary's room, she's cold, needs something warm and food –

– Fine, I'll help – he said without further ado, opening the fridge – What can it be? –

– Do you know anything about cooking? – I asked, frowning, while grabbing a pan and starting to make scrambled eggs.

– Something – he coughed – but I don't know what could help her recover faster –

– Do you have any meat? – I asked, and he nodded as he moved the blood bags and began to search.

He took a medium steak and placed it on a griddle, not taking his eyes off it, as if just by looking away, the food would burn instantly.

– This shouldn't be happening – he said, running his fingers through his hair.

– Don't you always kill? – I inquired, looking at him with a wrinkled forehead – What would be the difference now? –

– None of your business –

– Yes, of course it concerns me – I replied dryly, moving the kettle and the pan away from the fire and looking at him seriously – or you can do it all by yourself, seems like you're good at it –

– I don't think you want to challenge me – he said, glaring at me – put that on the fire –

– Alright, but I'll find out – I replied calmly.

A few minutes later, we had a terribly sweet tea and a plate of meat and scrambled eggs ready. We both went up to the room quickly, almost as if it were a competition; he arrived first, but only because I was carrying the tray with everything. We opened the door. The girl was sitting on the bed, with a confused and somewhat frightened expression.

She must have been between nineteen and twenty years old. She had large, brown eyes, surrounded by dark circles, and long, delicate lashes. Her dark brown hair, long and straight, was somewhat stuck to her neck and stained with dried blood. She had full lips, a perky nose, and was extremely slim. She wore clothes that highlighted more curves than she had. She was dressed in a tight, shiny black leather top; very short, high-waisted shorts made of the same stretchy fabric, and tall, dark boots.

Her eyes moved from me to Cedric, and as soon as she saw him, she quickly lowered her gaze, embarrassed.

– I'm sorry... – she began to apologize with a remorseful face, but I interrupted her.

– You don't have to feel anything – I smiled, approaching with the tray – Are you feeling okay? –

– I'm a little dizzy, I think I need sugar... –

– Here's a tea. I put a lot of sugar in it, and it's hot to raise your temperature a bit –

– Are you Godric's donor? – Cedric asked, without even approaching or giving her an encouraging smile.

– Yes... –

– And what are you doing here? – he asked, crossing his arms, while she began to drink her tea.

– I left Godric's room at night, and as I was leaving, a kid... –

– He's a vampire, don't talk about him as if he were just a silly human child – Cedric cut her off, somewhat irritated – So? –

– He caught me and dragged me here. I know he bit me, and then everything is very confusing... I think I asked for help, but he took too much blood –

– I apologize on his behalf. I know that's not in the contract –

– It's okay – she said as if almost dying wasn't important – If I had been close to death, would they have turned me? – she asked, biting her lip with a strange coquetry that bewildered me.

– No – he said, shrugging – if you had died, we would have had to burn your body to leave no traces – he continued very calmly – I'll tell Godric to remember that donors are accompanied to the door. It's obvious he forgot, and this won't happen again –

– Alright – said the girl, finishing her tea extremely quickly and starting to eat the steak we had prepared for her.

– When you finish eating, get out – he told her, opening the door to leave – April, take a shower... I think it's time. –

CHAPTER 7

I took the longest bath I had in a long time. The warm water ran down my back; I lathered myself several times and played with the foam between my hands until my fingers wrinkled a bit.

Then, I figured it was time to get out. I wrapped myself in a fluffy black towel, tied it around my chest, and with my hair still dripping, I left the bathroom. I definitely didn't have clean clothes anymore.

– Destiny? – I called out in the middle of the hallway, hoping she'd hear me.

A second later, she was in front of me, looking at me with a furrowed brow.

She was a truly beautiful vampire, that had to be admitted. Her dark, short hair was neatly styled, and her brown eyes observed me with a certain disdain. Her clothing was not at all my style. Black and white lace, loose dresses like those of a gothic princess, and a black collar tight around her neck, with a reddish stone in the center.

– You can't call me as if I were your dog – she pointed out, quite annoyed – What do you want?

– Cornelius told me I could ask you for some borrowed clothes – I said, scratching my forehead with some insecurity.

– What? – she inquired, looking at me as if I had just said something really terrible – My clothes?

– Please... Anything you dislike... I don't have any more clean clothes, and apparently, I'll be here for a long time –

– Well, that depends on your sister – she said with a devilish smile – fine, I have some old and not very expensive clothes – she sighed.

I followed her to her room. Her room was a bit smaller than Gary's and didn't have its own bathroom. That seemed strange, considering she seemed quite pretentious. Her bed was like mine but with velvety sheets that made you want to cover yourself up to your head; and everything was filled with small scented candles and roses.

– So – she said, opening the closet in front of the bed, revealing a neat row of hangers full of outfits.

She rummaged through the drawers for a while and handed me some underwear. They had nothing to do with me. I usually wore comfortable and somewhat sporty things, but everything she had seemed to want to highlight any attribute. She gave me two lace bras and matching panties, along with some pairs of stockings.

It's not that I liked wearing someone else's underwear... But, truth be told, I had no other choice. On the other hand, she was picking some dark outfits from the hangers, which didn't seem to match her current style.

A terribly soft, tight-fitting black wool sweater, a fairly short and loose dark red skirt that buttoned at the waist, some plain, boring T-shirts, and jeans that didn't seem to have much to do with her.

– I don't have anything else – she said, shrugging – get going –

– Wait... – I said while holding the stack of clothes she had just given me – Can I ask you a question?

– You already did, and the answer is no, go away – she said, opening the door for me to leave.

I left quite annoyed and went back to the bathroom. I put on a bra that noticeably lifted my breasts and made them look even bigger than they were. My body was like that of a wasp, a small waist, rounded hips, but not too wide, and my legs were somewhat athletic from how much I trained. I dressed in Destiny's sweater and jeans. They fit tightly even though she must have had one or two sizes more than me.

I looked at myself in the mirror. I didn't seem to be at my best, but that style suited me well. My hair was so fine and short that it was already finishing drying. I had it cut above my shoulders, straight, with the bangs on the side, falling a bit on my face. It was an almost white blonde, just like my sister Aixa and our mother. My face was slender, with rosy lips and cheeks. A slightly upturned nose and huge light blue eyes.

I brushed my hair to tidy it up a bit and went out again. I went down the stairs and headed to the kitchen to see if there was anything I could cook for myself, but Cornelius intercepted me at the foot of the stairs and gave me a fake smile, extending a hand to help me down.

I declined, of course, and stopped next to him.

– Let's have dinner, he told me, pointing to a door that must be the dining room –

– Am I... eating with you? – I asked, clearing my throat.

– That's right – he said as we started walking towards the living room.

When we entered there, the first thing I saw was a long wooden table. Dark and elegant, with plates, cutlery, and glasses already set. There were several chairs, many more than the diners who would sit on it.

At the back, there was a large fireplace, with the fire lit and crackling. Without thinking too much, I approached to warm my hands; it was the only room a bit warmer than the rest. Then, I looked up, over the fireplace, there was an immense painting portraying Cornelius in all his elegance, wearing clothing that seemed to be from eighteen hundred.

A few minutes later, while Cornelius took a seat at the head of the table, Cedric entered and settled to his right. He had a serious and somewhat tense expression. He glanced at me and then raised his eyebrows a bit.

– It seems like you took a bath–

– Yes, well– I said, shrugging my shoulders– you suggested it so enthusiastically that I couldn't help it– I sighed, rolling my eyes.

Cedric shrugged and focused on his empty glass while Destiny and Gary settled at the table. Then, someone else entered. He was a tall and very thin man. His silver hair was combed back, and his skin was as wrinkled as a raisin. He was certainly a human, but he wore an elegant butler's suit. What was he doing there? Why was he serving them so calmly?

The man started placing asparagus, mushrooms, and hake fillet on my plate. I wondered why he was serving me before the homeowners, especially considering that there was an omnipotent vampire by his side.

As soon as he finished, he left. I looked at the others with an inquisitive expression, but none of them seemed surprised.

– Aren't you eating? – Cornelius asked me with a wide smile.

– Don't you guys? – I said, hoping they wouldn't tell me their food was me.

Just then, the door opened again, and Godric entered, leading by the arm the donor who should have left at least an hour ago.

They both sat at the table, she between Godric and Gary. The boy looked at her and moved away a bit, but he couldn't take his eyes off her neck.

– What's happening? – I said, standing up and pushing the chair back.

– Sit down – Cedric ordered me, fixing me with an unreadable gaze.

– No, if you don't tell me what's happening. She's weak...– I said, furrowing my brow.

– It's better if you sit, dear – Cornelius instructed me with icy eyes– for the good of both of you–

I held his gaze for a few seconds that seemed eternal, and finally decided that it was best to sit down.

Godric reached out and moved the girl's long hair, exposing her pale and bruised neck.

– It seems like today you played the heroine, right? – he said to me, looking at me, while he caressed her neck with a finger– it seems like you care if someone else dies–

– Of course, I care. I'm not a monster– I said, spitting out the words and glaring at him.

Destiny stood up and approached the donor. She took one of her arms, without the girl putting up the slightest resistance. Without hesitation, the vampire showed her long white fangs and bit her wrist harshly.

– Let her go! – I exclaimed, standing up again, and as I did, my chair fell to the floor.

Destiny moved away from her a few centimeters. A line of dark blood dripped from her lips, and she looked at me with red, fiery eyes.

– Then tell us, April– Cornelius sang from his place, completely unaffected– where is your sister? –

It was obvious; that's what they had wanted from the beginning. They had found a crack in me, a weak point, an interest in saving someone about to die, and there they were, playing with that and looking for an advantage.

Gary extended a finger and took a bit of blood from Destiny's chin. He brought the finger to his lips and sucked it as if it were the last drop on earth.

– Gary is the youngest... He still struggles to control his thirst... But maybe today, we don't want him to control it–

– I don't know where my sister is– I said, staring at the boy, ready to jump on him if he bit that girl again.

– Mistake– Godric released and sank his teeth into the donor's neck.

The girl squinted her eyes in pain, but slowly she calmed down and let him suck as much as he wanted.

I took the knife I had for eating and didn't hesitate. I jumped onto the table and lunged at Godric. But before falling on him, a hand as hard as steel grabbed me by the neck and threw me to the other side of the room, dangerously close to the fireplace.

It was Destiny, who advanced toward me again. She took hold of my arm and stood me up, keeping me still.

Godric detached himself from the girl's neck and turned to look at us, with a thick, red smile.

– Tell us where your sister is– he repeated to me.

My eyes focused for a second on Gary and then on Cedric, who seemed tense but said nothing.

Destiny let me go and stepped back a bit. Then everything happened very quickly. With the impact I had when being pushed by Destiny, my forehead hit the floor brutally, and a small drop of blood was making its way down my face.

Gary couldn't take it anymore. Instead of going after the donor, he leaped with inhuman agility and lunged at me, showing his fangs. He effortlessly knocked me down again, ready to attack me, and then Cedric stood up, removing him before he could achieve it.

But that wasn't all; as soon as he moved him away, Gary collided with Destiny. She took him by the shoulders and dangerously brought him close to the girl, whose neck and arm were soaked in blood.

– To her– I heard Destiny tell him.

Gary, without hesitation, jumped onto the table. He crashed some plates to the floor in a movement and pounced on the girl, still on the table. She seemed surprised but let herself be bitten. The boy made such a disgusting noise that it made me want to vomit.

Cedric turned to me and looked at me with narrowed eyes.

– If you want to be a heroine, this is your moment– he said, biting his lip.

– Let her go! – I demanded, trying to push him, but he didn't even flinch.

– Tell me where your sister is– he demanded with a rough, commanding voice.

– In a church! – I blurted out without more, not even knowing what I was saying– she's in a church, but I don't know which one–

– You'll have to be a bit more specific– I heard Destiny's voice next to me as Gary kept sucking relentlessly–

– I don't know anything else– I spat out furiously, lunging again at Cedric to make him let me pass.

– Gary, enough– I heard him say, with a firm voice, but the boy was far from stopping.

Cornelius stood up, grabbed the boy by the hair, and pulled him up to detach him from the girl's neck. Gary kicked like an animal that had just been deprived of its food, but Cornelius didn't let him go.

The donor fell to the floor from the chair, completely unconscious, and I ran to her to check her condition. Her pulse was minimal again. She was cold, bruised, pale, and her breathing was almost nonexistent.

Cornelius left the room with Gary gripped by the neck. Godric pushed me aside and took the girl in his arms.

– Don't touch her! Let her go! Enough! – I said, pulling his arm to let her go, and he frowned at me.

– Calm down, beast– I heard Cedric say, taking my fist in the air to stop me– he won't kill her–

I felt that anger and helplessness were about to explode in my chest. I looked at him with a furious face, while Godric left with the unconscious girl.

– And now eat– Destiny said, looking at me with a strange excitement in her eyes.

She had loved all of that.

– Weren't you hungry? – she laughed, taking an asparagus from my plate and bringing it close to my face.

Cedric reached out, took her by the wrist, and pushed her away from me with a swat.

– Don't go too far, Destiny– he said to her, somewhat annoyed– she's not her sister–

– They're the same– she muttered, leaving the room.

– You told them to try to help the girl! – I exclaimed furiously, pointing at him accusingly.

– It's true–

– But you also wanted to save her...–

– What I wanted was not to have an unnecessary death in my house. Don't get confused; this isn't for the humans. This is to keep our name respectable–

– Of course– I said with disdain– What more could be expected from you? –

Cedric ignored me and simply left.

CHAPTER 8

As soon as I was alone in the dining room, I felt an uncontrollable fury. That donor was a complete idiot. While I was trying to save her, she let herself be bitten, all to become a vampire, something they didn't even intend to do.

As if that wasn't enough, she had revealed that my sister was hiding in a church, and even though I didn't know where she was, it was very likely that she was in one. Unintentionally, I was leading them directly to her.

I took my plate and brought it to my room to eat in peace, without anyone showing up to spill blood in front of my face. I chewed forcefully, with a furrowed brow, thinking, scheming, hating those monsters, and hating the stupid girl trying to be one of them.

Finally, I left the plate on the bed and couldn't stand it anymore. I left my room and knocked forcefully on Godric's door.

– Come in– he said from the other side.

I opened the door and walked in before he kicked me out. He looked somewhat confused to have me there.

– Can I talk to her? – I said, nodding toward her, putting my hands in the back pockets of my jeans.

– Why not? – he said, shrugging, and left his room, looking at me with a certain malicious amusement in his eyes.

As soon as he closed the door, I walked to the bed where she was sitting, drinking something hot. Her coffee-colored eyes landed on me with some interest. She had a fearful face, as if I were going to attack her, and she wasn't entirely wrong.

– Are you stupid or what? – I said, looking down at her seriously.

– Excuse me? – she inquired, blinking quickly, as if she didn't understand what I was saying.

– They almost killed you twice, and you let them do it so calmly... Are you suicidal or what? –

– You're like me– she responded in a low voice– you're a human in a house of vampires. I know you also want to become one of them–

– I don't want to be a vampire– I denied, scrunching up my face– I'm kidnapped, they hate me, and I hate them. That's it–

– You wouldn't understand then–

– Of course, I do... I understand that you want an eternal life. What I don't understand is that you're willing to kill people, live only at night, leave your loved ones behind... Why? To avoid aging? –

– There's no need to get upset. We have different points of view, that's all–

But that wasn't all. With a vein about to jump from my neck, I put on my most serious face and looked at her.

– If I hadn't given an answer to what they asked me, you'd be dead right now– I suddenly said– you owe me one–

– You're blackmailing me–

– Doing me a little favor is the least you can do after I saved your life–

– All right– she sighed, drinking a bit from the cup she had in her hands.

I admit I bet everything on a single possibility. There were very few who knew that vervain prevented vampires from manipulating you and also weakened them over time; it was something known within the vampire hunter group but not something any other human would know.

I took a dry sprig of vervain from my sock and showed it to her, studying the expression on her face. She remained calm, undisturbed, and I knew she had no idea what it was or what it was for.

– As soon as you leave, I need you to get more of this. A lot more– I began to tell her as I turned the twig between my thumb and index finger– and when you come back, the first thing you'll do is bring it to me. Godric will have to wait–

– Is that all? Do you want me to buy you a plant? – her eyes widened, and she looked at me with bright eyes– Wait! Are you a witch? –

– What? – I asked, looking at her as if she were an idiot.

– I couldn't believe it; she was enthusiastic about everything that wasn't human; it was simply annoying.

– No, I'm not a witch, I just need it– I continued.

– All right– she nodded, losing all the interest she had in me in a second– I'll bring it to you in two days; Godric told me not to come tomorrow–

When I went out into the hallway, Destiny intercepted me.

– You, come with me– she ordered me as she continued walking down the dark hallway in her high-heeled shoes.

I had no other option; I followed her in silence downstairs, with the cold sound of our steps on the marble, and we both stopped next to some plush dark red armchairs on the side of the stairs.

– We're all here now– she finally said.

Cedric and Godric turned to look at us, each with a glass of a thick red liquid that I assumed was blood.

– Do you want some? – Cedric said, offering me his glass with a malicious but amused smile.

– What's happening? – I asked, ignoring his unfunny joke.

– A while ago, you said your sister is in a church– Godric responded with his rough and irritating voice– In which one? –

– I think I also said a while ago that I don't know anything else– I replied, crossing my arms.

I felt the heavy gaze of the three fixed on me, but I showed no signs of weakness.

– You must know which church she could go to– Cedric told me, giving me a dangerous look.

– There is one... Near my house– if my sister had left, I was sure she hadn't taken refuge in the nearest church, but I wanted to mislead them as much as possible.

– Yes, I already know that– Cedric replied, unfolding a quite large map on the coffee table in front of the sofa– I marked the five nearest churches. We'll start with the one you mentioned– he said, pointing

to it even though he had already circled it with an indelible marker–
you're coming with us–

– What? – I asked, swallowing hard.

– You'll be our guarantee that if she's there, she'll come out to save
you– Godric replied, shrugging.

– To save me? – I asked, feeling suddenly like my legs were turning
into jelly.

– You'll see, let's not waste any more time– Cedric declared, folding
the map again and standing up, as calmly as someone about to go for
a walk.

About ten minutes later, I finally breathed outdoor air. It was cold,
and faint snowflakes began to fall. I looked up, and one fell directly
on my nose, making me sneeze.

Cedric was by my side, wearing a cloth coat, buttoned at the chest.
He extended a palm into the air and let some snowflakes settle on it.
I looked at his face from the corner of my eye. He was serious but not
nervous at all. His dark hair fell a bit over his face, and he left it there
without caring in the least.

– After a hundred years, even snow bores you– he finally said,
noticing I was watching and squeezing the hand and flakes he held.

– Are you a hundred years old? – I asked him, looking at him and
thinking that despite that, his skin was still smooth and flawless.

– Why? How old did you think I was? – he said mockingly, looking
at me.

Godric and Destiny joined us silently, wearing their coats. We got
into a black limousine that stopped right in front of the main gate,

driven by the same man who had acted as a butler a few hours earlier. Did they pay him a salary? Or was he just a slave at their disposal?

Finally, there I was. Locked in a limousine with three vampires. The journey was silent; surely they had a plan I wasn't aware of. I only prayed in my mind that my sister hadn't been so obvious as to hide there.

Half an hour later, the limousine stopped. The four of us got out, right on the edge of a small forest. I knew it well; it was near my house, in the town where I lived.

As a child, I had played there with Aixa many times. I knew where the brightest clearings were and where the tree canopies overlapped enough to prevent the rain from soaking you.

We walked among the mix of enveloping trees. They also seemed to navigate perfectly, although I had no idea why. How many times did a vampire try to get close to a church?

I felt very clumsy among them. They moved with incredible agility, without stumbling, avoiding low branches, pushing away leaves before getting too close. I, on the other hand, seemed like a clumsy troll that bumped into everything. My feet tangled with the roots protruding from the ground, my sneakers got muddy, I stumbled, and my clothes got caught on branches. As if that weren't enough, all the plants Destiny pushed out of her way, two seconds later returned to their place, slapping me from all sides.

When we began to glimpse the church, they started to move faster, and I had to quicken my pace not to irritate them.

It was a small and simple building. The outer walls were of a slightly worn white, and somewhat chipped in some parts. Its entrance was made of light-colored lightweight wood with darker knots.

At the side was the bell tower, with a giant golden bell, which remained silent at that time of night.

– Destiny and April will go into the church and desperately ask for information about Aixa– Cedric said quickly, looking at both of us.

– Destiny is going in? But...– I began to ask, and I saw her face light up a bit at my surprise.

– Crosses and all those spiritual symbols in churches weaken us, but they don't prevent us from entering, nor do they burn us as the movies say–

– Did you think we'd let you go inside a church alone and not come out again? – Godric asked, amused.

That was a low blow. I had no idea they would simply weaken a bit. Undoubtedly, Aixa must know, which meant she wouldn't have sought such a vulnerable place to hide.

A sense of relief washed over me. They wouldn't find her, but where did that leave me? Would I stay with them forever, or would I find a way to escape?

CHAPTER 9

Destiny and I approached the church door while Cedric and Godric remained hidden in the shadows of the trees. I reached out an arm and pulled a small bell that served as a doorbell. That church had been there for decades, and they hadn't even bothered to replace that antiquity with an electric doorbell.

We remained silent, waiting, and after a few minutes, we heard footsteps dragging from inside. The parish priest opened to us, with sleepy eyes. He looked at Destiny, and his face seemed to darken a bit until his eyes finally settled on me, and then he smiled.

– Father, we apologize for the hour...– I began, biting my lip.

– Can we come in? – asked Destiny, looking at him intensely.

There was one condition preventing her from entering, and that was that she needed someone to invite her inside. However, the priest didn't do it; he spoke directly referring to me.

– April? What are you doing here at this hour? – he asked, furrowing his brow a bit.

– I'm looking for my sister, Aixa...– I explained, trying to stay calm– she left a few days ago, and I don't know where she is–

– Is she your friend? –

– Yes, yes, I am– Destiny responded for me, somewhat urgently.

– Aixa hasn't come here...– he replied, and he genuinely seemed saddened, even too much– but wait. I have something that might help you– my heart skipped a beat.

Did he know something about finding my sister? Was he about to reveal something important in front of Destiny?

Out of the corner of my eye, I saw a smile forming on her face. The priest had gone back inside and had gone to get something, surely a clue. I looked back, Cedric and Godric weren't even visible in that darkness.

– Perhaps this will help you– the priest said again, reappearing with a somber face.

He quickly took something out of his pocket. A small glass jar. He removed the cap with a swift motion and threw it at Destiny. The jar exploded against her face. She let out a sharp scream as her skin seemed to burn. It was undoubtedly holy water.

I stood there stunned for a second as the priest lunged forward with a wooden stake, ready to kill her.

Then, Godric appeared, as fast as lightning, and violently pulled Destiny away. In the process, the tip of the stake pierced his arm, and he let out a scream of pain.

– Quick, April! Get in! – the priest grabbed my wrist and pulled me inside the church.

Before I could take a step inside, a hand grabbed me firmly by the other arm. I tried to free myself, but Cedric had too much strength, even with two against one.

– Get in! – the priest exclaimed, not stopping the pulling.

Cedric held me with both arms. The priest's feet slipped on the floor, getting closer to the exit.

– Enough, Cedric! – I shouted, trying to free myself from him.

– You're not going anywhere! – he gave a final tug.

The priest and I were thrown outside. I fell to the ground, at Cedric's feet. I didn't see where the priest landed; I only managed to see Cedric grabbing him by his pajama shirt and lifting him off the ground.

– Cedric, let him go! Let him go! – I shouted, getting up in a jump and trying to push him.

Godric grabbed me by the waist and separated me from him, leaving me immobilized despite my kicking and struggling, trying to save the man. Cedric, however, was faster. He plunged his hand into the priest's chest, not letting go, and pulled it out again, full of blood, with a heart between his fingers.

– No! – I screamed, opening my eyes wide.

I couldn't believe what he had just done. The coldness, the lack of expression, and the nonexistent guilt in tearing someone's heart out.

Godric let go of me, and I ran to the priest, lying on the ground, with his eyes open but devoid of light. I felt my eyes burning, and hot tears filled them. That man had only tried to save me.

– Why did you do it? – I yelled at Cedric furiously, turning towards him with tears streaming down my cheeks – You're a monster!

Cedric looked at me in silence, hands stained with blood. He clenched his lips tightly, holding my gaze.

– Why did you kill him? – I shouted again.

He looked away, let out a scoff, as if this were a stupid situation, and began to walk into the forest without saying more.

Godric and Destiny followed him, signaling me to follow.

I looked back at the priest, wiped away the tears with the back of my hand, and began to walk behind them.

The journey back in the limousine was strangely cold and silent. There was tension in the air. Destiny still had burn marks, Godric had a torn coat sleeve and was stained with blood dripping onto the seat, despite his attempts to stop it. Cedric looked silently out the window, as if there were a very interesting landscape in that darkness. I, on my part, had my eyes fixed on him. My white hair fell over my face, but I didn't care, and I didn't care about the stinging in my arms from how much they had pulled me.

I hated them, I hated them deeply and with all my being. They treated humans as if we were mere lifeless objects. They fed on us almost to death and ripped out our hearts as if they were made of plastic. Would they do that to my sister if they found her? Would they rip her heart out and then wash their blood-stained hands as if nothing happened? It was hateful, disgusting, monstrous.

When we arrived, I walked into the kitchen, ready to collapse on the small island in the middle. I sat on one of the stools in the darkness and buried my face in my hands, trying to breathe calmly. I needed to leave; I needed to get out of there somehow, find my sister on my own, and get far away from those vampires. Then, an idea crossed my mind. It was a dangerous idea, but I really wanted them to realize that humans were not just pieces in their chess game.

I opened the drawers where the cutlery was kept and took the largest knife I could find. I swallowed hard as a knot formed in my throat, and I began to walk towards the main hall.

Destiny was sprawled on one of the armchairs, drinking from a blood bag. Godric beside her was bandaging his wounded arm, and Cedric was going up the stairs.

– You! – I shouted, making everyone turn towards me – you have to let me go – I blurted out.

Cedric turned at the top of the stairs, hands in the pockets of his jacket. Godric and Destiny smiled, as if it were very amusing.

– I am the only way to find my sister. If you don't let me go, I'll stab myself with this. And you won't have a way to find her anymore –

– What's your problem? – Destiny asked, looking at me as if I were an idiot.

– My problem is that I'm not an object! And you won't treat me like one –

– April, put down that knife – Godric said, squinting his eyes – we know you wouldn't do that –

– Let me go – I repeated, lifting the knife and holding it with both hands.

– You're not going to leave... – I heard Cedric, who hadn't moved from his spot – put that down; you can hurt yourself, and it'll be for nothing – he sighed.

– No – I denied, fixing my eyes on his – it won't be for nothing –

It would be a lie to say that I didn't hesitate. My hands were shaking, my legs were like pieces of jelly, but the hatred I felt towards them and the fear that they could find my sister were too much.

I didn't want to help them hunt her down. I didn't want to give them the slightest chance, and I couldn't let them kill everyone just as a stupid warning to me. They had tried to extract information from me by torturing a donor, and they had killed the priest who had only tried to keep me safe. I knew they would kill the next person who stood in their way, just to scare me.

But I wasn't going to make it easy for them. I clenched my teeth and plunged the knife into my stomach.

I felt the metal, cold as ice, piercing my skin. Terrible pain tore through me. I took a gasp of air as I fell to the floor. Cedric's eyes, wide open, met mine. I saw him start running towards me. Blood ran through my fingers, my heart pounded hard, my vision was strange, flooded with shadows. My body loosened, lying on the floor, and everything turned black.

CHAPTER 10

I opened my eyes suddenly, with a muffled groan. My chest rose and fell several times, taking in air, as if I hadn't been breathing until that moment. I was in the enormous bed they had assigned me, still trapped in that detestable mansion.

– You finally wake up – said Cedric, catching my attention. He was sitting astride a chair, with his arms and chest resting on the back, watching me with a strange gleam in his eyes.

– How am I alive? – I asked, remembering that I had stabbed myself and was sure I had hit the mark. I looked at my stomach, felt it. The black shirt I was wearing was soaked in blood, but I felt no pain.

– I had to give you my blood – he said as if it were the most normal thing.

– Did you turn me into a vampire? – I asked, widening my eyes.

– No, it takes much more than a little blood for you to turn. It just served to keep you from dying. For now, we need you –

– Can't I choose to die either? –

– That wasn't what you wanted – he said, getting up from the chair and walking towards my bed – you wanted to be in control, feel that we weren't walking all over you. I must say you surprised me –

– It shouldn't have been a surprise; I warned you I would do it if you didn't let me go –

– True. None of us took it seriously. It's not something any human would do, there's no doubt about that –

– Does it matter that I surprised you? – I asked, furrowing my brow a little.

– It depends on what you wanted to achieve – he shrugged – I'll tell you something. Maybe we went too far with you; maybe what we did yesterday wasn't necessary –

– Of course, it wasn't – Cedric raised a finger as if asking me to let him continue.

– We are like that. We like to get what we want quickly, and we are willing to do whatever it takes to achieve it. A human, I suppose, can't have that same perspective –

– Of course not, because we are humans. You are monsters without feelings – a melancholic smile crossed his face for a second, as if my words had managed to affect him, even if only a little, but he quickly hid his expression.

– Yes, April – he nodded, looking at me with his deep violet eyes – that's what we are, and you can't expect anything else because we don't feel like you, and we don't value human life – he continued – we can't let you go because we really need to find your sister. And you really are the only one who can find her –

– I'm not going to help you – I denied, swallowing hard – you won't find my sister –

– You will, whether you want to or not – he said, running a hand through his hair – but living together will be better for you. We are monsters, but we don't dedicate ourselves only to killing and drinking blood. We also do more... Human things... Things that wouldn't make you want to stab yourself in the stomach at least –

– Are you telling me that you will... Will entertain me or something? – I asked somewhat bewildered.

– No – he said with a grimace – I'm telling you that we will try to treat you better and scare you less. When we ask for your help with your sister, you won't even notice –

– No more threats, violence, hearts ripped out of someone's chest? – I asked, feigning surprise that I didn't feel – I can't believe it – Cedric let out a sigh that seemed to be a resigned laugh.

– As long as you don't anger us... Or try to attack us with a fish knife – he said, rolling his eyes and recalling my attempt to push Godric away from the donor.

– You can't kill anyone again or almost kill, like that donor –

– Well, we won't... In front of you –

I shook my head. It was impossible; they would never stop killing. And what did he mean by not realizing when they asked me about my sister? Surely, they would try to hypnotize me. I had to be careful and remember to take vervain every day.

– Because of you, I had to be awake during the day – he suddenly said, getting up and heading towards the door – I'm going to sleep for a while; see you at night –

It was evident that I had been unconscious for more hours than I imagined. I took advantage of my solitude to take a bath and remove the clothes soaked in blood. I dressed in a burgundy long-sleeved shirt, leaving my shoulders bare, a fairly short black skirt, and dark stockings that covered my legs completely. I went downstairs. I was still processing that attempt at peace Cedric had tried to make. Would it be real? Or would I stumble upon a corpse in the middle of the room at any moment?

As soon as I entered the kitchen, I realized I had never seen it so full of life. The butler had the lights on, but through a large rectangular window next to the oven, the lights of the sunset still filtered through. The man remained silent while seasoning a chicken and surrounding it with vegetable slices.

– That looks good – I said with a smile, trying to appear pleasant. He turned to look at me, with a surprised expression but a small smile.

– Mr. Cornelius asked me to make an effort in today's meal; it seems there will be a guest – he told me, raising his eyebrows a bit.

– Is that good? – I asked, approaching slowly and inspecting what I could steal. Finally, I saw a container full of carrot slices. I approached and took a handful.

– It depends on who it is. Anyway, it seems that none of them intends to harm you... So, I wouldn't worry too much if I were you –

– Do you know them well? – I asked, nibbling on the raw carrot – Is there anyone else working here? –

– No, I'm the only one – he denied, as he returned to work – I've been in this house for many years, always serving the family –

– You know what they are, right? – I asked, and he nodded calmly.

– Yes, I know –

– Aren't you afraid of them? – I asked, and his answer hurt me even though I didn't know him at all.

– They took everything I had, my wife and my daughter... I have no reason to be afraid of them anymore –

– How did they do that? – I inquired, somewhat confused – Why are you still here? –

– Many years ago, I know I'm hypnotized. I do things to serve them that I know I don't want to do, but there are times when my body and my lips move on their own, without my deciding it –

– It's... It's a prisoner of all of them – I said, pondering it for a moment.

– If I could choose, I'm sure I would have left this place a long time ago. But I just keep cooking for them, keep driving their car, and keep doing everything they ask me to do –

– Isn't there something that can break the hypnosis? – I asked, thinking about sharing my vervain.

– No – he denied – there are things that prevent you from being hypnotized, but if you already are, there's no way to change that –

– But you could try to resist... –

– I could, it's true – he said with a somewhat muted voice – but I have nothing to do and nothing to lose. I'm old and tired... I don't have that much willpower –

– If you want, I can help you – I said suddenly, trying to sound friendly – I don't have much to do, and I know how to cook –

The eyes of that man gleamed in a strange way. No one in that house should have ever offered him help, and indeed, there were many things he had to do.

– Can you finish this and put it in the oven? – he asked me as he rinsed his hands and dried them on a dirty kitchen apron – I'll go set the table –

– Of course! – I smiled at him – by the way, I'm April – I said, extending a hand.

– Peter – he said, shaking my hand, and then he left the kitchen. Immediately, I took some sprigs of vervain that I had hidden. They were somewhat dry. I placed them on a cutting board and began to crush them with a knife until they were just powder.

I mixed it with the rest of the spices and finished seasoning the chicken. Vampires couldn't detect the smell of vervain, and they couldn't taste it either. But if I could do that for several days in a row, they would start to weaken, and maybe, if they found my sister, at least she would have a chance to defeat them.

I put the food in the oven, washed all the utensils so that no traces remained, and then went to the living room, where Peter showed me how to set a table according to the protocol.

CHAPTER 11

That night I sat down to eat with them again, without surprises in between. I was the last to arrive. Everyone had already taken their seats, and I looked for my place as far away as possible from everyone, settling only next to Gary.

Nothing Cedric had told me was going to make me feel more comfortable, and I was determined to make it known.

However, something caught my attention. There was an empty seat at the table, a seat that Peter and I had set up for a supposed guest who seemed not to have arrived yet.

– Are we waiting for someone? – Destiny asked as Peter entered with a huge tray.

– Yes– Cornelius nodded – I'm sure you'll be very pleased–

As soon as he said that, in a cold and indifferent tone, the doors of the room swung wide open.

A girl entered who looked every bit like a vampire. Her face was impassive. She had long, flowing, reddish hair. Her face was thin, full of freckles, her nose delicate and small, delicate lips, and fierce, proud eyes of a bright blue hue.

– Emily? – I heard Peter say, stopping his service to look at her.

– Hi, Dad – she greeted him with a soft, feline voice.

Hadn't he said that this family had taken away his wife and daughter? How come his daughter was suddenly there?

The vervain-filled chicken I was swallowing got stuck in my throat, and I hurriedly drank a glass of water to try to wash it down while that girl walked calmly to the table, as if she were a star on a red carpet.

– What are you doing here? – Cedric asked, furrowing his brow and dropping his utensils.

– Your daddy hasn't told you? – she asked with an exaggeratedly confused expression, while putting her hands on Cornelius's shoulders and giving him a kiss on the cheek – I thought you'd let them know–

– Not yet, Emily– Cornelius said as he pointed to an empty seat for her to sit – I wanted to surprise Cedric–

– What a surprise – he muttered, glaring at his father – Why does she honor us with her visit? –

– In a few days, there will be a gathering where they present the new members of the clans – Cornelius began to say as he calmly cut a vervain-filled potato and brought it to his mouth without realizing anything – it happens every hundred years, and this time, it will be at home–

– Do Godric and I have to return to our house then? – Destiny asked, dispelling my doubt that her resemblance to him was because they were siblings.

– No – Cornelius denied – your family will join you here on the day of the ceremony–

– Is Emily going to be introduced as a member of your family? – Godric asked, looking at the red-haired girl with some disdain – she's a half-breed–

– I know – Cornelius nodded, sighing – the Council already knows what happened. Our name is not at its best, but Emily will be very charming to everyone; maybe someone will be interested in her, and then it won't matter if she marries a pure-blood–

– If not, Cedric could do it... – she commented, looking at her nails with some disinterest – Dad, serve me chicken, please – she asked Peter, pointing to the plate – by the way, why are we eating this? – she said, putting her hand into Destiny's plate and taking a potato – I thought I'd at least be greeted with a donor or something...–

Destiny calmly lifted the knife she had to cut the chicken, and in a skillful movement, she stabbed it into the hand with which Emily had tried to steal her food.

– This is not really your home – she said, then, looking at her with a wicked smile – so behave, because I really hate half-breeds pretending to be at our level, more than humans themselves–

Emily bit her lips hard to avoid letting out a scream of pain. She pulled the knife out in one go, and blood began to stain the white tablecloth that Peter had placed very carefully.

– Ladies... – Cornelius began to say, rolling his eyes – behave – both decided to ignore each other and fix their eyes on him – none of you has been introduced, except Destiny, so during the next week, you will train a lot so that both the Leblanc house and the Briand house stand out as the best in vampire society.

– How does the presentation work? – Cedric asked, leaning a bit on his chair to listen.

– It will last three nights – Cornelius replied – the first day will be the presentation ceremony, a dance, blood, donors, and there you will have to establish all the relationships you can with new and old vampires – he began – on the second day, after a banquet, there will be a cricket competition, where your best physical qualities will be evaluated: speed, strength, and reflexes–

– Do you play cricket? – I asked, unable to interrupt – I didn't know that vampires entertained themselves with something like that–

– When you have eternity ahead of you, you must have several ways to entertain yourself – Cedric said with a grimace, and without understanding why, Emily suddenly looked at me with some interest, as if she had just realized that I was there and that I wasn't like them.

– On the last night, the oldest members present the positions of the houses, and alliances begin to form – Cornelius continued – you will have to train in cricket, reread all the books in the library, know how to dance perfectly, and have the most elegant outfits you have ever worn in your lives–

– We could use this as a way to clean the family name – Cedric said, running a hand through his dark and shiny hair, even though instantly some strands fell back onto his face.

– That's exactly what we'll do – Cornelius nodded.

Dinner ended without anyone realizing that they had ingested a good amount of vervain. I had very little left, but if everything went well, the donor would bring more the next day, and that way, I would manage to keep putting it in the food or wherever.

I helped Peter set the table because discovering that he was hypnotized and forced to do all the household chores alone had made me feel really sorry for him, and I wanted to make the work a little easier for him. I washed the dishes in the kitchen while he cleaned the tablecloth stained with his daughter's blood.

I didn't dare ask him about that; I was sure he didn't want to talk. His face, in fact, was much darker than that afternoon, and I didn't want to rub salt in the wound. Anyway, I had no doubts that one of those vampires had turned her, and if he detested those monsters, he surely felt as if they had taken her away.

– You don't have to do that – I heard a voice from the kitchen door – that's why we have a servant–

I turned around; Gary was watching me calmly, not approaching too much, and with Cedric's cat held by the tail..

– And you shouldn't grab a cat like that – I retorted, frowning, and watched as the animal shook wildly and scratched the boy's hand without managing to make him let go – people who mistreat animals when they're little are generally psychopaths when they grow up – I said as if it were an interesting fact.

– Maybe I already am – Gary smiled at me in a rather terrifying way. He let go of the cat, but I suspected he did it only because he had gotten bored of holding it.

– Let's play cricket, we need one more player. You have to play – he ordered me without further ado.

– I don't know how to play, and I'm pretty bad at sports –

– Everyone is waiting for you in the garden, move –

I never thought a nine-year-old would give me orders. However, he was a vampire child, quite twisted and disturbed, so I decided it was best to follow him. After all, running a bit wouldn't hurt me.

The garden of that mansion was incredible, there was no other way to describe it. It was bordered by rose bushes, and the flowers were open and red, shining in the moonlight. It was immense, with freshly cut grass, neat and with a scent of freshness and roses.

Everyone was there. They hadn't even changed their clothes, as if exercising were as easy as breathing, and they didn't need to be comfortable.

– April, put on these things – Cedric pointed to me, throwing a helmet for me to catch, similar to the ones rugby players used.

– How considerate... – Emily smiled, very close to us – Is she your new protegée, Cedric? –

– It's none of your business – he replied, while continuing to give me knee and elbow pads – but I need her to stay alive –

– Alive? – I asked, pointing to the helmet and furrowing my brow.

– A ball thrown by any of us can leave a hole in your skull – Destiny shrugged – you better not get hit –

– I would like to be on Destiny's team... Just to make sure – I said, swallowing hard and looking at her with some concern.

– Well, I'm with you – Emily said, joining us as if someone had invited her.

– Women against men it is – Cornelius nodded – I will be the referee. For those who don't know, cricket is the sport we practice the most. Before the ceremony, you must know how to play like true professionals and, above all, know the rules well. Cheating will cost you points in your houses, so you better do a good job –

Soon, I discovered that, in a real game, each team had to have eleven players. Two batters stood facing each other and had to hit a leather ball with a wooden board, which had been replaced with a metal one so that it wouldn't break every time they hit the ball.

The idea of the game was to hit the wickets, wooden sticks placed behind the batter. I knew I had absolutely no chance of scoring against them, and apparently, my teammates knew that too because they decided that I would be the last to bat.

Destiny took the batter's position, and on the opposing team, Cedric prepared to throw the ball. Seeing them in that way was strange and new. I knew they had an eternal life ahead of them, but I had always seen them only as creatures that went out to kill or gathered at night to plan how to terrify humans.

However, there they were, standing, looking at each other with a gleam of fun competition in their eyes. As if they really liked it, as if they too could have fun and be human from time to time.

Cedric threw the ball accurately, but Destiny's reflexes and strength did not fail. She hit the ball with the bat, and it shot out of the garden. Both started a little race where each went to the other's batting position, while Godric went in search of the ball.

It took at least forty minutes before Cedric finally managed to hit one of the wickets. The stick was torn from its place and fell to the ground with a rattling sound.

Then it was my turn. Destiny was eliminated. She stepped aside from the middle of the garden and stopped by the rose bushes, arms crossed, annoyed because Cedric had managed to defeat her.

– Change – Cornelius told the boys on the team – Godric pitches, and Gary goes to get it –

Receiving a ball thrown with Godric's force was like jumping into the water from a height of a hundred meters; upon landing, it would be like hitting cement.

I gripped the metal bat with sweaty hands, letting out a bit of air in an attempt to breathe with difficulty. Godric found my eyes under the huge helmet he was wearing and smiled with a certain devilish amusement. I just prayed that he wouldn't hit me in an unprotected area.

He raised his arm calmly, ready to throw:

– I'll go easy on you – he said mockingly and threw.

The ball flew through the air with unexpected speed, but despite that, I could follow it with my eyes. I clenched my teeth, concentrated, swung the bat back, and gave it a determined hit.

It was terribly painful. As soon as the ball hit the bat, it shook so much that every part of my body trembled. I took a few steps back to stabilize myself until I realized I had to run to Godric's position.

– Excellent – Godric laughed as he passed by me, running slowly to make me feel worse.

Emily managed to catch the ball so quickly that she didn't even let me reach the new position.

– We can't play with her; she's weak and slow – she said without more, returning to us with a furrowed brow.

She had made a high and tight ponytail, and even though she had run against the wind, not a single hair had come loose. I looked at her with narrowed eyes, thinking of an eloquent response, but Cornelius decided it was best to finish humiliating me.

– April, be a better referee – he said with a sigh, walking to the middle of the garden and taking the flat, metal bat from between my hands.

I hated it. It was the first fun thing I had done in days. I had even managed to catch Godric's ball, and they called me slow and weak.

– You're better than me at the game – Gary said, shrugging, and I was surprised that he said something so kind.

– Gary, no – Cornelius told him, looking at him with a stern face – we all know you're better than a human –

– Maybe he's better than me – I said, looking at him coldly – but he's also better than all of you, much kinder –

– No one wants to be kind to you – Emily mocked, raising her eyebrows and looking at me with some amusement.

– Neither with you, Emily – Destiny retorted from the rose bushes.

They both looked at each other with hatred for a moment. The air between them was so heavy that it could be cut with a knife. Then, Emily shrugged to downplay it.

– Do we continue or what? – she asked, returning to her runner position.

They did, and I stayed there watching without more, still wearing the helmet, knee pads, elbow pads, and a terrible desire to kill them all.

.

CHAPTER 12

The next day, I woke up before everyone else. I opened the curtains of my room to see the last rays of sunlight coming through the window. My body ached even though I had played very little cricket. The bones in my arms seemed to have felt the impact of the force with which Godric had thrown the ball.

After taking a shower, I calmly went downstairs and out into the garden. Peter was silently trimming the rose bushes. I approached him, trying to make some noise with my footsteps so that he wouldn't be startled when I reached him, but he continued his work calmly without noticing my presence.

– Hello – I greeted him with a grimace, tucking my hair behind my ears.

– Hello, April – he greeted me, not taking his eyes off the flowers – Do you want to tell me something? – he asked, and I looked at him with a furrowed brow, not understanding.

– What are you talking about? –

– I always eat the leftovers from the family dinners... – he began, and then I felt the blood drain from my face – the chicken had vervain, didn't it? –

– I don't know what you're talking about... – I tried to deny it like a fool, but he turned towards me with a pair of large pruning shears.

I didn't think he was going to stab me with them, but it did look quite disturbing.

– No problem with that – he told me, smiling at me sideways, allowing the wrinkles on his face to become even more pronounced – but you have to be careful; you can't just put it as if it were nothing –

– How did you know? – I asked, biting my lip.

– I'm not a vampire; I can detect the taste of that herb. Besides, I've been making that recipe for years; I would notice even the slightest change –

– I'm sorry... –

– Find a way to do it, and make sure I don't know how, because if they find out, they will interrogate me, and I won't be able to keep your secret – he asked me, turning back to the roses.

Then I felt that it was the right time to ask him the questions I had kept to myself the day before. I cleared my throat to gather courage and finally let it out:

– Don't you mind if I give vervain to your daughter? –

– Emily is no longer my daughter – he said with a somber face – my daughter died a long time ago –

And that was it, a conclusive and cold answer, but it was the only answer I knew he would give me. Peter was a man trapped in a house of vampires; it was logical that he hated them.

By the time I went back inside, the sun had completely disappeared, and I needed a new plan to continue getting them to consume vervain without realizing it. I sat on a stool in the kitchen, holding my face in my hands, not knowing exactly what I could do.

Food was not an option; Peter would notice, and they would release him as soon as they realized something was wrong.

– Good evening – greeted a silky male voice behind me.

Cedric had just entered the kitchen. I was quite impressed, but I managed to put on a poker face. He was wearing only gray sweatpants, barefoot, and his torso was exposed. When he turned to open the fridge, I noticed that his back was entirely tattooed. It was a black and white drawing of a pair of wings that extended to the middle of his arms.

I looked at his muscles tensing as he stretched to grab something, the smooth curvature of his neck... Cedric turned and looked at me with a playful side smile.

– Is something wrong? – he asked me, closing the fridge again, holding a blood bag in his hands.

– No – I denied, furrowing my brows and looking at the blood bag – Is there another game today? –

– No, there's something better... – as he spoke, he poured blood into a glass, and I couldn't help but feel nauseous.

– Something like what? –

– We're having a party with the donors – he said, shrugging – my father won't be here today; he has matters to attend to, so we'll take the opportunity to have some fun –

– You talk like a teenager, but I remind you that you're a hundred years old... – I said with a grimace.

That comment didn't even faze him. He rummaged in the pocket of his pants and pulled out a metal box from which he extracted a cigarette and put it between his lips.

– Do vampires smoke? – I asked him, somewhat bewildered.

It was strange, but I couldn't stop looking at him. Maybe it was because he was semi-naked or because at that moment, with just a pair of pajamas and slightly disheveled brown hair, he looked more human than ever. But I couldn't help but look at the lines of his lips as he lit the cigarette and those eyes between blue and violet studying his surroundings while exhaling a puff of smoke.

– No vice kills us... So why not? – he said, taking the cigarette between his fingers and walking towards me – I have something for you – he said, leaning on the bar while taking another drag from his cigarette and looking at me from above – it's for tonight. Follow me –

I followed him out of the kitchen without understanding. We approached the armchairs; he took a bundle of black fabric and threw it to me so that I could see it up close.

WHAT THE HELL?!

He had just given me a classic maid outfit, but something... Something short. It consisted of a kind of black dress with princess-style sleeves and a skirt that barely covered my thighs. Attached to the front was a white apron full of lace.

– Why would I wear something like this? – I asked him, looking at him with wide eyes, and he smiled amused.

– Because Peter is old, and this is too much fun of a party for him to be there in the middle –

– Do you want me to be the waitress of the party? – I asked, blinking like a fool and scanning my gaze from him to the maid outfit and then back to him – I'm not going to do that... –

Cedric approached me with confident steps and stared at me. I understood instantly, but I swear I couldn't believe it.

– You will, you will serve a lot of alcohol at the party and without complaints –

I was about to spit in his face. Cedric was trying to hypnotize me. For what? So that I could be a sexy waitress all night long? And the worst part? The worst part was that I couldn't reveal that I was taking vervain, so I had to pretend to be completely hypnotized.

With boiling blood in my veins, I nodded.

– I'll do it – I said, and he smiled with a malicious face and walked away from me.

CHAPTER 13

The outfit was terribly short. It covered me just below the thighs, so with just a little bend, it would have revealed my soul.

Luckily, Destiny had lent me a pair of black stockings that completely covered my legs. I put them on and felt a bit more secure. As soon as I left the bathroom, I heard someone ringing the doorbell. I rushed down the stairs and arrived just in time to see Godric opening the door to a group of donors who had just arrived. The first one was precisely the girl I had been waiting for.

I finished descending the last steps, and while Godric was indicating for them to enter the main hall, I approached the group with my most fake smile.

– I'll escort them – I said to him – so you can finish getting ready –

– Fine – for the first time since I knew him, he smiled at me.

Without hesitating too much, I hooked my arm with the donor I had been waiting for. She looked at me with some strangeness but said nothing.

– Do you have what I asked for? – I said feeling like a drug dealer, and she nodded somewhat nonchalantly.

While everyone entered the hall, I kept her arm firmly. I closed the door, and it was just the two of us facing each other.

– What do you need this for? – she asked me while taking off a backpack she had on her shoulders and opening it slowly.

– They're for making tea – I lied, quickly taking the paper bag she was handing me.

I looked inside just to make sure. There they were, hundreds of vervain branches; it had to be at least a kilogram.

– Can you make me one? – she asked me, looking at me curiously – I have to go change, but I'd like to try it –

I pondered it for a second until I realized something: if I prepared a drink with vervain for a donor... that meant the vampires would drink blood with vervain.

– What's your name? – I asked her, suddenly looking at her with more gratitude than ever.

– I'm Lucy – she smiled, shaking my hand, and I mentally thanked her for the idea she had just given me.

– April – I returned the smile – you've been very kind; I'll prepare tea for everyone –

Without waiting for a response, I ran to the kitchen with the vervain package in my hands. I heated a large amount of water, enough for the eight donors in the hall. I searched the pantry for some loose-leaf tea and found a box of black tea.

It wouldn't be anything special, and I didn't even know if it would taste good with a bit of vervain, but it had to be tried. After all, she and probably none of the present ones knew what taste that plant had.

I dismantled some vervain flowers and mixed them with a certain amount of tea. I filled the cups with sugar and placed them on a tray, ready to take them.

Before that, however, I hid the vervain package behind some groceries, so no one would discover it.

– I left the kitchen trying not to spill the contents of any cup and began to walk towards the hall.

– What are you doing? – Gary's voice intercepted me from the stairs, behind me.

I turned and looked at him, with trembling hands holding the tray.

– It's tea for the donors... They recharge energy before... They take blood out of them – I replied, struggling to keep calm.

Gary had a book in his hands; I wondered if he was preparing for his weekend presentation.

– Are all humans so kind? – he asked me with a small sinister smile. I didn't know why, but I felt a chill running down my spine.

– I don't think so – I said, hesitating for a moment – Could you be kind and open the door for me? – I said, pointing to the entrance to the hall with a nod of my head.

The boy sighed as if I had just asked him for something too heavy. He descended the last steps and opened the door for me.

Inside, the donors were finishing changing. There were both girls and boys. The girls wore black leather bodysuits, loose hair, and dark, intense makeup. The boys wore leather boxers and bare chests.

I was quite stunned. I swallowed hard and advanced, handing them the tea cups with a smile.

When I handed the last one, I felt strange. I hadn't even wanted to look at the donors so that my face wouldn't betray my fear. But I felt eyes fixed on me, staring at the back of my head.

I turned; a boy was looking at me. He was sitting on one of the arms of a chair, which had been specially placed for the party.

He had his chest exposed, and perfectly marked abs. His ashy blonde hair was short on the sides and a bit longer on the crown. His face was fine and delicate, with green eyes that seemed to pierce through me.

– I'm done – he said calmly, handing me the empty cup.

I walked toward him, and he gave me a look full of intention that I couldn't understand. I took the cup and noticed that inside there was a crumpled piece of paper.

Just then, the doors of the hall opened again. Cedric, Emily, Destiny, and Godric entered the room with a haughty look, as if they were kings going to meet a group of commoners.

Godric smiled at Lucy, settling next to her very calmly and took the tea cup from her hands.

– What are you drinking? – he asked very calmly.

My heart raced when she, with a flirty smile, began to speak:

– It's vio...–

– Violets! – I interrupted her, hurrying over to Godric and holding out my hand for him to give me the cup – I made it for them to have something before the party starts... It's better if I take the cups –

– Let me try – he said, shrugging and taking a sip of tea.

I thought I would faint right there. They would discover me, and they would kill me in a second.

– It seems common – he said, looking at me as if I were an idiot – it doesn't even have the scent of violets –

– I must have been mistaken... – I said, swallowing hard with a knot in my stomach – or Peter bought a very cheap brand.

Lucy looked at both of us with a furrowed brow, not understanding anything, but she kept silent.

– No one wants tea right now – Cedric interrupted us with a bored expression – April, you can start serving alcohol – I looked at him with my worst expression, and then remembered that I had to appear hypnotized, so I finally nodded, picked up the cups, and went to the kitchen.

It took me a minute to remember that one of the cups had a note. I took it; it was stained with tea and something sticky. I opened it with my fingertips and read:

"I know your sister; we will get you out of here."

It was like my soul returned to my body. I took a deep breath, with my heart pounding hard. It was a brief message, but it meant a lot. In a few words, Aixa knew they had me, and she wasn't waiting for them to find her. She was probably planning something with that boy. Would he also be a hunter? Could I really trust him?

I threw the paper in the trash after tearing it into pieces. I put crystal glasses, bottles, and ice on the tray and headed back to the hall.

The music was blasting. It was sexy electronic music, nothing like the serious and elegant air of the vampires I had seen that day.

I carefully placed the tray on a table and started serving some whiskey on the rocks. I observed the situation around me and felt quite uncomfortable. Cedric had a human sitting on his lap, and they were laughing. He had a self-sufficient expression, touching her face attractively, making her smile.

Godric was with Lucy sitting on his right and another curly-haired blonde girl on his left. The latter ran a small hand with slender fingers over his chest, while he looked at Lucy and shamelessly touched her knee.

On the other hand, Emily was lounging on a chair, and two male donors were dancing in front of her. Her face was at the level of their bulges, and I wondered if she was aware of it; probably yes.

Destiny reached me, with an arm around the boy who had left me the note, and asked for two whiskies. I served them, and both clinked their glasses in a playful toast. Was he acting, or was he happy to be there?

Cedric signaled for me to hand him a glass. I walked over to him with the ice tinkling in the glass and handed it to him with my best bitchy smile.

– Come, sit – he smiled, patting his leg.

The donor next to him looked at me curiously and gave me a strange expression. It was a forced gesture of kindness; she didn't want me to interrupt, and I didn't want to be there either.

– Leave me alone – I told Cedric, rolling my eyes.

I turned to leave, and then he took me by the arm and pulled me. He brought his face close to my ear and whispered in a velvety voice.

– That outfit looks very good on you –

I felt a strange tingling all over my body, as if his words and that lascivious look ran through me completely. I moved away quickly and went back to the table.

Little by little, everything became more and more uncomfortable. Cedric started biting one of the girls and then another. Godric focused on Lucy for a while, while the other donor sat on him. Emily was squeezed between two guys, and she bit them alternately. Destiny was already wiping her lips stained with bright blood, while letting her two donors touch her neck, legs, and waist.

My eyes focused on my sister's supposed friend. He was caressing Destiny's thigh but seemed tense. His jaw was tight, and his neck was stained with his own blood.

If he was a hunter, at that moment, he must have felt completely disgusted and furious. He disguised it quite well, but I could tell. His eyes locked onto mine, and he held my gaze when Destiny decided to bite him again.

I felt guilty; I was doing this for me. I was doing this to find out how he was and the best way to rescue me; I felt I owed him, even if it meant ending all of this. I took one of the empty glasses and smashed it forcefully against the floor.

Everyone paused for a moment, turning to look at me.

– I'm sorry – I said, bending down to pick up the broken glass.

I slid my hand over the glass until I felt a shard stabbing into my palm painfully.

With tight lips, I removed the glass, and blood began to drip down my arm to the floor. At that moment, the door to the hall swung open wide, and Gary stormed in.

– There's too much smell of blood in this house! – the boy shouted with red and bulging eyes.

Cedric quickly pounced on him to stop him. Godric turned toward me, looking at my hand full of blood. I noticed him swallowing hard, but he moved away from Lucy and ran to help Cedric.

– The human had to ruin it – Emily said, rolling her eyes.

– You can all leave; the party's over – Destiny ordered the donors, also irritated.

CHAPTER 14

I didn't have a chance to talk to the boy who had given me the note. As soon as they said the party was over, Emily herself took care of pushing them out of the hall.

– I'm not stupid – I heard her say, stopping in front of me while I finished picking up the glass shards from the floor.

The others were locked in another room with Gary, trying to calm him down.

– Huh? – I asked, standing up with the glass shards in my hand.

– I saw you, you cut yourself on purpose. Why? –

– No, it was an accident. I was thinking about something else, and... –

– I don't want lies – Emily quickly took my hand full of glass and forcefully made me close my fist around them.

I felt thousands of stings in the palm of my hand and let out a painful groan.

– I was disgusted!   I shouted without hesitation – I couldn't keep watching them... Take the blood of those people – she seemed satisfied with my answer, loosened my hand a little, but quickly tightened it again.

– We are vampires; you'll have to get used to this kind of thing – and then she let go.

Some glass splinters were embedded in my skin, and blood was flowing incessantly from the wounds. It hurt like hell. I hurried to throw them away and ran to the kitchen in search of something that could help me remove the glass shards.

I had no doubt; Emily was a bitch. Confirmed.

– You're killing me – I heard a voice behind me.

I turned around, Cedric was hugging himself with shining eyes, leaning on the door frame.

– I'm sorry... – I said, unable to remove the pained expression from my face – Is there a pair of tweezers or something? –

– Do you have splinters? – he asked, walking towards me and extending a hand for me to show him mine.

– Some... –

– I'm going to help you – he sighed, looking away from my blood with difficulty – just because this scent doesn't help Gary calm down –

– Do you think it's a good idea? I don't want you to bite me –

– April, I can't bite you. My father has forbidden us, and I know that if I bit you, I wouldn't be able to stop –

He let that out with a strange expression. He looked at my neck with a certain desire, with eagerness; he even bit his lip to restrain himself.

– Why not? – I asked him without further ado.

– Because I find something special in what's forbidden – he said, smiling playfully – and apparently, you are the only prohibition I have –

I couldn't explain why, but I felt my heart racing suddenly. I looked at him for a moment in the eyes, resisting his heavy gaze, but finally looked away.

He walked to one of the cabinets and pulled out a small plastic first aid kit. He opened it, rummaged in it for a few seconds until he finally found a small pair of metal tweezers, similar to those used for plucking eyebrows.

Both of us sat on a stool, and I extended my hand so that he could remove the glass splinters.

– Why does Gary have so much trouble controlling himself? – I asked while watching his focused face.

His dark and thick eyebrows were furrowed, forming a wrinkle right in the middle. Occasionally, he moved away and took a deep breath, away from my blood, to try to control himself.

– He's young. Vampires take about fifteen years before they can control themselves well – he cleared his throat, and his face darkened a little.

– What's the problem then? – I inquired not understanding very well.

– The problem is that he's twelve... – he said, and I opened my eyes somewhat surprised.

Seeing him so thin and small, I had thought he was only nine, but apparently, I was wrong.

– And he has too much trouble controlling himself. At this point, he should be able to avoid getting desperate like this –

– Maybe he just takes a little longer... It doesn't mean he won't achieve it... –

– There is a predetermined time for him to achieve it – he replied, abruptly removing the last piece of glass.

– What if he doesn't make it? –

– He'll turn into a different creature. It would be frantic, addicted to blood... He would lose sanity, wouldn't even resemble one of us –

– A different creature? – I asked.

– Yes, come – he said, lowering from the stool.

He put my hand under the tap, and a cascade of icy water soaked my skin. I kept it there for a while, and when the blood finally stopped flowing, he wrapped my palm with a bandage.

– Do you want to see it? – he asked me then, pointing behind him with his thumb.

– To Gary? – I asked, blinking like an idiot.

Why would I want to see the psychopathic kid?

– To the creature... – he said, rolling his eyes.

– Do you have one here? – I felt my blood drain from my face just imagining encountering a bloodthirsty and deranged being.

Cedric looked at me again as if I were an idiot, left the kitchen, and gestured for me to follow him.

We went up the main stairs and walked to the left, in the same direction as Cornelius' study. Everything there was darker and even more unsettling than the other corridor.

Cedric opened a door as my heart pounded, ready for a two-headed, twenty-fanged monster to jump on me.

But no, all that attacked me was a soft scent of paper, ink, and old leather.

He turned on the light and motioned for me to enter. As soon as I did, I was amazed. It was an immense library, full of tall, well-maintained and shiny wooden shelves. There were some leather armchairs grouped around a lit fireplace and a long table full of books and scattered sheets.

– This is... – I had no words to describe it.

I imagined running and jumping on a huge mattress of books. I loved to read, loved the scent of the pages, the smell of ink that every word carried.

– It's paradise – I concluded, unable to close my mouth due to excitement.

– Yes, well. Whenever you want, you can rummage through the books; there's everything... Even some over two hundred years old –

Without hearing anything he was saying, I began to walk among the shelves, observed the worn spines of some books, their golden printed letters...

– April... – Cedric looked at me as if I were a five-year-old who had just been given a pony.

I must say I felt like one.

– This is the creature – he held out an open book to me.

So, I remembered that he had taken me there for a reason. I approached and took the book. There it was, the drawing of a creature somewhat similar to a human and partly not. It had longer, white hair down to the knees; the back curved in a strange hump, and two rows of pointed teeth protruding from a long mouth that stretched almost to the ears.

The image didn't have too many details, but that was enough. I wondered if it was possible for such a perfect and elegant child to transform into something like that.

– It would suck if he turned into this – I exclaimed, slamming the book shut and trying to suppress a shiver.

– Yeah, well... What great comfort you just gave me –

– Did you want comfort? – I said, wrinkling my forehead and looking at him with a malicious smile – I'm a kidnapped human... It's not like we're friends or anything –

– Don't mention it to him – he said, suddenly getting serious – please –

Well, well... So keeping secrets from him and asking me for comfort...

– My silence has a price... – I smiled maliciously.

– Screw off, April – he said, squinting his eyes and leaving the library.

CHAPTER 15

– April, come with me – Gary said, appearing out of nowhere.

I was in the library, rummaging through various books, looking for one that caught my attention.

– What's happening? – I asked, closing the one I had in my hands.

– I need your help with something; you're the only one not thinking about yourself today – he sighed, narrowing his eyes.

I decided to follow him without further ado; I was bored, had already had dinner, and had nothing better to do. We went down the main stairs and encountered an immense display of fabrics, people, and worktables.

– What's all this? – I asked Gary, and he sighed in annoyance.

– A circus, that's what it is –

– I mean... – I tried to get him to continue talking.

– Today, we're going to choose fabrics and designs for our clothes for the weekend presentation – he clarified – everyone is very focused on theirs, so you'll have to help me –

I nodded even though I had no idea about fabrics and elegance. Destiny and Godric had shiny eyes at all this. They caressed different fabrics, brought them close to their faces in front of a mirror, and finally discarded them, continuing their search.

– Why did you ask her for help? – Cedric asked, suddenly approaching the table.

– Because you're too busy – Gary sighed – come on, April, look at these –

Cedric stood by a stack of fabric rolls while we moved away from him. We looked for a while. A woman showed us some models of suits that she had drawn in a folder.

– This one is nice – I said, pointing to one with my index finger – Do you like it? – I asked him.

Gary nodded. He didn't even seem very interested in finding something that would make him look good.

He responded yes to everything. I chose a shiny black fabric for the jacket, a dark red one for the shirt, and silver chains to decorate the buttons.

Finally, the woman who was with us almost dragged him away to take his measurements.

My eyes landed on Cedric for a moment. He didn't seem interested at all. He kept his arms stretched out while a man took his measurements, looking at the floor as if he were completely thinking about something else.

I walked slowly toward him and snapped my fingers in front of his eyes to bring him out of his reverie.

– That color you chose is pretty ugly – I said, pointing to the fabric next to him, of a horrible khaki color – Haven't your hundred years helped you develop a sense of taste? –

– Excuse me? – Cedric blinked as if he couldn't believe I was saying something like that – I didn't know you were a fashion expert –

– Why not this one? – I said, taking a purple and opaque fabric – Any color is better than the one you chose –

The man taking his measurements gave me a satisfied smile.

– She's right; that tone is very nice – he said, turning his gaze back to Cedric.

– I like the one I chose – Cedric said, shrugging proudly.

– Fine – I said, looking at him defiantly – I suppose even Peter will look better than you –

– You're unbearable – Cedric sighed, holding the bridge of his nose with his thumb and index finger – I'll use the purple one – he finally told the man.

I wanted to smile at him smugly, but just then, someone rang the doorbell. Peter appeared like lightning to open the door, and a group of guys peeked into the mansion.

They were donors; I recognized Lucy and the guy who had given me the note.

I couldn't let him escape; I had to talk to him as soon as possible, find out what they were doing outside or if he knew a way for me to get out of there.

– Let's take a break for lunch in five minutes – Cedric said to the rest.

The donors sat on the sofas by the side of the stairs and silently watched their respective vampires, who seemed happier than ever to have new outfits. How important was this presentation? Would they be weaker because of the vervain for that weekend?

Then I remembered.

– I'll prepare something hot for you while you wait – I told the donors, and then I ran to the kitchen.

Peter wasn't there; he continued helping in the hall with everything possible. I calmly chose a red fruit tea and mixed it with a slightly larger dose of vervain. Sugar and hot water... I went to the hall, handed each one a cup, and kept one for myself.

– Is it cold outside? – I asked, bringing up the worst conversation in history.

– A bit, yes – Lucy responded, warming her hands with the warm cup.

– I love the cold... – I said with a grimace, gesturing a lot with the cup.

I had sat right next to my sister's friend. He watched me with some interest, as if waiting for me to do something magical so we could talk privately, but I could only think of one thing, the simplest and the one that would make me look like an idiot.

– It's always freezing in here – I exclaimed, gesturing dangerously with the cup, and then, a large part of the content spilled onto his legs.

– Damn! I'm sorry! – I said, jumping to my feet and waving my hands to apologize as I spilled more tea.

– April, are you stupid? – Destiny inquired from the other end of the room – Did you have to stain mine precisely? –

– I'm sorry! Come on! I'll help you clean up! – I said, grabbing him by the wrist and dragging him to the farthest bathroom in the mansion.

As soon as we stopped, I noticed he was laughing at me under his breath.

– You're a terrible liar, you know? – he said in a deep, masculine voice.

– I do what I can – I shrugged.

I wet a towel and handed it to him to clean his jeans.

– I have a lot of questions – I said without further ado.

– Hi, I'm Daniel, nice to meet you. How can I help you? – he said, rolling his eyes.

– There's no time for polite conversations – I muttered, frowning at him – Do you have a weapon? A stake? Something? –

– No, I can't go in armed just like that – he said, scratching his forehead – but listen. There have to be weapons inside this house. You have to find out where they are –

– Why would they have weapons against themselves? –

– They keep them as trophies from vampire hunters they managed to kill – he explained in a low voice – find them, and if you can get rid of one of them without the others knowing, do it without hesitation –

– And my sister? – I asked – Is she okay? Where is she? –

– She's okay – he said – she's hiding in the vampire hunters' institute –

– In what? – I asked, widening my eyes.

– It doesn't matter now. Aixa is safe; that's all you need to know –
he said, looking down the hallway to make sure no one was listening
– we're preparing to attack them, but we need you to keep making
them take vervain, okay? –

– Yes, no problem –

– Try to make them not sleep, expose them to the sun for some
reason, that way they'll weaken much faster –

– I'll do what I can... – I said, biting my lip nervously.

How was I supposed to make them wake up during the day?

– And listen... – he handed me a paper – these are places you can
send them to look for your sister – there will always be hunters
waiting for them –

– Understood – I nodded, putting the paper in my pants pocket.

– We went down the stairs again. Destiny looked us up and down,
and finally, she approached Daniel and took him to her room.

– Why did it take you so long? – Cedric's voice seemed to cut
through me like a sharp blade.

I turned, quickly thinking of an answer, and finally, I looked him
straight in the face.

– I told him what they were choosing fabrics for, and... He said he
wanted to be a donor at least one of those nights –

Cedric narrowed his eyes and approached me slowly. He stooped a
bit so that our gazes were at the same height, and he stared at me
intently. His deep eyes studied me with curiosity and challenge. I
could even feel, for a moment, his cold breath on my face.

– Should I believe you? – he said without stopping to look at me, and I swallowed hard as my heart raced.

– You can trust me – and I knew it was the biggest lie I had ever told in my life..

CHAPTER 16

On Wednesday, I woke up earlier. I took a shower, washed the clothes I had been wearing for those days, and put on a pair of jeans and a dark red sweater again. I spent more time than necessary in front of the bathroom mirror, combing my short whitish hair, and noticed that my face was losing much of its rosy hue. I took off the bandages from my hand and looked at my palm. It was strange. The cuts had been deep, but my skin was only slightly pinkish at those points, no wounds healing, no pain of any kind...

Would the blood Cedric gave me when he stabbed me in the stomach still be effective?

It was impossible; by now, it should have been completely expelled. I shrugged, perhaps they just hadn't been as deep as I remembered. I went downstairs, and Peter handed me a brimming plate. It had red meat, asparagus, and two hard-boiled eggs.

– Eat, you look very bad – he said with a smile – you need protein or a bit of sun...

– I think so – I replied with a grimace, attacking the plate with hunger.

We chatted for a while; I helped him wash the dishes and even tried to get a laugh out of him, but it was difficult. That man was rough and held a lot of anger inside; you could tell by just exchanging a few words with him. I didn't blame him; after all, he was a slave in the service of the creatures he detested the most. As the sky darkened, I began to hear noises from the upper floor. Before they appeared, I took a quick look at the paper Daniel had given me, where the places to send the vampires were noted. I chose one and put the paper back.

– What do you have there? – I heard Godric's thick and cryptic voice entering the kitchen.

I turned to look at him, startled. He was pointing at the pocket of my jeans.

– It's nothing – I said with a grimace, trying to buy some time – Peter gave me his turkey recipe – I lied.

– Is that true, Peter? – Godric asked him.

– No – the man denied, very calmly.

Damn hypnosis, thanks for resisting so much, Peter. – I'll ask again – Godric said with an irritating smile on his lips – What do you have there? – I kept my lips sealed. I didn't know what the hell to answer, and his gaze was still fixed on my pocket. Without further ado, he approached me and took the paper. I stretched my arm to take the paper and pulled. He pulled too, and I applied more force. Our gazes met for an instant, like invisible rays being exchanged, and finally, he took the sheet from my hands. He opened it, and his dark, gloomy gaze, so lustrous, ran over the sheet for a few seconds.

– What are these places? – he asked, frowning and looking at me with confusion.

– Places I like – I shamelessly lied, as if he were an idiot. At that moment, Destiny entered the kitchen and watched as we both studied each other with our eyes.

She was perfect, as always. So well-dressed with her ruffled dress and lace stockings, that dark hair perfectly combed. She looked like a porcelain doll, but a demonic one like "Annabelle."

– What's going on here? – she asked, pretending that her fingers were scissors, cutting the air between us.

– Look – Godric passed her my paper.

Destiny looked at what was written for a moment, and then her eyes, identical to Godric's but a little colder, focused on me.

– What are these? – she asked me.

– Places... – point for April, always so astute... In a millisecond, Destiny had slammed me against the opposite wall and held me by the neck.

– Tell me what it is – she ordered me, with no intention of hypnotizing me, just wanting to force me.

– They're nothing – Destiny squeezed my neck even more.

I felt my breath cut off, and my throat creaked. Could she be breaking some important bone? I tried to speak, but I couldn't even do that. I needed to save the little air I had to survive. At that moment, a face appeared beside us. A thick and strong hand grabbed Destiny's wrist and violently pulled her away.

– What are you doing? – I heard Cedric's voice, but it seemed distant.

As soon as the hand let go of me, I fell seated on the floor. My vision was full of black spots and stars that indicated I had almost fainted.

– She has to learn to answer the questions she's asked – Godric intervened, supporting his sister.

I raised my eyes a bit, trying to take in some air. Everyone moved and argued around me, and there I was, lying on the floor.

– I have a deal with her, and I warned you – I heard Cedric responding – you almost killed her. Do you think she can be of any use to us dead? –

– Oh, thank you, Cedric, you're a hero – I said sarcastically, while trying to get up.

– So, with your so kind deal – Destiny replied, almost spitting the words – ask the pet what's written on that paper –

Cedric turned to me, raising his eyebrows.

– What is that, April? – I kept my lips sealed, saying nothing.

Cedric lifted my face by the chin and then stared into my eyes, ready to hypnotize me.

– What does that paper say? – he asked me again.

– These are possible places where my sister might be –

– Why would you write them down? – he asked me, genuinely confused.

– To remember not to mention them – I lied again.

Then Cedric let me go, pleased, and looked at Godric and Destiny mockingly.

– See? Much easier, and the hostage is still alive – I hated him. For a millisecond, I wanted to laugh at him for believing my pathetic lie. They thought themselves so superior that they couldn't even suspect that I might not be hypnotized. Fucking idiots.

LI pushed them all away with a shove and walked towards the living room. I sat down angrily on one of the armchairs at the foot of the stairs. Only then did I notice that Gary was sitting there, with the cat resting on his lap. For the first time, he was petting it without any malice.

– Are you friends now? – I blurted out, trying to appease my anger with him.

– I don't want to be a psychopath like you said – the boy replied.

Oh, I wanted to die. Have you ever seen those moments of weakness when you say something and feel like all is not lost? That's how I felt.

Maybe Gary was good... He considered my opinion in choosing his clothes, invited me to play cricket, and even listened when I lectured him... Maybe he was good, as much as a vampire could be, right?

– We're going to the church in the middle of the town – Destiny warned me, coming out of the kitchen and walking towards the stairs – come with me, April –

I followed her reluctantly to her room. She opened the doors of her closet and started pulling out black dresses that seemed even more ominous than what she usually wore.

– Put this on – she said, tossing one to me.

– Why? – I asked, while she took another one and leaned it against her body to see how it looked.

– Today in the town, it's the witches' festival. We'll have to walk among the crowd and blend in as much as possible –

I took off my clothes and started putting on the dress while looking at her with strangeness.

– Do you think we'll go unnoticed with these clothes? – I said, wrinkling my forehead.

– We're going to dress up as witches –

– Can't you go as a vampire? – I said, trying to hide a smile.

She rolled her eyes and started changing. In the mirror, I noticed that the dress looked quite good on me. It was tight up to the waist and then loose until a few centimeters above the knee. The collar was white with ruffles and a red satin bow. Who wore that kind of clothing every day? She had a similar one in white and red.

– Why are you wearing white? – I asked her while she handed me a small suitcase full of makeup.

– I'm a white witch... or something like that – she sighed, and for the first time, she smiled at me. Incredible, considering that a few minutes earlier, she had tried to kill me.

– Where are we going? – Emily suddenly entered Destiny's room and stared at us.

– You're not coming – Destiny replied, applying intense red lipstick.

– I'm not going to stay here babysitting Gary while all of you go to a party –

– It's not a party – Destiny said, rolling her eyes and handing me her lipstick.

Wow... What was happening to her? – Yes, I know. You're going to hunt for your little sister – Emily smiled at me mockingly – lend me one of those dresses –

– You're not touching anything in my closet –

– Fine... I'll fix myself up –

She left the room like lightning. I focused on outlining my eyes in black and shading them with dark eyeshadow. It strongly emphasized my light eyes. I looked pretty but also eerie and too much like one of them.

– I think I have some hats... I've dressed up as a witch several times – Destiny muttered, touching her chin – I'll go get them –

– Fine –

At the very moment Destiny left, I made up my mind. The image of Gary petting the cat, feeling remorseful for being sadistic, had touched some sensitive chord in me. Remembering that maybe this same child could turn into that horrifying creature, with white hair and a monstrous mouth, didn't appeal to me at all. I went out into the hallway and walked up to Cedric's door.

– Come in! – I heard him say from inside.

I entered, saw him, and strangely, my heart skipped a beat. He was dressed in tight leather pants, hair tousled and wet with gel, and without a shirt.

– Should I come back later? – I asked, pointing towards the door with my thumb, and he smiled at me, somewhat mischievously.

– I'm going like this – he said, shrugging.

– It's cold... –

– I don't feel it at all –

– Do you think that will make you go unnoticed? – I asked, wrinkling my forehead – What are you dressed up as? –

– As a very desired and sexy wizard – he smiled – in fact, help me – he said, pointing to a jar of creamy paint resting on the edge of his bed.

I approached the jar. It was black, and I didn't understand what he could use it for.

– You have to make lines on my chest – he instructed me very calmly – I can't do it alone –

– Why would you want black lines? – I asked, dipping the tips of my fingers into the paint.

– Just do it – he said – from the shoulders down –

With somewhat trembling hands, I brought the tips of my fingers to his shoulder and carefully rested them. I could feel his gaze fixed on me as I traced the line down his chest. His skin was so smooth, and his muscles firm. My fingers kept going down his abdomen, slowly, and I stopped at the level of his navel.

– The line should disappear into the waistband of the pants – he pointed out.

I looked up at him. He observed me with slightly raised eyebrows and a lascivious smile.

– I can hear your heart, April – he bit his lip, and I was about to run away – calm down, they're just lines –

– I am very calm – I emphasized without moving my fingers from where they had remained.

Cedric took my hand with one of his and made my fingers slide down to his groin. I felt electricity throughout my body, and once I was sure I had managed to draw them, I stepped away from him a few steps.

– Thanks – he said very satisfied, looking at me with intention, and I looked away.

– I was only looking for you because I wanted to suggest that Gary come with us –

– I don't think so... – suddenly, he seemed somewhat puzzled.

– If he needs to learn to control himself, it's best for him to try it surrounded by people. Anyway, we'll be there for a short time, right? –

– And why would you want to help us? – he asked me with some curiosity.

– Just... I don't want him to become the creature you showed me –

– We could give it a try –

A few minutes later, we were ready. Gary seemed more excited than ever, like a real child going to a party with his school friends.

Destiny had found three hats, one for her, one for Emily, and one for me, but I gave it to Gary because he had almost no costume, except for his usual elegant clothes.

I didn't even want to look at Cedric as he joined us. Godric wore pants similar to his, but he had been kind enough to put on a long leather jacket and a golden necklace with a huge stone, as I said. And then there was Emily... She wasn't wearing a dress but a black bodysuit that didn't cover even half of her buttocks, fishnet stockings, her bright red hair like fire, loose, and the hat Destiny had given her.

– How cute, Cedric – she said with a seductive smile.

– I know – he shrugged, as his only response.

Let's go – Destiny sighed, and we left the mansion..

CHAPTER 17

I had attended the witches' party in my town many times. Since we were little, my sister and I had started the tradition of dressing up as witches every year, with pointed hats and a spider drawn on the cheek, made by our mother. Everything was the same as always. Despite being outdoors, the clock tower was considered the entrance. There were two smoke machines installed there, one at each end, releasing white vapor that was tinted with the colored lights piercing through it.

We looked like the typical group entering high school with wind-blown hair and sensational background music. Or at least, they did.

Cedric walked in the middle with disheveled hair and his torso exposed, looking like a god from Olympus crossing the earth. To his right, Godric also looked magnificent, with his dark eyes and the long wizard's jacket waving through the smoke. Emily walked with determination, the last thing she did was go unnoticed. Her orange hair waved in the wind, and her light and intense eyes pierced anyone who looked at her. Destiny, to Cedric's left, looked like a gothic princess: so elegant, graceful, and refined... She was perfection.

Behind them, Gary and I walked. Dull, we looked like two second-hand magicians. He had a deformed spider on his cheek, which I had drawn for him on the car journey. I had drawn one for myself, but I wasn't even sure if it resembled an arachnid. To top it off, when we walked through the smoke, I started coughing as if I had tuberculosis.

The group of gods turned to look at me as if I were an idiot, and finally, they resumed their march. The journey to the church was not too long, but it was difficult to advance because of the crowd in the way.

There were stalls on the sides of the street, like a fair, where they sold strange objects. Gary suddenly seemed dazzled, and although Cedric didn't want to stop, he couldn't leave him behind, so he had to wait while the boy scanned every object at each booth with his eyes.

– Godric, buy me this necklace – Destiny told her brother, pointing to something at a booth.

Without waiting for any invitation, I approached to look. It was a strip of black velvet that clung to the neck, interrupted in the center by a silver hoop.

– It's nice – I said, taking it and putting it around her neck – it will suit you.

– I know – she said, shrugging her shoulders.

– I like it too – Emily joined, and I could see the irritation in Destiny's eyes – Godric, buy one for me too.

– Forget it – Godric rolled his eyes – I'd rather buy one for the human.

To my surprise, he pointed to a similar one to the vendor, with the pendant of a half-moon, and gave it to me.

– Th...Thank you – I said on the verge of mental collapse; I couldn't believe they even gave me something, which I liked.

– How kind of Godric – Cedric approached us and looked at the other vampire with narrowed eyes.

– Look what I have! – exclaimed Gary, who had arrived at the same time as Cedric.

He raised a hand in front of us. Between his index finger and thumb, he held a tea spoon.

– Oh wow, Gary! – Emily mocked, opening her eyes wide – I've never seen a spoon...

– No, look – he denied with shining eyes.

He waved his hand up and down, and when he left it still again, the teaspoon was bent.

– That's awesome! – I said with an encouraging smile.

– You'll have to teach me how to do that – Destiny smiled at him, resting a hand on his crown.

Obviously, it was a spoon made for magic tricks. Godric and Emily didn't even bother to pretend interest and resumed the march, and for the first time, I wondered if the fact that vampires were so cruel and horrible was due to how they were treated from a young age.

– He never came to a place like this – Cedric told me, walking beside me and watching as his brother ran to another table full of objects in front of us.

– He's handling it well, he doesn't even seem to care that he's surrounded by potential food... – I said, shrugging my shoulders.

We passed by a living statue. Gary asked Cedric for money to make it move. As soon as he left it in a box at the feet of the "statue," the woman, all painted silver, started a friendly dance and left a handful of shiny plastic stars in Gary's palm.

– What nonsense – Godric said, looking at him.

– Yeah, right? – said Gary, suddenly embarrassed.

I was behind him and saw how he let go of the stars and dropped them to the ground. Without thinking, I crouched down and started picking them up.

– What are you doing? – Cedric asked me, stopping by my side.

– Later, he'll want them again, and he won't have them

– We don't have eternal life to keep plastic stars – he told me with a grimace – we don't feel like humans –

– And I suspect you don't feel because you don't want to... Maybe Gary does want to keep them –

– Wait – he said to me as I finished picking them up and stood up – What do you think you're doing? –

– Collecting...–

– No – he interrupted me with a confused expression, but trying to clarify – you're starting to doubt that we are monsters... or at least that he is...–

– You are monsters, I'm sure of that – I replied, frowning.

– Oh really? – he smiled at me smugly – but you're trying to change us. You're trying to find something good in us...–

– And is there anything good? – I asked, wrinkling my forehead and opening my eyes wide.

Then his face darkened a bit, he looked towards the others, who were still walking very calmly, and then turned his eyes back to me.

– No, there isn't. So leave us alone – he said, walking away.

Finally, we began to leave the celebration and the crowd behind. The street became quieter, and only our footsteps were heard on the slippery cobblestones.

When we reached the end of the street, we stopped in front of a church.

– We'll do things simply – Cedric began to tell us – April, you will go with Gary to knock on the door. Maybe we'll be lucky, and they won't realize he's a vampire–

I hesitated for a moment. Most likely, hunters would be waiting for us. That meant that as soon as they opened the door, they would kill Gary... Even though he was a vampire. Did I really want him to die?

– Why not Emily? – I blurted out.

Better her than Gary, right?

– Why her? – Godric inquired, raising an eyebrow.

– Because... She is very striking. Whoever opens the door will be impressed, and then they won't pay attention to the fact that she's a vampire...– I lied, trying to keep my heart rate normal.

– Why are you helping us find your sister? – she snapped, studying me with her eyes – Do you two get along so badly? –

– Last time, they attacked Destiny as soon as they opened the door and ended up tearing a man's heart out. I don't want anyone to get hurt...– that was not believable at all.

– Are you planning something? – Destiny crossed her arms.

– No – I denied, looking her in the eyes.

– We'll do what I said – Cedric interrupted us – April, Gary to the door. Ask for Aixa, if necessary, hypnotize whoever it takes–

Both of us advanced reluctantly, while the others hid in the shadows of the houses. Gary knocked on the door of the church, and both of us fell silent, waiting to hear some noise from the other side.

Finally, the door opened very slowly. A man who must have been around fifty years old looked at both of us and then smiled.

– Can I help you with something? –

– We're looking for my sister... Aixa Fontaine...– I said, looking at him intensely in the eyes, as if I could convey that something was wrong, but he simply didn't get it.

– Aixa...– he scratched his beard, thoughtfully – I think... Yes, she's here! Wait! –

My heart pounded as loudly as a machine gun. Was my sister there?

– Gary...– I tried to whisper to him, trying not to let the others hear me – please don't hurt him–

The boy gave me a strange look. Was he hesitating? I saw his nostrils widen as he breathed nervously. My hands began to sweat.

The door was still ajar... Gary was serious, and I wasn't going to risk my sister, trying to trust a vampire. I quickly stretched out a foot, ready to step inside the church, but before I could do it, someone grabbed me by the fabric of the dress and threw me backward.

– I knew you would do something stupid – I heard Cedric's voice as I felt his hand gripping me.

Right at that moment, the man who had opened the door appeared again.

– What's going on? – he asked, looking at both of us.

And then... Behind him, I saw a face, a very familiar one. My sister's.

She pushed the man away with a slap and stopped a few inches from the door, taking shelter inside that place.

– April! –

– Aixa, don't come out! – I shouted to her.

Cedric held me a little tighter while looking at her with fury.

– You better come out if you don't want me to kill your little sister! –

Aixa looked at him with hatred, with contempt; her blue eyes, darker than mine, sparkled with fire.

– They won't kill me! – I shouted to her again.

And then, it all happened very quickly. While Emily, Destiny, and Godric were preparing with Cedric, a group of guys came out of the church, armed to the teeth. They wielded stakes, wooden bows and arrows, crucifixes, and vials of holy water attached to a belt.

Aixa also came out of the church, but everything was so fast and unexpected that before Gary could move away from them, they had already smashed a vial of holy water on his head.

The boy screamed in pain as the water burned his scalp and facial skin. Using that moment of weakness, Aixa and another one of the guys grabbed him forcefully, while a third one aimed a stake at his chest.

– Don't move, or I'll kill him – the guy said, looking in our direction.

– I think you misunderstood...– Cedric said mockingly – we have the hostage, and you will do what we want–

– You can't believe we ruined your game, right? – Aixa observed him defiantly, raising her chin – let go of my sister, and we'll give you this one–

– I'm sorry, no – Cedric raised his eyebrows in a malicious smile and threw me into Destiny's arms.

She dragged me so fast that I didn't even understand what was happening to me. In an instant, my body was suspended in the air, and in the next, my feet were at the edge of the bell tower. I looked down and paled; it was really high, and Destiny was squeezing my shoulders.

– You have two minutes to return the boy, or she will fall from the bell tower, and her neck will break – I heard Cedric warning them.

– If you do that, we'll stake the boy – Aixa replied.

– Are you really going to risk proving it to me? – Cedric had a malicious gleam in his eyes.

– Do you want to prove it yourself? – she inquired, even angrier.

– Very well, it's a pity – he shrugged and stretched out an arm to get Destiny's attention – do it –

– Wait! – Aixa shouted, opening her eyes wide – Okay! Don't hurt her! –

– Very well...– Cedric reached out a hand to them – give him to me now –

– Let him go, please – she pleaded, releasing Gary's wrist.

As soon as the hunter removed the stake from his chest, the vampire ran towards Cedric and stood behind him. He turned again to Destiny and nodded. I thought he would bring me down, and he did... by pushing me off the bell tower.

I fell, like a sack of potatoes and at full speed. I heard my sister's voice screaming in horror, and the cold wind shaking me as I approached the ground.

Four meters... Three meters... Two...

Strong hands caught me. I kept my eyes closed, thinking that I would continue falling due to the force of the drop, but Cedric's strong and muscular arms held me.

It was strange, but I knew it was him even before I saw him. When I opened my eyes, he was looking at me with his unbearable sideways smile and an air of superiority.

– Did you think I would let you fall? – he whispered, so only I could hear.

I didn't have the strength to respond. My whole body was trembling from the adrenaline I had just felt, and my heart seemed to explode in my chest.

He looked up at the others who were watching us, motionless, still not understanding what had happened.

– We're leaving – he shouted to the others.

– Wait! – my sister exclaimed – let her go, I'll go with you! –

Cedric still had me in his arms; I turned my eyes to him. I wanted to beg him not to touch her, not to harm her, but he gave me a look that I couldn't decipher and smirked at Aixa.

– I'm sorry, I think I'll keep her a little longer,,,

CHAPTER 18

– What's your problem, Cedric? – Destiny roared as soon as we crossed the entrance of the mansion.

I stood in awe, watching her look at him with a savagery I hadn't seen until that moment.

– We had her! She volunteered, and you let her escape! – she continued shouting.

– I have a better idea, that's all – Cedric sighed, sitting on the arm of one of the armchairs.

– You didn't have to have a better idea! You had to follow the plan we had made! – she retorted, while Cornelius calmly descended the stairs.

– Your son, the idiot, let the hunter escape –

– Come on, he didn't let her escape – Emily interjected, looking at Cedric mockingly – he just wants to get the human first –

– I'm still here! – I reminded her, looking at her perplexed.

– Cedric? – Cornelius looked at his son inquiringly – What do you have to say? –

As a response, he took his time. He furrowed his brow as he took a cigarette and held it with his lips to light it.

– The only thing I have to say is that when I deliver the hostage, I'll make sure all the hunters who thought of defying me die bleeding – he took a drag from his cigarette, and as he exhaled smoke, he looked at me with narrowed eyes – and if she wants to have sex, there's no problem –

Destiny lunged at him with fury. Cedric fell on the couch, and she, on top of him, began punching him in the face.

– You're an idiot! This could have ended today! –

Cedric pushed her, and she went flying backward, almost colliding with me on the landing. Her eyes were red, her body tense, and her perfect black hair, slightly disheveled.

– I don't feel like being questioned; you're in my house – Cedric reminded her, getting up a few meters away from her.

– And do you think I'll shut up because this is your house? – Destiny laughed dryly, indignant – then screw this, I'm leaving, and we'll discuss it outside, where I have freedom of speech –

– Stop, both of you – Cornelius' voice interrupted them, cold and serious – no one will leave, and no one will discuss it outside – he said, approaching Destiny – you have every right to be angry, all of you. Our house is very proud and vengeful, and I regret to say that I have passed this on to Cedric. I can't blame him for wanting to kill a group of hunters; they're just disgusting – he said very calmly.

– She has to die. And the faster, the better –

– This is stupid! Who says something like that? Well, I do... – They could put aside revenge, and it would just be over –

– Did anyone ask for your opinion? I don't remember – Emily scoffed, tilting her head as if she didn't understand.

– We didn't ask for yours either – Godric retorted, giving her a threatening look.

Cornelius pinched the bridge of his nose between his index and thumb, searching for patience somewhere within him.

– This is not revenge – Destiny turned towards me – it would be nice to kill your sister just for fun, but this goes beyond –

– I don't understand... –

I heard Emily muttering something under her breath, but I couldn't understand what she said.

– Your stupid sister killed one of ours. There is a possibility of bringing him back to life, but for that, we need her blood –

– What? Wait... You can't bring someone back... –

– No, if I already said she's stupid – Emily rolled her eyes, and before anyone could respond, she started going up the stairs.

– It can and will be done – Godric replied, pushing a strand of his long hair, which fell over his face.

– Are you sure it was her? – I asked, feeling my legs turn to jelly.

It felt very strange. Once again, doubt lingered in my head. I had thought they wanted revenge, that they didn't mind shedding blood just for pleasure, but there they were. They intended to kill her, yes, but it was to resurrect someone important to them. Wouldn't I have wanted to do the same for my parents or Aixa?

– Is there no other way? – I said, looking at all of them.

– No, there isn't – Cedric replied, lighting another cigarette – I'm sorry, Destiny – he said, exchanging a glance with the vampire.

– Go to hell – she replied, walking away to her room.

– She'll get over it – Godric sighed – but we had a plan, Ced... Was it that hard to follow it? –

Cedric gave me a quick look and then turned his gaze back to his friend.

– You're right, I'm sorry –

– Now, son, I hope you find a way to kill the hunters. We need to try not to lose any of us along the way –

Cornelius shrugged with disinterest and went back upstairs to his study.

– We can't attack while there are so many things against us. It's likely that next time there will be more, and they'll be waiting for us – Godric reclined in the free chair and took off his shoes with his feet.

– I'll see what I can come up with – Cedric sighed, smoking calmly – I'll check the library to see if I find anything –

I didn't want to pay attention to either of them. Now that I knew their reasons, I hated them even more because despite the means they used to achieve their goals being wrong, they were trying to save someone, and it angered me that I couldn't blame them.

I approached Gary, who was very silent by the door, and I held out my closed fist to him.

– Here – I said and released the party stars onto his palm.

His eyes gleamed for a moment, but that feeling quickly faded. He nodded without saying anything and put them in his pocket.

The next day, I woke up around noon. I quickly ate something and started looking for the weapons that Daniel had asked me to find.

Not only did I need to get them as part of the plan, but I also needed to have them in my hands, a reminder of why I hated those monsters and that I only had to think about destroying them.

According to what he had told me, they kept them as trophies. Which one of them had already killed a vampire hunter? Gary was ruled out. He had been caught too easily. Cornelius was the oldest, but he was too terrifying; I was scared even thinking about entering his room and being discovered. Destiny was the second oldest. She was irascible, somewhat violent, and hated humans. I was sure she had killed at least a dozen.

I mustered courage and climbed the stairs, wearing the dress she had lent me the night before. If she woke up, my excuse would be that I had come to return it.

I opened the door to her room very slowly. I tiptoed inside and closed it behind me. As soon as I turned, I looked towards her bed and almost had a heart attack. She was sitting, looking at me.

– What are you doing here? – she asked me, her face strange.

– I came to return the dress – I blurted out quickly – Why are you awake? –

Goodbye, the only chance to search her room...

– I don't know – she said, furrowing her brow and running a hand over her forehead.

That gesture seemed casual but wasn't. Destiny was drenched in sweat, her lips were somewhat dry.

– Are you okay? – I asked, approaching her a little.

– I don't know... No – she continued sweating.

She got up abruptly from the bed.

– I'll take a shower – saying this, she left her room without even looking at me.

She was unwell, there was no doubt about it. A little over a week ago, she had started consuming verbena... Could it be that?

For a moment, I stood planted in the middle of the room, wondering if it was really my fault. Anyway, that didn't matter, did it? They were vampires, to hell with them.

I left her dress at the foot of the bed and decided it was time to look for the weapons in her room. I opened the wardrobe, quickly moved her clothes, rummaged through her shoes and some closed boxes, but there were only papers and dusty ornaments.

I walked to her bedside table, opened the drawers, rummaged through them trying to make as little noise as possible, but there was nothing there either.

I got down on my knees on the floor and looked under the bed. Nothing. I moved the only picture hanging on one of the walls, but there was no secret hiding place behind it.

I clicked my tongue in frustration and left her room. If she had weapons, they weren't there.

In the hallway, I crossed paths with her again. She was wearing a dark towel tied around her chest, and although she looked a bit haggard, she seemed to feel better.

– Are you okay now? – I asked her, stopping in front of her.

– Do you care? – she asked, furrowing her brow.

Yes, she was definitely better. I passed by her and continued down the hall until I entered the other corridor. I went to the library, entered, and then I jumped, again.

Cedric was there.

– Did everyone wake up early today or what? – I asked him, confused.

He completely ignored me and kept flipping through the pages of a volume with yellowed sheets.

– What are you reading? – I asked again.

– I said it yesterday – he sighed without looking away from the book – I'm looking for a way to kill all the hunters –

– Oh well... – I said, biting my lip.

– Are you going to help me? – he asked, finally lifting his gaze.

He didn't look good. Like Destiny, he was tired, still disheveled, and seemed stressed.

– Yes, of course. I'll start looking with you right away – I mocked sarcastically and walked towards the chair in front of the table where he was working.

He offered me his cigarette box, and I shook my head.

– Good girl – he said, smiling at me.

– Did you get any sleep? You look terrible – I pointed out with a grimace.

– Are you worried about me? – he said maliciously, his eyes gleaming.

– No, I'm not interested –

– Of course you are; you got nervous when I asked you to draw the lines on my chest yesterday –

– I'm sorry; vampires are not my style – I shrugged, pretending to look at one of the books on the table.

– And what is your style? Boring, mediocre, and easy-to-kill humans? –

– It's none of your business – I shrugged, and he leaned a bit forward, pressing his palms on the table and looking me straight in the eyes.

– Yes, it is. I'm curious – he said very calmly – the offer I made you yesterday about having sex was true... –

Dear universe, have mercy on me. My heart skipped a beat.

– Well, no – I denied, holding his gaze – pass–

Cedric smiled amused by something that evidently only he understood and leaned back, sitting down again.

I stood up, determined to ignore him and find some interesting reading in the library.

CHAPTER 19

It was around nine in the evening when Cedric decided to close the book he had been reading for hours. He looked up, somewhat tired, and glanced at me.

– Get ready, we're going out – he said, standing up.

– Are we going back to the church? – I asked, feeling the blood drain from my face.

– No, the two of us are going out – he clarified, pointing at both of us.

I opened my mouth to reply, but he was already leaving the library. Well, I didn't have anything better to do anyway. I had read all day, and they didn't seem to have many entertainments other than preparing for the stupid social presentation. I went to my room, put on the same tight jeans I wore the day I was kidnapped, a dark and tight T-shirt that left my shoulders bare, and a pair of laced boots that Destiny had lent me. I looked at the necklace Godric had given me, on my bedside table, and finally decided to wear it. I went down the stairs. He was waiting for me below and offered me his hand with exaggerated elegance, as if he were a gentleman.

– Spare me the good guy act – I asked, rolling my eyes and passing by him without taking his hand – What are we going to do?

– Have fun – he replied, snapping his fingers, and Peter appeared with a coat in his arms.

Cedric took it; it was blood-red, thigh-length, and with a warm hood. I thought he would put it on, even though he already wore a leather jacket. However, with a disinterested gesture, he slid it over my shoulders and opened the door for me to pass.

This was getting stranger and stranger... Peter came out with us, disappeared into the darkness, and a few seconds later appeared in front of the entrance, driving the limousine.

– What's this about? – I asked when we were both seated inside.

– I don't know what you're talking about... – he gave me a sly smile that made me want to slap him.

– You're being nice and taking me out of the stupid house –

– I was bored – he shrugged – that's all –

I remained silent and looked him over. Ripped jeans at the knees, braided boots, a black shirt with the top buttons undone, and a leather jacket. His brown hair was perfectly combed to one side again, and his face was immaculate, with no trace of a beard. Besides, he filled the air with the citrusy and woody perfume he had applied.

Twenty minutes of silence later, we got out of the car. He offered me his arm, and I didn't take it. Come on, he was very attractive, but he was a vampire and had me kidnapped – we weren't friends either.

We stopped in front of a fairly small place. Outside, it had neon Japanese letters that blinked a bit. He opened the door and let me in. Inside, the place was dimly lit, with a bar on one side, overflowing with people taking turns to order. There were some small square tables against the walls, with high stools.

– What is this place? – I asked, quite confused.

– The paradise of Japanese food – he said, putting a hand on my back to make me move with him.

– And what are we doing here? –

While we were in the car, I had imagined going to a church, a cemetery, or an abandoned castle. That place was... Very human, simple, and pleasant for hanging out.

We sat at a small table against a column. An oriental waitress smiled ear to ear at us and handed each of us a menu.

– Have you tried Japanese food? – he asked me while opening his menu and flipping through the pages.

– No... – I said, reading all the strange names that appeared there.

– I'll make it easy for you – he said, pointing with his finger to one of the dishes – if you like chicken, you can order this one, it's very good –

– Well... I guess I can trust you at least to choose the food – I shrugged and closed the menu, intertwining my hands on the table – Are you going to tell me what all this is? –

Cedric ignored me and signaled the waitress to come over. He ordered two "chaw mien," two Coca Colas, and also two measures of sake.

– Look, I don't know anything about Japanese food, but as I understand it, sake is alcohol –

– And? – he said, looking at me challengingly.

– You don't need to get me drunk; you can just tell me what you want, and that's it... Anyway, you're good at hypnotizing me –

– I'm not going to do it today – he shrugged, leaning back in the chair and looking at me with a devilish smile – I'm sure I won't need it –

Around us, there was low rock music, along with the laughter of everyone crowded at the bar, pushing each other aside.

The food arrived very quickly. In white cardboard boxes, they handed us the chaw mien, along with some Chinese chopsticks that I had no idea how to use. Cedric took them very calmly and took the first bite of the fried noodles. He brought them to his mouth and chewed animatedly until he realized that I was trying to figure out how to hold them.

– It's not very difficult – he said, showing me his hand and how he held them securely between his fingers..

– Yes, well, it's easy for someone with a hundred years of experience... – I sighed as I picked up one, and the other slipped away.

– You're clumsy – he sighed, trying to hide a smile – I'll ask for utensils for you.

He asked the waitress for a fork, but she explained that they didn't have that kind of utensils. However, she offered me something else, something even more embarrassing than asking for a fork in an oriental food place. It was a small blue plastic square with two notches, and she explained that the Chinese chopsticks could be placed there as "help" to eat more normally. I followed her instructions, feeling ridiculous and clumsy, and started to eat.

– Now you look like a five-year-old – Cedric laughed again.

– Yes, very funny... – I sighed, rolling my eyes.

There, far from his luxurious mansion, his cold father, and his group of followers, he even seemed human. He didn't maintain the same cold elegance as when he dined with the others at home, nor did he sit as straight as when he settled into the limousine... He was normal.

– I need your help – he finally said after eating more than half of his noodles.

– You finally say it – I said as I opened my can of Coca-Cola and took a long sip – What do you want?

– You're good with Gary, I've noticed... – he said, running a hand through his hair.

– Was he nervous? Did it cost him so much to ask for a favor?

– I had never seen him so happy as at the fair... Doing, I don't know, childish human things –

– But you know he's not a child, really –

– Of course, yes, he's a monster like all of us, right? – he sighed, stirring his chaw mien absentmindedly – And are you better than all of us?

I was about to tell him yes. But was that true? I remembered what I had felt seeing Destiny sick from the vervain... I despised them because they killed humans, but I wanted to kill them.

– Maybe we're not as monstrous as you thought – he said, as if reading my thoughts.

– Of course they are; they want to kill my sister; I won't forget that –

– Listen, I want your help for Gary to learn to control himself. He needs to manage to stop thinking about blood, to feel something more than just the pressure of restraining himself all the time –

– Let's see... – I frowned and crossed my arms over my chest – You're going to leave me without a sister, but I have to help you so you don't lose yours? – I asked mockingly.

– But that's what you wanted – he said, becoming serious – you were the one who wanted to save him in the first place. It was your idea to take him to the party yesterday; he didn't even ask you. But you were right; it worked, and maybe you can do something more –

– No – I was irritated – I'm not going to help you so that later you retract and kill her –

– Then I propose a deal – I took a bite of noodles into my mouth and chewed while still looking at him – your sister for my brother –

– And what does that mean? – I asked confused.

– It means that if you manage to get my brother under control, I will make sure no one touches your sister –

– Of course, and at the right time, I suppose Destiny will kill you, and then she will kill her. You won't betray her –

– The vampire we want to revive was my friend, but if I have to choose between my brother and him, I choose my brother –

– And the others? –

– I'll find another way... I'll find something to resurrect my friend without killing Aixa. That's what I've been looking for all day –

– You lied to them, didn't you? – I said suddenly lighting up – you said you stayed with me because you preferred to have time and kill all the hunters –

– You caught me – he said, shrugging with a sigh – I preferred to stay with you before trading you because I realized you can help Gary –

– If I agree... We'll first have to find another way to resurrect that vampire. I'm not going to try to save Gary just for you to back out later and kill her –

– Very well, then we'll need a witch – Cedric smiled at me and raised the sake shot to toast – come on, April, seal the deal – he said sarcastically.

I raised my shot, we clinked glasses, and both drank it in one go. I felt the liquid burn my throat. It wasn't as disgusting as tequila, but it was very strong.

– Tomorrow, all the vampire families will come. It's the last day I have to have fun, and then it will all be about helping Gary, talking to witches, and dealing with you, so... – he said as he took off his jacket because of the warmth of the drink – let's order more –

I didn't refuse. I didn't feel like it. I had a new spark of hope within me, and it had just ignited.

We approached the bar. Cedric, with his nonexistent patience, pushed half of the guys crowding there and pulled my wrist to get me closer too. We ordered two more shots and then two more. On the fourth, Cedric was smiling, and for once, it wasn't a smug, annoying, or seductive smile; he was just doing it because he felt like it. Finally, he bought a bottle, and we settled back at the table.

– Let's play something – he said with bright eyes and a small lock of hair in his eyes.

I blame the drunkenness of the moment as a justification for reaching out to him again and putting the lock back in place.

– What's the game? – I asked, laughing, without knowing why.

– Once each, we'll ask each other questions; if the other answers, the one who asked drinks, if not, the one questioned drinks –

– I don't want to ask you things – I said squinting like an idiot.

– Well, now that we're allies, I do – he said, and I saw a devilish look in his eyes.

– Start – I said as I poured a shot of sake.

– Do you want to sleep with me? – he said with a sideways smile.

– No. Drink – I said, sliding the shot across the table in his direction.

– It's not fair to lie, April – he said, biting his lip.

– It's the truth. I don't want to do it – I laughed a bit, feeling dizzy – Why did you choose Japanese food?

– Is that what you're going to ask? – he said, furrowing his brow.

– Come on, answer – I demanded as he began to pour a measure of sake for me.

– I like to travel, and of all the trips I've taken, Japanese food fascinated me the most – he handed me the drink, and I drank it a bit disgusted.

– How cultured... – was all I said.

– I'm going – he smiled at me – Godric or me?

– Your questions are stupid – I laughed – your dad –

– What??? – Cedric opened his eyes wide, and I started laughing as if having an epilepsy attack.

– Cornelius is very sexy – I laughed.

– Really? – he wrinkled his face – he's my father...

– And he looks the same age as you. That's quite weird – I shrugged – You, Godric looks like a girl with his long hair, shinier than mine – Cedric was satisfied and drank his shot. Did he want spicy questions? Well, I'd give them to him.

– What's going on between Emily and you? – I asked, pouring myself a shot and drinking it in advance.

Cedric snorted a bit, as if talking about it was stressful.

– Pass –

– You're not going to pass – I refused – I already drank the shot –

– You did it on purpose to force me to answer – he said, narrowing his eyes – very well – he poured himself a shot and drank it to gather courage – I was very much in love with her when I met her. She was Peter's human daughter, sixteen years old, and we liked each other right away. We were boyfriends until she turned nineteen and asked me to turn her to spend an eternity of love and unicorns. I did it, and as soon as she learned to control her blood thirst, she left me –

– What? – I asked, opening my eyes wide and drinking for his tragic story.

– That's right. The bitch used me for years just for me to turn her. I argued with my father, tarnished the family name by creating a hybrid, and it was all for nothing –

– Oh – I said, placing a hand on my heart – they hurt poor Ced's heart –

– You're an idiot – he sighed, rolling his eyes, while I laughed at him.

– It's my turn to ask. Tell me about a romantic failure of yours – he asked, pouring himself another shot.

– Hmm... I fell in love with a two-hundred-year-old vampire named Cornelius, but I think I'm going to kill him – I said, laughing, and he rolled his eyes again.

Sorry, I had discovered how to horrify him, and I had to take advantage of it to the fullest.

– I don't know – I said, wiping a tear from laughter, while everything began to spin – I've never been too interested in those things... –

– Wait... Are you a virgin? –

HA, if he was expecting the sweet and virginal human girl, he was very wrong. Well... I had sex only once; I wasn't very experienced, but...

– No – I smiled at him – you wish. Hey, since you're paying, I'll order another bottle – I said, standing up.

The alcohol hit me all at once. The room spun quickly, and I collapsed to the floor.

– It's better if we go home – I heard Cedric's voice as I tried to get up and fell to the ground again.

– Are you going to get up, or are you going to sleep here? – his voice sounded distant.

Was I looking at him? Oh no, I had my forehead against the sticky floor. Cedric grabbed me tightly and held me by the waist so that I wouldn't fall again.

I rested my head on his chest, while everything kept spinning. I tried to focus on moving my feet at his pace. Uff, his shirt smelled too good. What if I unbuttoned one? Would he get angry?

– What are you doing, April? – he asked, containing his laughter.

Apparently, while I was thinking, I had already unbuttoned one.

– I already figured out how you lost your virginity – he laughed.

I don't know when we went through the main door. Did Cedric pay?

– If we left without paying, we should run – I said, opening my eyes wide.

– Yeah yeah... – he sighed – whatever you say –

– You're annoying –

– You're clumsy, and you don't know how to drink – he seemed to be laughing, but I wasn't sure.

At some point, I felt like I was lifted off the ground and put into the limousine, which I didn't know when it had appeared.

– Wait! – I exclaimed, hitting my head on the window – we bought another bottle and didn't drink it –

– You fell before ordering it, April... –

If he said anything else, I didn't notice. I closed my eyes and fell asleep, sprawled on the seat..

CHAPTER 20

– April, open your eyes, come on...–

I mumbled something nonsensical and stirred a bit.

– Come on, April, I need you to be awake for two seconds...–

I opened my eyes, feeling heavy eyelids, and focused on a face near me.

Cedric was shaking me a bit by the shoulders, looking frustrated. It was dark around us... We were still in the limousine.

I managed to sit up in the seat and looked at him.

– I need you to walk on your own to the entrance, and then you can crawl on the floor if you want – he asked, running his fingers through his hair.

– Sure...– I nodded, feeling my stomach churn, and things started to spin around me again.

Cedric helped me out of the limousine and held me as we slowly made our way down the gravel path.

– Can you do it? – he asked me in a low voice, probably so that it couldn't be heard from inside.

I nodded as a response. He studied me for a moment, buttoned my coat, and smoothed my hair a bit, which was quite disheveled. He turned the key in the lock, and we entered as quietly as possible.

– It seems you finally deign to appear – Cornelius stood in front of us and glared at his son – Where did you go? You can't just take her away; the idea was to keep her here –

– I needed some fresh air, and I took her for a walk – Cedric replied, huffing – calm down, we're back, and we're both safe –

– I don't like disobedience – his father reminded him, frowning.

– Well, I'm a hundred years old... It's time you get used to it, right? –

– Oh, let them be...– Emily stood up, rising from the couch where she had been watching us – it seems Ced is desperate and needed a date with someone –

– That's not true – he said, rolling his eyes – I wanted to have fun; we'll have three days of pure ceremonies and elegance –

– Whatever – Cornelius seemed really upset – I need to talk to you alone. Emily, April, please go to your rooms –

Emily shrugged and started to climb the stairs to her room. I understood what Cornelius was saying, but I couldn't take another step without falling.

– Go to your room, come on...– Cedric said, clearing his throat.

I nodded, while my stomach shook, and saliva began to accumulate in my mouth.

– April? – he placed a hand on my back as an incentive to obey him.

I raised my head, looked at Cornelius, and unable to avoid it... I vomited on his shoes.

– Get her out of my sight! – the furious vampire shouted.

– Sorry, Dad, we'll talk later – Cedric seemed to want to laugh, but he didn't.

He slid an arm around my waist, and I grabbed him by the neck to be able to walk. We didn't go upstairs; we walked towards one of the doors on the ground floor and entered.

It was a fairly large bathroom, but I couldn't see too many details. I collapsed on the toilet and began to vomit everything I had drunk, while tears streamed down my eyes from the retching.

– For God's sake, April! I'll never make you drink again –

– Help me – I asked him with a choked voice.

– Vomit for you? – he laughed.

Of course... After all, he was a vampire; he had no idea what it was like to deal with humans, or at least not with a drunken one who needed help.

– Hold my... – I vomited again before finishing the sentence, but apparently, he understood.

Carefully, he crouched down next to me and took my hair with one hand, gently pushing the strands away from my face.

I stayed in that position for a while longer until I felt I was only spitting bile. Then, he lifted me carefully and washed my face with cold water.

– Ready? – he sighed, handing me a towel that slipped from my hands.

He picked it up with a sigh and sat me on the toilet lid to dry my face himself.

– I'm sleepy – I mumbled as my eyes closed on their own.

– And now I have to deal with my father and his stupid sermons because of you – he put the towel aside and effortlessly picked me up, holding me in his arms.

He opened the door, left the bathroom with me on his back, and finally, I fell asleep.

The next day, I woke up with a terrible headache. I was dressed like the night before, but Cedric had taken off my shoes and covered me with a heavy gray blanket.

I got up, took a bath, and went downstairs. The main hall was in complete chaos. There were vases full of red roses, human employees scurrying around finalizing details, and stylists who had been there for days with suits and dresses, going up and down the stairs beside me.

I finished going down and headed to the kitchen. Everyone was there, drinking calmly from blood bags.

I looked at them and finally decided to sit on the only available stool, next to Godric.

– It seems you were partying last night... Destiny said, looking at me amused.

– You could say that...– I replied, scratching my forehead and looking at Cedric guiltily.

– And it will be the first and last time. When she drinks, she's even more unbearable – she said, winking at me and finishing her last sip of blood.

– Are there any aspirins? – I asked them with a grimace, and everyone seemed amused by my pitiful situation, except Emily.

They pointed out that there were some in the first aid kit, so I went to get one and swallowed it with a glass of water.

– So, April...– Destiny cleared her throat to get my attention – despite your sorry state, today you'll have to be at the party... In fact, you'll have to be there for all three days.

– How? – I asked, blinking as if it were very difficult to understand.

– We're not going to risk them finding out that we have a kidnapped human in the mansion, so you'll pretend to be the donor for the Leblanc family–

– And the rest won't want to bite me? – I asked, confused.

– No– Destiny denied– the first two days, every vampire house has its own donors–

– It's just for precaution. They don't want to risk hosts or any other vampire feeding the donors with vervain or holy water to weaken you–

– Why would anyone do that? – I asked, furrowing my brow.

– So that you lose in cricket matches– Godric replied, shrugging– drinking blood with vervain or holy water weakens us–

I felt that something was wrong... Something was very wrong, and it was my fault. I had given them vervain all week. Did that mean they would lose the matches? Would it make them look bad in front of all the vampires?

I swallowed hard; guilt felt like a heavy stone placed on my head. I had been weakening them all these days with the idea that they would be weak to face my sister, but... I had never planned to sabotage them, and I didn't even know if that made me happy.

– Relax– Emily mocked, seeing my face– no one is going to bite you these days; that's why we're drinking this horrible bagged blood now–

– In fact... I think it would be very strange for her to be a donor and not even have a bite mark– Godric reminded them.

They fell silent for a fraction of a second, and then everything happened very quickly. Godric leaned over me, with invisible speed, and I felt a pinch on my neck. I let out a surprised groan and opened my eyes wide. Everyone was just as surprised as I was, seeing what he had just done.

– What are you doing? – Cedric shouted, sparks flying from his eyes.

He lunged at Godric and pulled him off me. He slammed him forcefully against the floor, knocking him off his stool with a loud crash, and started punching him in the face.

I was too shocked. Blood started to ooze warmly from my neck, and I tried to stop it with the palm of my hand, staining it red.

– Stop! – Emily ran towards them and pulled Cedric to move him away from the other vampire.

– What's your problem, Cedric? – Godric shouted angrily, blood streaming from his nose and mouth– Someone had to do it. Did you want to do it yourself? –

– No one had to do it! – he replied, almost spitting out the words as he resisted the urge to lunge at him again– You're an idiot! –

– Cedric, calm down– Destiny exclaimed– Godric was right; it was very strange not to notice even a bite mark–

– He doesn't have to touch her! – he yelled.

Godric laughed maliciously as he wiped his nose with the back of his hand.

– Why is it a problem for you? – he taunted with gleaming eyes– well, let me tell you that her blood is delicious– he turned to leave the kitchen, and as he walked away, he spoke again– I've never tasted anything like it.

CHAPTER 21

When the vampires began to arrive, a chill ran down my spine. I had seen them, I had met them, I knew they weren't as terrifying as they had been described to me, but being an unarmed human inside a mansion filled with hundreds of vampires was still terrifying.

The vampires arrived in groups, probably divided according to the house they belonged to. The women wore long dresses that reached the floor, even covering their shoes. They looked more majestic than the other. They exposed their pale skin with pronounced necklines, bare necks, and hair tied up or curled, cascading delicately.

I stood next to Cornelius, who seemed very calm, with a glass of bubbly champagne between his fingers. Each group that entered approached to greet him, and they didn't even seem to notice my presence.

Before the dance began, I had been asked to put on a simple dark blue velvet dress that hugged my waist and then fell loose a few inches above the knees. It was supposed to be the Leblanc family's color, and as their donor, I was supposed to wear it.

In the background, a piano played a calm and elegant melody, like the entire party. No one danced; they only drank, laughed occasionally, covering their lips with their hands, or whispered while indiscreetly watching others.

– I need you to stay here for a moment. I'll go introduce the new vampires– Cornelius asked, and I nodded.

The vampire left, approaching the foot of the stairs. There, Peter handed him a rather thick envelope, and he opened it carefully. He tapped a microphone a few times, as if everyone there didn't have an all-powerful ear to hear him, even if he spoke softly, and began:

– Welcome to these three days of celebration where we honor the new members of the vampire community. It's an honor to receive you in my abode, and I hope you feel very comfortable– everyone applauded him for his wonderful hospitality.

I rolled my eyes; I hated that everything was so formal and boring. Couldn't they stop talking and just dance or have champagne? The answer was a resounding "no."

Cornelius began to call out one by one to all the new vampires. As they heard their names, they descended the mansion's wide staircase, which had been covered with a fiery red carpet.

– They're so pretentious– I heard a voice behind me.

Daniel was behind me. He had slightly tousled blond hair, a annoyed expression on his face, and was dressed in a white suit with a wine-colored tie.

– How elegant, you look like a cake topper– I said with a grimace.

– Thanks, April, you look good...– he sighed– By the way, thanks for telling Cedric that I wanted to offer myself as a donor for the event... Destiny's family, the Briands, were very happy to drag me here–

– Well, I had to say something, I'm sorry– I said as he took two glasses of pink champagne from a waiter's tray.

– Want some? – he offered me one.

– Actually... I still have a hangover; it's better if I don't– I said, feeling nauseous just smelling the alcohol.

– Well, more for me– he smiled, taking a sip of his glass– I'll need several when I have to be the appetizer for all the Briands–

Among the vampires, it was Gordic's turn. He appeared in a navy blue suit and a white shirt. He began to descend the stairs with a proud smile, amidst the applause of all the vampires who seemed to adore him. For me, he was just an idiot who had bitten me by surprise.

– Am I the only one who finds it horrifying that parents and children look the same age? – I asked as I saw Godric joining his parents and Destiny at the foot of the stairs.

– It's disgusting, another example that they're just monsters– Daniel said with disdain.

– Yeah, disgusting...– as I said those words, Cedric appeared at the top of the stairs, and a part of me wanted to wash my mouth for what I had just said.

How was it possible that a creature like that could be so horrible? He descended the stairs seriously, wearing his black suit and the purple shirt I had indicated he should wear. The clothes clung to his body, and his dark shoes shone as he descended each step. He had his hair styled to the side, and his eyes looked straight ahead, with that bluish-purple color that... Did I like? HA, impossible.

– Hey, maybe we should go outside; I have some things to ask you– Daniel said, bringing me back to reality.

– Cornelius asked me to stay here...– I said while tucking a strand of white hair behind my ear.

– And why would you obey? – he was right.

Without even checking if anyone was watching us, we walked to the kitchen and finally went out into the garden through the back door. The night was cold and dark. The moon shone in its waning crescent, and countless stars were visible.

– So, April, have you found the weapons I mentioned? – he asked, burying his hands in his pockets.

– Not yet, sorry... I've searched for them, but I don't think they have them in their room–

– Well, it's a very large house– he nodded– I'm sure they don't hide them because they display them proudly. You should look if there's a room where they are in plain sight–

– Something like a trophy room? – I asked, clicking my tongue.

– Of course, they have enough space to have a place like that–

– You're right... Hey– I said looking at him directly– we went to one of the churches where you said my sister wouldn't be, but when we got there, she was there–

– I know...– he sighed, scratching his forehead– I told her I would have a group of hunters waiting for the vampires and you, but as soon as I mentioned you, she wanted to go to the church, she wants to save you, she's quite desperate– he explained– what I don't understand is why Cedric didn't want to make the exchange when he had the chance–

– About that... Listen– I cleared my throat– maybe there's a way for no one to get hurt. I talked to him. They wanted to kill Aixa to revive a vampire she killed, but now he wants to find another way to revive him if I help his brother in return–

– April, no– he said, placing his hands on my shoulders and looking me straight in the eyes– we're vampire hunters, we kill them, we don't make deals with them–

– Sure, I know, but... Maybe they're not as bad as we think– I said feeling ashamed for defending them– maybe we think they are very different from us, but in reality, we could coexist...–

– Don't go on– he asked me– listen, they are creatures similar to us, but you must remember that they are not the same. Their first instinct is to kill humans; they don't want peaceful coexistence with us, they just want our blood– he sighed– if they didn't need you, they would have killed you already. They would have killed Aixa...–

– But maybe not all of them are the same–

– Of course they are, April. They are vampires. They are monsters. Everything about them attracts us: their scent, their appearance, their voice... They are predators, and they only see us as their prey, as stupid blood bags or servants–

I remembered Godric, biting me without any hesitation, just not to be looked down upon by others like them. I remembered Emily sticking glass shards into my hand, Destiny despising me with her words, Cornelius forcing me to watch as they drank from the donor... They were not good; that was not human at all.

– You're right... I'm sorry– I said, lowering my gaze.

– I know it's difficult to live with them. They will try to manipulate you in a thousand possible ways, but always remember, they are not your friends. I am, and I will remind you of that every time I can– he said, lifting my face by the chin and giving me a genuine smile– relax, we'll get you out of here–

– We should go back before they realize we're not here– I said, starting to walk towards the house.

Daniel nodded, and we went back inside.

In the main hall, the vampires had finished descending the stairs and introducing themselves. Some had started to dance with each other. I scanned the dance floor. Gary was dancing with a beautiful vampire girl. She had a blood-red spaghetti strap dress, skin as white as snow, and a bunch of cute coppery curls. However, he didn't seem too excited; they probably forced him to invite her to dance.

Then my eyes stopped at another couple. Cedric was dancing with... Emily? The cunning woman looked incredible, wearing a sweetheart neckline dress with bare shoulders. The top was tight against her body, with black lace flowers. The lower part below the waist was a mix of gray tones, flowing with her dance steps. I hated her a bit, just for looking so good. Just for that, not because she was dancing with Cedric; after all, if he was foolish enough to want to be hurt again, it was none of my business.

– Could you allow me a dance? – a guy stopped in front of me.

I looked at him strangely; he was a vampire who had reached his maximum growth age. His hair was almost as white as mine, combed back and tied in a short ponytail.

He wore a black suit with a tail and silver embroidery, giving him a majestic air. His eyes were honey-colored, large and hard; there was something strange about him, something as chilling as Cornelius or more.

– Is that allowed? – I asked, raising my eyebrows and blinking as if I were stupid.

– Of course, whatever I want is allowed– he said with a fake smile.

He extended a hand, and I couldn't help but take it. I could feel the eyes of most present on us, and that only made my heartbeat faster.

– How rude, I haven't introduced myself– he said as he placed a hand on my waist and took my palm with the other– my name is Thomas Dumont, and you are...? –

– April Fontaine– I said, swallowing difficultly. What was all this about? –

– And tell me, April, haven't we met before? – he whispered.

– I don't think so– I said, squinting my eyes to look at him – Why? –

– I don't know... It's just that you seem very familiar to me– he bit his lip, scrutinizing me as we continued moving to the rhythm of the music.

– So, did you ask me to dance just because I seem familiar to you? – I couldn't buy that– Couldn't you have just asked me? –

– Of course, but then I couldn't have done this– in a quick movement of his hand, he pulled me to lift my arm to the level of his face.

He rested his nose on my skin and closed his eyes to smell me. What the hell?

– What's wrong with you? – I exclaimed, taking my hand away from his.

– You're not human, right? Your scent is... Incredible...–

– Excuse me, Thomas– Cedric's firm voice cut between us, and he placed a hand on my shoulder– the song ended. Do you mind if I dance with her? –

– Of course– Thomas looked at him with a tense smile and then fixed his gloomy eyes on me– pleasure to meet you, April Fontaine–

Cedric quickly pulled me away from him; his hands firmly held my waist, and I placed my hand on his shoulder as we held each other with the other.

– What were you doing dancing with him? – he asked with a furrowed brow.

– He asked me to. Who the hell is he? – I replied, also annoyed.

– Thomas Dumont is the most powerful vampire in the entire room. He's even the leader of our Council–

– And why did he want to dance with a donor? – I asked, looking at him with narrowed eyes– it doesn't make sense...–

– I have no idea... What did he tell you? –

– That I'm not human... Is he an idiot? Of course, I am! –

– Of course, you are... He was probably speaking in a double entendre– he said calmly, though twisting his face a bit to look at him once again– by the way, the color of my family suits you very well–

– Yeah, right– I said, rolling my eyes– lucky you didn't wear khaki, you would have looked really ugly–

– Any color looks good on me– he said as he made me spin and then took me by the waist again to press me against his body– but you already know that..

CHAPTER 22

The next day, I woke up much better. The hangover and stomachache were gone. What remained, however, was a feeling of horrible discomfort, knowing that in all the adjoining rooms, there were hungry vampires eager to smell and bite me.

Someone knocked softly on my door. I opened it. Gary stood in front of me with a furrowed brow. I let him in, and he handed me a stack of freshly ironed clothes.

– It seems that now I'm also a servant of the house– he grumbled– Peter is very busy, and my father asked me to give you this–

– What is it? – I said as I took it.

– Clothes with the house colors for today– he pointed, shrugging.

– Great– I said as I unfolded a dark blue hoodie, leggings, and a woolen hat– I'll look like a smurf–

– A what? – he asked, wrinkling his forehead.

– You know... Those blue cartoons–

– But this clothes is blue...– he looked at me as if I were stupid, and I sighed, annoyed.

– I get it, better no jokes with you... It's evident you don't have an ounce of humor–

– Your jokes are stupid and inconsistent– he grumbled.

– Fine– I sighed– Can you leave? I'm going to change...–

Before I could say anything else, Gary had already left my room. I put on all the outfits he had given me. I looked ridiculous, and the woolen hat was too big for my head, so it easily slipped off.

When I left the room and went to the bathroom, I headed to the kitchen to find something to eat. However, I found it packed with chefs peeling and chopping vegetables, sautéing food, and taking huge trays out of the oven. The aroma of all that enveloped me, making my mouth water.

– Out of the kitchen– a woman ordered me, dressed in a white chef's jacket and a very tall chef's hat– you will eat with the others–

– Mmm… Okay– I sighed, turning back.

As I turned around, I met Cornelius. He was wearing a loose blue T-shirt, black sweatpants, and a sun hat that wasn't needed at that hour.

– April, with me– he ordered as he unhooked a bag from his shoulder and handed it to me without interest.

I took it as best I could and followed him to the backyard. Everything was ready there. There were some metal stands for the spectators, and in the ground, the cricket wickets were nailed, which the cricket ball had to knock down.

– It seems like you caught the attention of many people yesterday– Cornelius suddenly said, glancing at me without stopping his walk.

– It wasn't really my intention– I quickly tried to clarify– I don't know why Thomas asked me to dance…–

– Well, I don't know either. And I don't know how you managed to make my son decide to dance with you–

– I think… I think he just wanted to keep Thomas away…– I said, clearing my throat– he seemed to want to bite me–

– And then? – he asked, pointing to the stands, signaling me to leave the bag he had given me– even if Thomas wanted to drink from our donor, I don't find a reason for my son to challenge him and push him away–

– I guess he wanted to defend the family name– I said, shrugging– after all, isn't it a bit tarnished? – I continued defiantly.

It was evident that that comment, coming out of a human's mouth, had just enraged him. However, he smiled falsely and kept watching me with narrowed eyes.

– Well, I hope that's it… You know, with a half-breed in the family, we have enough, and we don't even know how to get rid of her; I wouldn't want to get rid of another one–

Point for Cornelius with that wonderful explicit threat.

– Well, I have no intention of being a half-breed, don't worry– I replied with a forced smile.

– Maybe I want to get rid of you even if you're not a half-breed–

– As far as I know, I serve to help you find my sister. So better leave me alone and spare me the threats– I moved, ready to pass by him and leave, however, his hand rested on my shoulder, and with a swift motion, he sat me on the stand.

He brought his face close to mine; I could feel his gaze burning my skin with the fire of his anger. I had crossed the line.

– Maybe you're useful for now, but I think I'm going to consider giving myself the pleasure of killing you slowly, even if I can't resurrect one of my own–

His eyes were not at all like Cedric's; they were black, cold, and evil. He was all of that.

– Today, you won't use any kind of protection... So if a ball deviates in your direction, well, it'll be a pity– and with that, he stepped away and started walking again towards the mansion.

An hour later, the feast before the matches began. I had no desire to enter, but I was obligated to do so.

– April– Cedric took me by the arm and dragged me to the side of the stairs to prevent me from entering the dining room.

– What's happening? – I asked him in a low voice, so no one could hear us.

– We already drank blood bags today, but at some point, Gary, Emily, and I will have to pretend to drink from you. We'll get close, but none of us will bite you–

– Gary will get close to me and won't bite me? – I asked, feeling my heart race.

– He drank a lot today. Enough not to want to try another drop... He should be able to control himself– he explained, running a hand through his hair.

– Well, do whatever it takes to prevent him from biting me– I asked him– if he bites me, you'll have to take it off or I'll start screaming a lot and embarrass all of you– I threatened him very calmly, and he smiled sideways, mocking.

– Sure, April, whatever you say– I moved to go into the dining room, and then he quickly put an arm against the wall to stop me.

I looked at him strangely, and then he smiled maliciously.

– You don't look good today– he whispered – but at least wear the hat properly; it's cold outside– he took the ends of my hat and placed it properly on my head until it reached my eyebrows.

I felt my cheeks turn red, but I simply looked at him with a furrowed brow, passed under his arm, and entered the room.

Cornelius stood up once the two seats were occupied. He tapped the crystal glass he held in his hands with a spoon, drawing everyone's attention.

– With this banquet, we begin the second day of the presentation ceremony– he started– I hope everything here is to your liking, and know that at any time you can ask your donors to feed you–

Then he sat down, and the servants appeared to start filling everyone's plates. There must have been around two hundred, maybe more. I looked around for Daniel; he was very stiff in his seat, while Destiny caressed his neck with a finger and said something about "going straight to dessert." Wow... Where had all his elegance gone?

Gary was sitting next to a vampire boy with dark skin and cotton-like hair combed in a perfect circle, while on his left, he had the same girl he had danced with the night before. She laughed about something, while he stared at his empty plate, as if that tableware were the most interesting thing in the world.

I continued scanning the guests until my eyes met Thomas's. He was quite far from me, but he discreetly observed me while some vampire said something to him, very excited, which seemed to interest him not at all.

Just like the day before, he wore black and silver clothes, so I assumed those were the colors of the Dumont house. The only strange thing was that only he wore them. Did he not have a family? Was he there alone? How sad.

– Blood bag, here– I shifted my gaze from Thomas and focused on the annoying voice I had just heard.

Emily was looking at me from the other side of the table, snapping her fingers to get my attention.

– Come, dear, I'm hungry– she said, snapping her fingers again, as if I were a disobedient dog.

I stood up, even though I hadn't tasted a bite yet, and walked over to where she was. She didn't even move from her chair, observed me with an amused smile, and extended the palm of her hand.

– Your arm– she indicated, hurrying me.

I rolled up my sleeve, and I extended my wrist to her. She quickly showed her teeth, white as pearls, and placed her mouth on my arm, wrapping her teeth with her lips, so as not to actually bite me.

She stayed like that for about a minute, making strange noises as if she were drinking and enjoying it a lot, while she drooled all over me. As soon as she let go, she wiped her lips with a napkin, and I quickly covered my arm so that no one could see that there was no fang mark.

– Go, little bag, you're done– she laughed, and as soon as I turned to leave, she gave me a pat on the butt.

Cedric looked at both of us, holding the bridge of his nose, as if he were embarrassed by Emily's behavior.

– Come here, April– he asked me before I reached my seat again.

No one wanted to let me eat, huh?

I stopped by his side, ready to roll up my sleeve, but he gave me a devilish smile.

– No, sorry. I like it from the neck– he pushed the chair back a bit and patted his leg– sit–

I wished I could rip his head off or have a hidden stake in my pocket to stab him over and over. I cleared my throat, uncomfortable, and finally sat very straight on his lap.

– Let's see what we have here...– very amused, he brushed my hair off my neck with his cold fingers.

He caressed my skin with the tips of his index finger, and I felt shivers from his touch. Slowly, he brought his face closer to my neck. I could feel him smelling me, his warm breath on my skin. I sensed that he opened his lips, very close to me, and then... He ran his tongue over my skin, and I felt electricity run through my entire body.

He pressed his lips against my neck, not pretending to bite me but rather kissing it very gently while releasing a little pleasure moan, which I assumed was for everyone to believe he was drinking my blood.

I could feel his wet kisses traveling along the curve of my neck; he reached my earlobe and bit it gently. If he kept doing that, I would be the one to let out a moan, and it wouldn't be fake at all.

– Your heart is beating very fast– he whispered in my ear– if you want me to bite you, you just have to ask for it.

!

Then he moved away from me a bit, and while staring into my eyes, he wiped his lips in a feigned gesture of cleaning the blood.

– Because I do want to do it– for the first time, his tone wasn't mocking.

His eyes went from my eyes to my pink lips, and he finally looked at me again. I swallowed saliva, still with goosebumps and a sudden wave of heat flooding my body. As best I could, I swallowed saliva, unable to say anything in response, with shaky legs, I moved away and returned to my seat.

I started eating in silence, just like the rest of the donors. The food was delicious, but my stomach had tied itself into a knot, and I couldn't finish my plate.

Gary called me when he saw that I had left the utensils. I extended an arm, and fortunately, the boy had no preferences about where to bite.

We exchanged a look; I noticed he was somewhat scared, but I tried to smile at him to give him courage. He placed his lips on my wrist carefully, but I could feel his agitated breath on my skin. It was too hard for him. The flares of his nose widened as he breathed in my scent more and more.

I remained as calm as possible, but then something happened. Something very painful... Gary's teeth sank into my skin, over my marked veins. I let out a breath of pain and covered my mouth in surprise. Gary started sucking my blood eagerly, and I felt it flow out of my veins, hot and thick.

– Enough, you're going to dry her out– Cedric's voice echoed over the rest, in the middle of the hall. He had stood up and advanced toward his brother quickly– Gary...– he waited a fraction of a second for the boy to stop, but he didn't, so he grabbed him from behind and pulled him away from me with a jerk.

– No! No! – Gary began to scream.

His chin was stained with my blood, and even the blue shirt he was wearing had gotten dirty. His eyes were wide and red. He wasn't looking at me; he was looking at my arm, looking at the blood coming out of it.

Cedric dragged him out of the room, and I stood there, covering his bite, while two hundred vampires had their gaze fixed on me..

CHAPTER 23

A few minutes later, Cornelius concluded the banquet before his last name was further tarnished.

Slowly, everyone headed towards the backyard. Cornelius was organizing the teams; they were all mixed up since vampires measured their skills individually, and each one had the chance to elevate their house's rank.

I settled on the bleachers with a cup of coffee loaded with sugar because evidently, I had lost a lot of blood in less than a minute. Truly, a part of me doubted whether I could help Gary overcome those cravings. How could I do it if I was a temptation all the time? It was like trying to help a tobacco addict by smoking a cigarette, impossible.

– It seems the youngest Leblanc has some control issues– I heard a voice to my left.

Thomas Dumond settled beside me on the bleachers, with a satisfied smile on his lips.

– It's a pity. If he becomes a blood-addicted monster, the councilors will have to hunt him down, decapitate him, and burn his body... It would be the only way to get rid of him–

– Why are you telling me all this? – I inquired while taking a sip of my coffee and warming my hands with the cup.

– Because you're not a donor– he said as the first cricket match began– I think no one noticed, but seriously... Cedric, kissing your neck and arousing you like that in front of everyone, how lacking in elegance–

– Excuse me? – I frowned– yes, he bit me– I pulled my sweatshirt back a bit and showed him some tiny pink marks left from Godric's bite.

– Yes, of course– he smiled, following the ball with his eyes– whatever you say– he shrugged –anyway, I know you're not a donor, but for some reason, you're here with them, and if you're keeping the secret, I suppose it's because you care... So... It's really a shame that poor Gary Leblanc turns into an abomination–

– Well, don't worry, he won't become that– I said irritably, trying to focus on the match.

Destiny was playing alongside others I didn't know. Unlike the rest, she was at a total disadvantage: she was slower and threw the ball with less force. She had trained hard. What was happening?

In the second match, Cedric played against Godric. Both seemed very determined to compete despite having trained together. They moved in their positions, preparing for their turn. However, when it came, they were terrible. Godric was extremely agitated after the first run, even sweating, which was too strange for a vampire. Cedric, who in training had been faster than lightning, ran just a little faster than a human making their maximum effort.

– What's happening to them? – I asked Thomas, confused.

– Well... Since they haven't drunk from you... I don't know who they might have drunk from, but it's clear they've consumed vervain– he leaned back on the bleachers and watched the match with bright eyes– it seems this year will be easy to come out on top. To think that the Leblancs worried me, it's clear they're not what they were when Cornelius played cricket–

I couldn't believe it. I had doubted whether the vervain I had been giving them would take effect in just a week, and it was clear that the answer was yes, unequivocally yes. Because of me, their vampire abilities had significantly decreased, and everyone was noticing.

Gary also competed against other children and newly turned vampires. That was the final proof I needed to know that everything was my fault. Unlike the others, he still maintained his speed, strength, and reflexes. He didn't drink from the donors, so he hadn't tasted the blood I had manipulated. He was clean and still strong.

When it was Emily's turn, Thomas stood up and entered the field. They were on the same team. Only then did Daniel, dressed in white, settle beside me.

– Did you see that? – he said without taking his eyes off the match– The vervain you're giving them is taking effect. Keep it up, and when we face them, you won't have an escape–

– Yes, I noticed– I nodded remorsefully.

I felt dirty and mean. They weren't kind to me; Gary had even come close to draining me of all my blood. However, I didn't want to see them defeated; I didn't want to see them dead, and I didn't want to be the one to condemn them. But I couldn't tell Daniel all that because then it would mean I was on the side of a group of vampires, and if I stopped giving them vervain, they would kill a bunch of hunters.

– What's wrong with you? You look pale– Daniel suddenly said.

– No, nothing, just thinking...–

– Is your bite okay? I wanted to kill Gary, but it would have been too obvious...– he sighed with a grimace.

– Yes, I'm fine now. Hey, do you have any idea how I can try to help him control himself? – he looked at me somewhat doubtful– I mean, as long as I'm here, I'll have to help him... Plus, I don't want him to keep biting me... You know–

– Of course– he nodded– well, I suppose if he's addicted to blood, he should manage it like any other addiction, meaning... gradually reducing it–

– But he feeds on blood, he can't stop eating–

– Well, obese people are addicted to food, but they need it to live. This could be similar... He should develop the habit, for example, always drinking the same amount... And undoubtedly doing other things besides just thinking about controlling his thirst. A distracted mind is easier to manage...–

– You're right– I smiled– I had thought about distractions, anyway–

– Anyway, April, try not to get too involved. Your guard is dropping; it's not good that you keep getting closer to them–

– Sure– I nodded, trying to appear much more convinced than I actually was– it's under control–

Just as I finished saying that, a ball came flying from the field and hit Daniel's shoulder squarely. I saw in slow motion as his shoulder twisted backward at a strange angle.

He let out a groan and bit his lip while squeezing his eyes shut, trying to control the urge to scream.

– Oh shit! – I shouted for him.

He held onto his shoulder.

– Someone call a doctor! – I screamed, looking horrified in all directions.

Destiny quickly appeared in the bleachers and pulled me away from him.

– No one is going to call a doctor– she told me while looking at Daniel's contorted face– he's my donor; I'll take him to the hospital–

– I can manage on my own! – Daniel exclaimed as he continued to writhing in pain.

– Shut up, blood bag– she sighed, putting him on his feet and pulling his healthy arm to make him follow– let yourself be helped–

I knew that letting a vampire help you was even worse than having a broken shoulder. I sat there, watching as they both left. When I turned around, Godric was standing next to me, watching the scene with his hands in his pockets.

– You know that was meant for you, right? – he said very calmly.

– What? – I asked, astonished.

– Emily threw the ball, but if my hearing doesn't fail me, I can say with certainty that Cornelius asked her to give it to you. You're lucky that today we're doing everything wrong... Otherwise, the accuracy wouldn't have failed, and the one with the broken shoulder would be you.

– Well... I guess I should have expected it– I said, glaring at Cornelius, while he, from afar, also observed me.

– Do you know why? – Godric asked me.

– No, I don't know– I lied– anyway, you bit me, so just leave me alone–

– Yes, I bit you, and I don't regret anything. I had never tasted blood like yours, yes, similar, but not like yours... And certainly not in a human–

– What do you mean by not in a human? – I asked, furrowing my brow, and he shrugged.

– I don't mean anything; just that it's surprising... It's like searching for copper and finding gold– he chuckled to himself.

– Well, you won't taste it again, understood? – I warned, and he shrugged.

– Don't worry, seeing Cedric's hateful face once is enough. Besides, I have my own donor; she's hotter than you and much more willing... For everything..

CHAPTER 24

It was the last day of that absurd ceremony. The vampires were gathered, chatting in groups in the main hall.

They seemed to enjoy it or at least pretend very well. Once again, waiters distributed glasses of champagne, but also glasses of blood. I suppressed a gag just by looking at them and walked among the different groups, looking for Daniel, in case he had come despite the broken shoulder.

– Come on... Calm down... We'll find a way to fix it– I heard Destiny say to Godric, in a corner of the room.

– We are the shame of our family– he said, shaking his head.

He seemed visibly distressed, staring at the floor with his thick eyebrows furrowed.

– What's wrong with him? – I asked Destiny, putting my hands in my pockets.

– What was missing. Our status is already so low that humans think they can be our friends– Destiny sighed, holding the bridge of her nose.

– Are you going to tell me or not? – I asked, narrowing my eyes and studying both of them.

– The rankings are out– Godric said as he took a glass of blood from one of the waiters' trays– our family is second to last–

– What? – I asked, widening my eyes– I'm sorry... I guess–

– We are losing our abilities. Is it a disease or something? – Godric said with a grimace.

– We are vampires, Destiny cut him off- we don't get sick. If we do, it's because something weakens us...–

– Could someone have poisoned them for the competition? – I innocently inquired.

– Impossible... We only drank blood from our bag reserve– Destiny denied, biting her dark red-painted lip– I'll investigate what happened; I'm sure there must be a good explanation for this–

– If you're in second to last place, who did worse? – I asked them.

– The Leblancs– said Godric bitterly– not only will I be a low-ranking vampire, but I'll be the right hand of a vampire worse than me–

– Cornelius is powerful– Destiny interrupted him– his score was one of the highest after Thomas Dumont and the rest of the councilors–

– Yes, but it wasn't enough to compensate for the scores of the others– he retorted, running a hand through his hair in frustration.

I started walking again among the people. I didn't understand why they attached so much importance to a senseless ranking.

Daniel was nowhere to be found; it was obvious that he couldn't make it, and everyone was so busy lamenting that I had nothing better to do than wander aimlessly through the hall.

– You– Emily's annoying voice reached me.

– What do you want? – I asked, looking up at the sky.

– Cedric asked me to find you while Cornelius gives him and Gary a super boring lecture on how they are the shame of the family– she explained while grabbing my wrist and dragging me behind her.

– Do you know what he wants? – I asked her, but she shook her head.

We left the house and headed towards the backyard.

Gary was serious, looking at the ground and kicking an imaginary stone. Cedric was listening to his father, sitting on one of the stands from the day before, smoking, and Cornelius gesticulated like crazy.

Emily waved an arm to get Cedric's attention and pointed at me with her thumb.

– Dad, I have to go– she interrupted, getting up and starting to walk.

– Where do you think you're going? – Cornelius exclaimed with wide eyes.

– We came in last, I don't think anyone cares if I'm not there– Cedric replied, shrugging as he caught up with us.

– Peter is too busy to drive– Emily informed him as we approached a back door of the mansion, quite similar to a garage curtain.

– Then we'll take the motorcycles. April, can you ride? – Cedric said as he pulled the curtain and lifted it.

– No... I've never ridden one...– I said, scratching my neck nervously.

– Well, then...– Cedric turned on the light, and the garage was completely illuminated.

All kinds of motorcycles were stored there. Some were large and heavy, others smaller, and even two scooters. He took down two bunches of keys from a hook and threw one to Emily, who caught it in the air.

– Well, my favorite– she said, smiling flirtatiously– it seems you still remember–

– I just want us to get there fast– Cedric clarified, rolling his eyes– have this, April– he said, throwing me a helmet that I tried to catch and dropped to the floor.

I could never get things right, huh? I picked it up from the floor, put it on, and tried to buckle it without success...

– Let me see...– Cedric stopped in front of me and took the helmet straps to fasten it under my chin– don't look for excuses to get me closer– he said, winking at me and smiling on the side– I like it when they are direct–

– Next time, I'll just leave the helmet unfastened– I muttered under my breath, knowing that he would hear me anyway.

– Emily, you lead us– Cedric continued as he approached a heavy black motorcycle that looked ready for a race.

– Okay– Emily sat on a bubblegum pink motorcycle and waited for us to do the same.

Cedric settled onto his motorcycle. His body seemed to fit perfectly there. Dressed in a white shirt, a leather jacket, and his dark hair, he looked like a magazine model.

With enthusiasm, he turned the key in the ignition and revved up the motorcycle.

– Get on – he said, patting the seat behind him.

– Is... Is this a joke? – I asked, swallowing hard.

– Better leave the blood bag here and let's go find the witch on our own – Emily sighed, inspecting her nails with disinterest.

– Are we going to find the witch? – I asked, looking at Cedric, and he nodded.

As soon as I knew it, I gathered all the courage I had and sat on the motorcycle.

– You better hold on to me – he said, and by his voice, I knew he was smiling.

– Of course not – I replied as I grabbed the handles on the sides of the seat.

Emily took off in front of us, and as soon as Cedric accelerated behind her, I leaned back, thinking I would fall backward onto the ground.

– I told you... – I heard his mocking voice.

"Damn stupid vampire," I thought as I wrapped my arms around his waist.

The feeling of riding on a motorcycle was new to me but very exciting. The cold night wind seeped into my helmet, slapping my face. Cedric's fresh, woody scent seeped into my nose and filled my lungs as I clung tightly to the front of his shirt, feeling his hard and defined muscles beneath my palms.

Why was I fixating on that? I don't know, but hugging his body felt even better than the incredible freedom I felt as we rode against the wind.

We left the mansion, passed through the forest, and exited the town. Emily kept advancing in front of us through a road surrounded by fields.

Half an hour later, we entered the neighboring town and gradually slowed down until we stopped.

I had visited that place several times when I had participated in sports tournaments with the school. It reminded me that I was missing classes. I didn't care too much, but I had always hoped to finish school with my classmates; I didn't want to repeat a grade.

– I need you to get off so I can do it – Cedric reminded me, pulling me out of my thoughts.

I got off, and he followed. He secured the motorcycle with a chain, and Emily did the same.

– It's this way – she indicated, starting to walk down a cobbled street.

We stopped in front of a light blue house that must have been two stories tall. It had a gabled roof with brown tiles, dark wood doors and windows, and a bunch of neglected plants at the entrance.

Before Emily rang the doorbell, the front door opened, and a guy appeared dragging two suitcases and a bag under his arm.

– Where are you going? – Emily put her hands on her hips and stared at him with a furrowed brow.

– Tell me he's not the witch you told me you knew... – Cedric seemed horrified just by looking at him and ran a hand over his face, trying to stay calm.

– Of course... They've arrived – the guy ran his gaze between Emily and Cedric, pressing his lips with resignation.

– You better come in, Declan, we need to talk to you – Emily told him, advancing in his direction.

The guy made a grimace as a protest and went back into the house. I entered first, looking around with curiosity. It seemed like an old house, filled with mahogany furniture. There was a battered armchair next to a dusty fireplace, and on the opposite side, a small kitchen with cupboard doors somewhat crooked.

– Take off your shoes – Declan asked me while looking at something behind me.

I turned around too and saw Cedric and Emily glaring at him furiously from the outside.

– Oh, how absent-minded – he said with a mischievous smile – come in, come in –

The three of them moved forward, glaring at him. Emily jumped on the couch, putting her feet on the armrests and taking off her shoes with a shake, tossing them into the air.

– Come on, Declan, don't look at me like that – she smiled very calmly – you're used to my clothes all over the house, right? –

– Yeah, well, what do you want? – he scratched his forehead uncomfortably.

I had to admit he was very attractive. He had dark, chocolate-colored skin; his black and curly hair was almost shaved, and his eyes looked like jet beads. His face was extremely symmetrical, with full lips, a round nose, and thick eyebrows.

– Finished looking at him? – Cedric stopped in front of me, with a furrowed forehead and his hands in the pockets of his jeans.

– Sure, yes, I'm done – I said with a fake smile.

– We want you to help us resurrect a vampire – Emily replied, sitting up in the chair – Can you, Declan? –

– Witches don't get involved in vampire affairs – Declan sighed while heating water in a kettle, resigned.

– Yes, sure – Cedric scoffed – we know your games. Tell us what you want, and give us the answer we're looking for –

– Are you ever kind to anyone? – I asked Cedric, blinking repeatedly.

– I am kind to you – he said, raising an eyebrow, and I snorted, looking away – So, Declan?

– I think they came before with the same request, and I told them the answer –

– Come on – Emily stood up and walked barefoot until she reached him.

She placed a hand on his chest and slowly lowered it, looking into his eyes.

– Last time, it didn't work... We need you to be more effective this time – her hand stopped at the waistband of his pants, toying with the elastic, while she purred each word.

I looked at Cedric, searching for the slightest sign of jealousy, but he seemed amused.

– I already told them how to resurrect a vampire – Declan replied, unable to stop looking at her – there is no other way –

– Come on! – I heard myself exclaim – there must be something that can be done, we really need it –

Declan looked at me with an uncomfortable grimace.

– I'll do whatever it takes, just help us – I insisted again.

– Look, she's asking you nicely... You don't want me to ask in my way – Cedric leaned on him.

– You know you can't touch me without starting a war, so spare me your threats – Declan warned him – maybe... There's something I can do –

– Mmm... That's good – Emily ran her tongue over his neck, and I felt completely out of place.

– Do you want us to come back later? – I asked, clearing my throat, cheeks burning.

– Relax, April – Cedric grinned at me playfully – if you want, I can... –

He approached my neck, but before he could lick it like at the banquet, I pushed him away, pushing his chest.

– Better stay away – I said, looking at him with a stern face – What did you come up with? – I continued, addressing Declan.

– There are some books they brought me... They belong to a recently deceased witch, an ancestor... –

– Yes, yes, get to the point – Cedric sighed, crossing his arms.

– Maybe there's something about resurrecting vampires in there, but I'll need your help, there are many books –

– Of course – I nodded, feeling hope rekindle in my chest – let's start now –

– Okay, but before that, let's establish my payment – Declan smiled.

CHAPTER 25

– Each of you will give me a sample of your blood – Declan said, looking at us with bright eyes.

– What? – I asked, blinking like a fool.

– It will only be a little, relax – he clarified with a smile – it's more like my insurance –

– I don't understand – I said, looking at Emily and Cedric for an answer.

– Witches use our blood for spells. With the samples, in case we want to harm him, he'll do it to us first – Cedric explained while taking a cigarette from his pack.

– If it's just for that, go ahead – I nodded, extending my hand to him.

– Later – Declan smiled at me – we're not in a hurry. I think it's better if you sleep here; we won't be able to go through everything in one night. Besides, I sleep at this hour; I'm not a night owl –

– Where are the books? – Emily asked, looking around.

– I have them in the loft. Will you help me? –

– No – said Cedric as he sat on the armrest of the chair.

– I'll go – I said, walking behind Declan and glaring at Cedric.

We climbed the stairs to reach the second floor. There were three doors, but I didn't ask. I focused on silently following him until he stopped. He tiptoed and pulled a small notch in the ceiling, opening a trapdoor, while a ladder unfolded before us.

Declan began to climb, and I waited for him to reach the loft so I wouldn't get a kick in the face as I followed him.

– Stay there – he told me from above – I'll pass you the boxes with the books, and you can take them downstairs –

– Can't you snap your fingers and make them appear in the room? – I asked, smiling.

– I could, but they control the amount of magic I use; I can't exceed in trivial things –

– Do they have a meter or something? – I joked as he handed me the first box.

It weighed more than I had lifted in a long time, but I felt like I could handle it. I went down to the living room, already out of breath, to leave the box and went back up to where he was.

– Magic is unique, although it renews very slowly. All witches only extract what we need; we can't overdo it because someone might be left without it until it renews –

– I thought it came from you... –

– No, we are the ones who can channel it, but magic has no owners; it is shared, it's for all witches – he said, descending with the last box and coming down with me through the ladder – that's why we use potions and magical objects –

Declan lit the fireplace while the rest of us sat on the floor and started taking books from the boxes. There were really a lot, impossible to finish them all in one night.

– Will we help you or will we look on our own? – Cedric asked Declan, watching him move from one side of the kitchen to the other without joining us.

– I regret to say I haven't had dinner. I can't read on an empty stomach –

– Well, give her something too – Cedric requested, pointing at me with his chin – she's human and hasn't eaten –

– Human? – Declan looked at me as if he suddenly saw me with different eyes – If I had known, I would have treated you better from the beginning! – he smiled, and I looked at him raising an eyebrow.

– Well, if being human will get me some food, then... What's on the menu? –

– I'll make something special! – the witch seemed fascinated, with sparkling eyes.

– No, nothing special – Emily cut him off sharply, do something quick and help us with this once and for all –

We immersed ourselves in the books in search of a way to resurrect vampires. We flipped through dusty pages with a musty smell, thin as the paper in bibles.

Declan sat next to me with a plate of oven-baked spiced potatoes and chicken thighs. Cedric looked up, and I knew he was studying my face even without looking at him, just by how heavy his gaze could be on me.

– So... Why a human with two vampires? – Declan asked, taking a bite of a potato while grabbing another book from the box – Is she your new girlfriend? – he said, looking at Cedric and chewing while smiling.

– No, I'm his hostage – I said with a grimace.

– And also my girlfriend – Cedric smiled at me with a sidelong grin, stretching and taking a potato from my plate.

– If it were true... It would be quite toxic – Declan laughed, shaking his head.

We continued searching through the books until our eyes began to bother us from fatigue. Occasionally, Declan stirred the fireplace to prevent it from going out, and the crackling of sparks and the popping of small logs could be heard beside us.

I felt that there was something pleasant about all this. The warmth of the fire, the old books... I opened my eyes as soon as I felt my head drooping; I was falling asleep.

– The sun is coming up – Cedric said, rubbing his eyes.

– I have a guest room, but it only has a queen-sized bed, so... – he looked at Emily with bright eyes, and she smiled diabolically.

– If you hear any noise, don't be scared – she said while taking Declan by the wrist and starting to climb the stairs – we're brutal –

– Great, something tells me we won't sleep – I sighed, rolling my eyes.

– Then we'll have to do something else... – Cedric said, starting to climb the stairs.

I went after him. Emily and Declan had just closed a door, and immediately there was a dry thud and their giggles.

Okay... Too much information.

I entered the guest room and crossed my arms, leaning on the door frame. Cedric had taken off his shirt and was lying on the bed, hands crossed beneath his head.

– I'm not going to sleep with you – I said, biting my lip, frustrated.

– Then you can stay on the small dusty chair downstairs, surrounded by moldy books – he said, looking at me very calmly – sounds great –

– Fine – I nodded, advancing to the bed and sitting on it – don't even think about getting close, understood? –

– Of course – he gave me a sidelong smile and closed his eyes – turn off the light, I'm sleepy –

I got up, turned it off, and lay back on the bed. It was comfortable, with clean, white sheets. I covered myself with a thick quilt and closed my eyes too.

I could hear Cedric's breathing beside me. It didn't sound calm, and I could sense his tension even without seeing him.

– Is something wrong? – I asked without opening my eyes.

He didn't answer, continued breathing like that for a few more seconds, and finally turned and buried his face in the pillow.

– Cedric? – I propped myself up with my elbow and put a hand on his shoulder.

As soon as I touched his skin, I felt an electric shock running through my body. I pulled away, my heart pounding forcefully against my chest.

My eyes were adjusting to the darkness, and I could see his tense silhouette and his head buried in the pillow. Finally, he turned towards me. I wasn't sure about the expression on his face, but his voice came out velvety and somewhat muffled.

– You smell too good – I didn't know what to respond... He seemed exasperated, as if my perfume bothered him.

– I'm sorry... – before I could finish the sentence, Cedric took the arm I was holding and pulled, making me lose balance.

My face smashed against his firm shoulder, but it didn't hurt.

– What the hell! – I exclaimed, surprised, when he buried his face in the hollow of my neck.

As soon as I felt his deep breath on my skin, I shivered, but I only thought of one thing, and that was that I didn't want to move away.

I felt him breathing in my scent.

– You're going to drive me crazy, April... – he said softly.

He placed a hand behind my head, pressing me a little more against him, as if he could absorb all my scent by getting closer. However, when I thought he would let go of me, his fingers gently caressed my hair, in a gesture that almost seemed affectionate.

– Can I bite you? – he asked me.

I didn't respond immediately. Was I stupid? Yes, probably, but I could feel his lips brushing against my neck, and I remembered his tongue passing over my skin on the banquet day. At that moment, I didn't want him to stop; I wanted him to continue, even at that moment.

I swallowed saliva, tried to move away, but every part of me begged me to stay by his side, glued to his shoulder.

Then Daniel came to my mind, reminding me that they weren't human, that they were bad, and their instinct was to kill. I remembered that my parents had died at the hands of a vampire, and now they also wanted to kill Aixa.

"They are lowering your guard; you have to stay away," Daniel had told me. Well, they were right; at that moment, my guard was low, I even wished for what? For him to bite me? Was I crazy?

– April? – Cedric had his mouth very close to my ear.

– You're not going to bite me – I said, forcing every muscle in my body to move away from him – I'm going to sleep on the couch – I continued, jumping off the bed like a spring and taking my pillow.

Cedric took my hand, stretching on the bed, and furrowed his brow; he seemed confused.

– Stay – he asked me with a choked voice – please –

I felt my legs turning to jelly. I swallowed saliva and studied him with my gaze. What the hell was happening to him? I had never seen that expression on his face.

He was conflicted, as if he were arguing with himself without saying anything. He lifted his gaze, his eyes met mine... And I was weak, just for a moment, I was weak. I let go of the pillow and got back into bed, and he didn't let go of my hand until I fell asleep.

CHAPTER 26

When I woke up, I was alone. My stomach felt empty, and it growled. I left the guest room, opened a door, expecting to find the bathroom, and there it was.

I washed my face and tried to convince myself that I had been stupid during the night. I desperately needed all of it to end once and for all.

I went down to the living room, and the scent of toast and coffee enveloped me. It was night, but that fragrance reminded me of breakfasts at home when my mother woke up early and prepared everything along with freshly squeezed juice.

– Good morning! – Declan greeted me, handing me a cup, smiling – looks like you're adapting well to vampire customs. You slept many hours.

– Yes, I was getting used to it... – I said, unable to help but stare at the toaster.

– They're ready now – he laughed while taking a sip from his green cup – it's seven-thirty, so I thought it would be good for us to have a snack.

– Can I stay here? – I joked – I haven't had more than one meal a day for a long time.

– It shows, you're a toothpick – the bread popped out of the toaster.

Declan took them and placed them on a plate. Then, he took cream cheese from the fridge, and we both sat down on the couch to eat.

– Where are they? – I asked with my mouth full.

– They went "hunting," as they call it. So in the meantime... Why don't I read your cards?

– Why don't we keep looking for the spell? – I replied with a strained smile.

– Come on, it'll only be until they return.

– Fine – I sighed – I always thought all that about cards was a lie.

– Usually, it is, but I'm a witch. You can trust me – Declan put his hand in the pocket of his jacket, stood in front of me on the floor, and I positioned myself at his height – I'll shuffle them so you can see there's no trick.

– All right – it amused me a bit.

– Let's see... – he spread the deck in front of me, facing down so I couldn't see the drawings – pick three.

I took three cards from the middle. He put away the rest and turned the ones I had chosen.

– Interesting... – he said, looking at the cards with a strange gleam in his eyes.

I looked at them, clearly not understanding anything, but they all seemed very normal.

– Am I going to die tomorrow? – I asked, furrowing my brow.

– No, relax – he laughed – however, all your cards... have a peculiarity – he slid his fingers over them and then took the first one and handed it to me.

The card had a drawing of a minotaur, its legs were hairy and black, and its chest extremely muscular.

– What is this?

– The minotaur represents two halves, a creature half monster, half human... You may encounter this type of creature or may have already encountered it.

– Isn't it supposed to show the future? – I asked while handing him back the card.

– It's confusing in you – he scratched his chin – but yes, it must be for the future... The cards don't speak of the past – he handed me the next one – this is day and night.

As expected, the card was divided in two. On one half, there was a shining sun, and on the other, a full moon against a dark blue background.

– What does it mean?

– This card speaks of a decision you will have to make...

– Between day and night? Something like: Do I want lunch or dinner for my birthday? – I mocked, quite skeptical.

– If you're not going to take this seriously, I'll stop – he said, glaring at me.

– No, no, I'm sorry – I laughed – please continue.

– It means you'll have to make a decision between two completely opposite paths.

– And which one should I choose? – I asked.

– I can't tell you that. I just have to warn you that, at some point, you will have to make that choice.

Finally, he handed me the last card – on it, two roses were drawn, one white and one black.

– Why are they all half and half? Am I incomplete or something? – I asked, frowning.

– You're not incomplete; it means your future is not yet decided. You have many decisions to make... Like that one – he pointed to the card with his chin – it means two loves, it seems they won't make it easy for you, and you'll have to choose one.

– I don't like anyone – I said with a grimace – doesn't it mean something else?

– Hmm... I think, maybe, the confused one is you – he smiled at me with his full lips.

At that moment, the door opened, and Cedric and Emily entered. Declan gathered his cards and put them in his pocket.

– Haven't you started yet? – Emily said, crossing her arms.

– No, you'll have to help – I replied, shrugging and getting up from the floor.

Cedric took a stack of books, sat on the couch, and left all the material he planned to review next to him, making sure no one could sit next to him.

Emily took a book and began to flip through it with a bored expression.

– Do you have whiskey? – Cedric asked Declan.

– No, I'm sorry, I only drink wine.

– How sophisticated – Emily smiled maliciously.

I finished my coffee as I started searching through a new pile of books. There were spells of all kinds: to change the shape of objects, turn humans into stones, animals into people... But there was no mention of anything regarding the possible resurrection of a vampire.

As the hours passed, everyone's faces darkened more and more. I didn't want to lose hope, but there were fewer and fewer books to search through, and we hadn't even read the word "vampire" anywhere.

– I'll start making dinner – Declan declared after a while, stretching and cracking his back – I have to go shopping; I'll be right back.

– Hold on – Cedric closed one of the last books – April will go.

– What? – the warlock raised an eyebrow and crossed his arms – What's the problem?

– We're not finding anything, and before we arrived, you planned to escape from us. You're not leaving until we find what we're looking for.

– And your hostage isn't going to escape? – Declan looked at him as if he were an idiot.

– Write down what you need, and Emily, go with her – Cedric replied.

– Fine – the warlock almost spat out the words – I never break a deal.

– Well, last time you didn't do what I asked. Excuse my distrust.

The warlock quickly wrote down what he needed and handed me the list. I left the house with Emily on my heels. It was already dark outside, and there were hardly any people on the street.

We walked to a supermarket that still had its lights on. We entered, and I took care of grabbing everything from the shelves because apparently, Emily was too much of a vampire to deal with things like that.

– Will you pay, or did Declan give you money? – I asked her, stopping in one of the aisles.

She looked at me strangely and shrugged.

– I'll pay...

– Perfect – I nodded and took a bag of sour candies, too expensive for the quantity it brought – we'll add these.

She rolled her eyes, but didn't say anything. We advanced to the checkout; the man put everything in a bag and handed it to us.

– Thank you very much – Emily smiled at him and stared into his eyes – you'll give us all of this for free.

The man nodded, confused and clearly hypnotized...

We left the store, and she threw me the bag of candies.

– I already feel bad for taking it – I said, looking at her guiltily – Is this how you get everything? Furniture? Food? Servants?

– Not everything – she said, taking the bag from my hand, opening it, and biting into a strip of sour candy – but most of it.

I sighed; it was already done... The man wouldn't remember, right? And the candies were very delicious... I took one and put the whole thing in my mouth. My principles subjected to a treat.

We returned to Declan's house and went inside. Cedric was standing in the middle of the room and gave me a smile.

– Did you buy candies to celebrate? – he asked, approaching and taking one.

– Celebrate what? – Emily asked, closing the door.

– We found the spell – Declan said with shining eyes.

A feeling of relief ran through my body. My sister was safe; we just had to follow that spell to the letter, and the vampires wouldn't try to kill her, in addition to freeing me.

– What do we need to do? – I asked them nervously.

– We need a blood moon – Declan explained – and blood, of course.

– What? Whose blood?

– Your sister's. But we won't have to kill her; it will only be a few drops because she was the one who killed him. But the light of the blood moon will complete the blood that doesn't come out of your sister.

– So... you need her, but you won't kill her? – I swallowed hard; my sister wouldn't agree to something like that. She would never want to help them.

– I know she's a hunter, but giving us a bit of her blood will save her from Godric and Destiny hunting her for life – Cedric said, seeing my doubtful expression – you can convince her, April, I know you can.

– She won't... – I felt like breaking everything. Couldn't it be my blood? I would have done anything to end that issue, but I was sure Aixa would only look for a way to kill them and end up dead.

– I'll convince her – I nodded – but let me see that spell, to make sure.

I reached out, and Declan handed me a small leather-bound book. There it was, the spell we were looking for and a hundred more spells, specially made to deal with vampires. Why hadn't we started with that?

– Okay – I nodded, returning it to him – we'll do it, and... – I turned to look at Cedric – I'll start helping Gary.

He nodded; he wasn't smiling, and didn't seem more relieved. I supposed that after all, we still didn't know if we could save the boy from becoming a monster. I could save my sister, but could he save his?

CHAPTER 27

"For this, I'm going to need everyone's collaboration," I began speaking. Cornelius, Cedric, Emily, Destiny, and Godric watched me in silence. I knew they were all skeptical about hearing what would come out of my mouth, but Cedric had explained to them why it was important to help Gary and that he really needed all the help he could get.

"We must make Gary feel... like a human child," I continued. "He needs hobbies, friends to distract himself with, new things... He needs the same as any twelve-year-old child."

"He's not a human child; he doesn't need that," Cornelius reminded me, crossing his arms. "None of us were raised as humans, and we managed to control ourselves perfectly."

"Yes, but none of us had the same problem," Cedric reminded him. "Doing other things won't make him less of a vampire; we just have to try."

"And what do you propose?" the father asked with an irritated expression.

"In two days, it will be his birthday, right?" I said, scratching my forehead. "We'll throw him a party... with vampires, but vampires his age, not a hundred years old."

"We don't celebrate birthdays like that," Destiny interrupted. "It should be an elegant cocktail where the best families are invited. They should do it, especially now that his family is last on the list of houses."

"We're last anyway; nobody will want to come. If we can get at least the families with kids Gary's age to approach, it would be a first step to climb up," Cedric reminded her.

"How do humans celebrate a thirteen-year-old's birthday?" Godric asked, somewhat puzzled.

"It depends... How much money do they have?" I said with a devilish smile.

"Whatever is necessary," Cornelius sighed resignedly.

"Well then... Destiny, can you take care of sending an invitation to all the vampire kids?"

"Can I make it elegant, or does it have to be a cartoon card?" she asked, raising an eyebrow.

"Make them as you prefer and send them," I nodded, conceding her some ground so that she wouldn't feel too opposed.

"Godric... Could you decorate?"

"I'll have to buy more roses; we used all the garden ones this weekend," he replied as he took out his phone, searching for who knows what.

"No..." I made a face. "He's a child. Why would he want roses as decoration?"

"It's elegant..." Destiny seemed on the verge of collapsing, just thinking about doing something without too much glamour.

"It doesn't have to be an elegant party. Godric, find out what Gary likes and make it the theme of the party," he nodded, looking at his sister, on the verge of fainting.

"Cornelius... Could you go buy... some things?" It was uncomfortable to ask for something, even if it was something for his son and even though they had expressly asked for help.

"What do we need to get?" he asked, running a hand full of rings through his hair.

I quickly wrote on a piece of paper everything we needed and handed it to him. He checked it, frowned, pursed his lips, and decided it would be better not to say anything.

"Cedric, could you take care of the gifts?" I said. "And I'll make the cake."

"And me?" Emily asked, pointing to her chest with a finger.

"You just don't bother," I said with a fake smile, and I saw everyone trying to avoid laughing, not very successfully.

"Cornelius, I'm going with you," she said, getting up. We all left to do our respective tasks. Cedric followed me to the kitchen, sitting on a stool and watching me as I began to gather everything I needed for a birthday cake.

"Do you need anything?" I asked while sifting the flour.

"What are you supposed to give for a birthday?" he asked.

"You never give things for his birthday?"

"We never give each other anything. We already have everything we want, and if we don't, we buy it ourselves."

"How boring. It's nice to give a gift. Sometimes giving it is even nicer than receiving it."

"Yes, sure," he laughed, rolling his eyes.

"I think I won't help you," I shrugged. "So you'll know what it's like to give a gift."

"Come on, April... I don't need to know, I really don't care. Tell me what and I'll go buy it."

"Cedric, that's not what we're looking for," I stopped to look at him with flour-covered hands. "What we're looking for is to convey support to him, to convey understanding, to make him feel something other than coldness from all of you. He can't overcome this alone; he needs you."

"I didn't say I wouldn't give him anything," he frowned irritably.

"Yes, but you pretend not to make an effort. Any gift won't do for Gary. You said you have everything you need. You have to give him a gift that means something to him... Something that will stir emotions in him. You're his brother..."

"Vampires don't get emotional... We don't feel things like you," he reminded me, crossing his arms.

"Of course you do. It's just that you don't want to feel any of that," I didn't know if it was true, but I was sure it was. "Vampires also fall in love, right? That's why you turned Emily... That's why you want to resurrect a dead vampire. If you didn't feel anything, you wouldn't do it."

"I don't feel anything," he seemed annoyed, he was denied to agree with me, and I was denied to leave him alone.

"No," I let out. "You're afraid to feel that it's something else."

Cedric released air in a kind of bitter laugh. I didn't stop looking at him, hoping he would say something more, but he didn't. He remained silent, hands clenched on the edges of the kitchen island.

"Then let me help you," he said without looking at me, in a voice so low that I almost didn't hear it.

"What?" I blinked as I brushed a strand of hair from my face and smeared flour on my cheek.

"Let me help you prepare his cake. It's something that would make him happy."

"Do you know how to make it?" I asked, raising my eyebrows.

"No," he said as he stood up and stood next to me.

"Are you asking me to teach you something?" I asked, as the corners of my lips curved into a playful smile.

"Fine, shut up," he sighed, rolling his eyes.

We started cooking in silence. I weighed things, and he mixed them slowly, under my watchful supervision. I knew he had to use an electric mixer, but I didn't tell him and let him stir by hand because he had to enjoy my small victory.

When he finished mixing everything, we put the mold with the mixture in the oven and washed our hands.

"It wasn't that difficult, right?" I asked him as I handed him a hand dryer.

"I felt like a servant," he said, as if having Peter do everything was the most normal thing in the world.

"Well, I managed to find out what Gary likes the most," Godric said cheerfully entering the kitchen. "You're all dirty. What happened to you?" he said, pointing to both of our clothes.

"Cedric learned to cook... It seems he's very energetic," I said with a grimace, looking stained with egg and flour.

"Why did you cook?" Godric asked him, furrowing his brow a bit.

"What does Gary like the most?" I intervened.

I didn't want them to question it... In fact, I didn't want them to question the first human thing Cedric did.

"Killing," Godric replied very calmly.

"And according to you, how are we going to decorate his birthday? "I asked him while trying to remove the stains from Destiny's hoodie. "With knives or something like that?"

"Well, what did you expect? It's Gary; he wouldn't choose unicorns," Cedric laughed, looking at me as if I were an idiot, and I sighed, resigning.

"Okay... Just avoid using real blood, or we won't be able to distract him," I asked Godric, and he left very calmly with a notepad under his arm.

By the time we finished baking the cake, the doorbell rang. Peter opened it, and a group of donors entered. Of course, there couldn't be a night without blood involved, right?

Cedric asked me to accompany him to the main hall where they were.

"Stay here; I'll go call the others, and we'll be back soon," he said as he ran upstairs.

Damn... I didn't have time to make them a vervain tea; I needed something quick.

I ran to the kitchen and looked inside the pantry. I found a packet of cookies. I put them on a plate, took the brown paper bag in which I hid the vervain, crushed it as small as I could, and sprinkled it over the food.

"Eat something before... you know," I said, passing them the plate.

"Great, how kind," Lucy smiled happily, putting one in her mouth.

My intention was no longer for them to be killed, but I hadn't convinced my sister not to try to kill them, and I wasn't going to let anyone hurt her, so I couldn't just let them regain their strength because there would be no way to stop them.

Gary came down with the rest. It surprised me... He would stay there watching as the others fed.

"Who wants to take a little risk today?" Godric asked, looking at all the donors. "Whoever does it might be one step closer to becoming a vampire..."

Lucy was the first to stand up and move toward him. That girl was crazy, no doubt.

"What do I have to do?" the girl asked, very determined.

"You see, my brother is a bit eager with blood, but he's learning to control himself," Cedric said with a malicious tone. "We need him to try drinking from a human."

"What?" I said, opening my eyes wide. "You're rushing things..."

"We have to hurry, April," Cedric replied without looking at me. "The sooner he controls himself, the better."

"But without risking anyone!" I exclaimed.

"I have no problem with that," Lucy smiled at me, as if there was no reason to reject that proposal.

I really didn't understand. Gary had already bitten her before and had almost killed her twice. Wasn't she really afraid?

"April, do you have to tell Gary something?" Cedric asked me.

"Something like what?" I asked, frowning.

"I don't know... That thing you do. Say words of encouragement or something like that."

"Well... Gary, don't kill her," was all I could say; I was completely caught off guard.

Before my eyes, Lucy rolled up the sweater she was wearing, exposing her pale arm. Gary advanced toward her with a serious expression; if he was afraid, he didn't show it at all.

I approached them, as if preparing to jump on him if necessary, to prevent him from leaving the donor without a drop of blood. The boy opened his mouth; I saw his sharp white fangs for a moment until they sank into the girl's wrist.

It was intolerable to watch that. I smelled the blood, heard the sound of Gary sucking desperately, and felt nauseous. I had never been bothered by blood before, but watching vampires feed was something I couldn't bear. Gary kept drinking without stopping, and her face showed some weakness.

"Gary, enough, control yourself," I told him, placing a hand on his shoulder.

The boy pushed me away with a slap, without removing his lips from her.

"Gary, I told you to stop! You don't want to kill her!" I said again, raising my voice.

Cedric, Destiny, and Godric didn't move, and the rest of the donors didn't either. Did they think they would let him kill her?

"Gary!" I jumped on him, on a thin, short child.

I grabbed him by the waist and threw him backward with all the strength I had. His head moved away from her for a moment; he turned toward me with lips and chin soaked in blood. Lucy stepped back and leaned dizzy against the couch. I could only see the blood from her chin. Dark and thick, it dripped onto the white floor. I didn't know why, but I felt my throat dry like never before. Was I thirsty? What the hell was happening to me?

I walked toward him, still looking at his chin stained with red. I reached out to him, looking at me with wide eyes, breathing heavily, and with the tip of my finger, I wiped a little of the blood. I observed my finger while my stomach twisted into a knot, my throat scratched asking for something I didn't know what, and then, saliva began to swirl in my mouth, and I vomited.

CHAPTER 28

"Oh no, that's disgusting," I heard Destiny exclaim.

"I'm sorry..." I said, looking up.

"Godric, call Peter to clean this up," Cedric ordered him next to me. "Gary, go to your room and clean yourself up."

I didn't understand anything; everyone was moving around me while I looked at them bewildered. Cedric put a hand on my back and pushed me a bit to move away and go upstairs.

I entered my room followed by him, and he closed the door behind him.

"Are you okay?" he asked me, as I sat on the bed.

"I don't know what happened to me..." I swallowed saliva. "I'm so disgusted watching them eat, but..."

"But?" he asked, sitting next to me.

"Cedric, how does the transformation into a vampire happen? I drank your blood, that should've... It should've done something to me because I feel strange."

"You're not turning into a vampire, April," he said, shaking his head. "To become one, you have to die having drunk my blood. I only gave it to you to heal; you weren't dead at any moment," he reassured me. "Besides, it was many days ago. If you were turning, you would have already drunk blood, and..."

"But I was thirsty," I blurted out without daring to look at him. "It's the truth, I... I felt so disgusted, but at the same time, I felt a stupid need to lick the blood... My throat was dry, and..."

"Do you want to try it?" he asked me confused, and finally, I looked him in the eyes.

"No! For God's sake, it's blood... It would be like cannibalism; I'm human... But why did I feel that? Why did Thomas Dumont say that I'm not?"

"I don't know, April," he sighed, running a hand through his hair. "Listen, you're human, I know it... The sun doesn't affect you, you need food to live, your blood smells incredibly good... You're human."

"And then what's happening to me?" I exclaimed frustrated, standing up.

I felt my eyes stinging with the urge to cry, but I refused to do it. I wasn't going to cry in front of anyone.

"Godric bit me! Maybe it was that? Do they have some venom in their saliva or something?"

"No, April, it wasn't any of us. Stop blaming us," he said, frowning. "I don't know what's happening to you. I know you're human! Maybe... I don't know... You're sick or something..."

"I'm not sick!" I said, raising my voice. "Something is happening to me... I want to go home! I want to go now!"

"You know I can't let you go," Cedric also stood up, facing me.

"I can't stand it anymore!" I shouted angrily. "That sound they make when they drink blood, and you... Looking at me with that face, I don't even know what you're trying. And everyone wanting me to do things, and I'm letting my guard down with you all, and look what happens! How did I wish to drink blood? What the hell are you doing to me?"

"Listen to me!" Cedric's voice broke my words and split the room in two.

He took my face in his hands and forced me to look into his eyes. He didn't seem angry, but he was serious.

"We'll figure out what's happening to you," he told me, calmer. "But you have to calm down, okay?"

"I can't," I said with my face still in his hands. "Cedric, I don't know what's happening to me."

"We'll find out, but you have to trust me. Can you do that?"

Could I do it? Of course not, just like he couldn't trust me. We were enemies; I lied to him all the time, and surely he did the same. I couldn't trust, I would only calm down when I found evidence.

"I can't," I said, swallowing saliva, and I can swear his expression hardened a bit. "You have to show me that I can trust you."

"I will, April," he smiled somewhat sadly. "I'll find out what's happening to you."

From that moment on, as soon as he crossed the door of my room, I didn't see him again until two days later when Gary's birthday arrived. I knew he had spent the last two days locked in the library. He didn't show up for dinner, not to finish decorating the cake, not to see the donors.

That day, everyone woke up a bit earlier than usual. It hadn't darkened yet, but everyone was standing, with the curtains tightly closed, decorating the entire house for Gary.

"What is this supposed to be?" I said, looking at Godric with a furrowed brow.

"A blood waterfall," he told me very calmly.

He had turned the typical chocolate waterfalls into one of blood and seemed very proud of his work.

"And according to you, how does this help a blood addict?" I said, scratching my forehead.

"Well, he has to feed anyway, right? It's his birthday..." Godric stuck a finger into the cascade and licked it, not taking his eyes off me. "Do you want to try?"

I glared at him and focused on hanging plastic knife decorations on the stairs.

"God, I've never seen something so poorly decorated," I heard Destiny's voice as she came down. "Where do I put this?" she asked, showing me an electric saw.

"That's not..." I began to say horrified, but Godric cut me off and took the saw with a macabre smile.

"This is for dinner," he replied.

"What are you planning?" I asked, putting my hands on my hips. "He's twelve, and he's not supposed to be a serial killer."

"Well, if he wants to control himself, he has to overcome temptation, right?" replied Godric, who seemed extremely amused by it all.

"If you ruin it, I'll stake both of you," I warned them, as if I could really do anything against them.

"I've already set up the speaker in the dining room," Emily informed us, pointing back with her thumb. "What music should I play, birthday expert?" she said to me, holding her phone in her hand.

I approached and searched for a pop song list.

"This will be fine," I said, handing it back.

"Diu, pop isn't elegant, sophisticated, or going to raise the prestige of the house," Destiny said with a wrinkled face.

"Well, it doesn't matter; it's a birthday," I retorted. "Okay, everything is ready."

When Gary came down that night, I couldn't believe it. His eyes widened, bright and excited, as he descended the stairs and saw everyone waiting for him below. The guests were also there. A group of thirteen vampire children dressed as Victorian-era aristocrats, which didn't fit at all with the party.

"Happy birthday!" we all shouted at once, and I felt a great relief because I had made them practice that at least a dozen times so that it would come out as a cheerful exclamation.

"What is all this?" Gary asked, looking in all directions.

"A surprise party," I smiled at him. "Thirteen years aren't always fulfilled, right?"

They started with the first part of the birthday. In the backyard, I had asked Cornelius to set up two soccer goals, which I had asked him to buy beforehand. I had drawn the entire field with white spray paint.

I divided the young ones into teams and asked Cedric to be the referee because I couldn't see how fast they were running, and I couldn't call any fouls.

"Do you think this will help him stop thinking about blood?" Godric asked, stopping next to me, while watching the group of vampires running with the ball.

"It already worked," I said with a half-smile. "He didn't even notice the blood cascade... And now he's not thinking about how much he wants to drink."

"You're smart, aren't you?" he said, nodding and trying unsuccessfully to hide a smile.

"I don't know," I shrugged. "You tell me."

They played for about two hours. They didn't sweat, didn't get tired, and the goal nets had holes from the force with which they kicked. Cedric called them all to finish the game. Gary ran towards us with bright eyes and a smile, not at all psychopathic, plastered on his face.

"Dinner time," said Cornelius, starting to walk again towards the mansion.

The birthday girl, who had danced with Gary, was glued to the birthday boy, hooked on his arm. He didn't even look at her; he just kept walking, pulling her to move faster.

"Are you already friends with Godric?" I heard Cedric's voice beside me, deep and masculine.

"What?" I said confused.

"I saw you laughing; it seems like you get along..." He looked ahead, as if there was something really interesting to see on the horizon, but he seemed a bit tense.

What was that about? Was he jealous, perhaps? I shook my head and didn't even bother to answer. I walked faster than him to get out of his sight. As if I needed that.

The table was set for all the guests. There was all kinds of food – salads, fries, and a huge turkey that needed carving.

"Well, since the birthday theme is 'killing'..." Godric began as he entered with the saw into the room. "Gary, I give you the honors."

Gary took the saw with a smile and looked at me.

"To her?" he asked very calmly.

"What? No! Gary, what's wrong with you?" I said horrified, stepping back.

"To the turkey, Gary, to the turkey," Cedric laughed, holding the bridge of his nose between his fingers.

Gary shrugged, pulled the cord, and the saw started roaring. He approached the turkey and began cutting it with excited eyes. Feathers scattered everywhere, but no one seemed to care except Cornelius.

Apparently, he couldn't stand it because he turned on his heels and left the room. It wasn't his thing, and he couldn't tolerate the laughter, the non-elegant parties, and so much humanity together.

Peter took care of serving the remaining food on everyone's plates, along with the side dishes, and then everything went awry: when he finished serving, he took the blood cascade and planted it in the middle of the table.

Gary's face darkened. His eyes widened. I walked up to him, took him by the shoulders, and asked him to breathe and focus on his plate. It was obvious he wouldn't listen to me. He pushed me away and lunged at the table, straight to the cascade. He opened his mouth and began gulping down all the blood that fell.

His clothes, his face, his hands, and the table began to soak in the thick red liquid, and soon other vampire kids joined him, though not with the same eagerness.

"Cedric, do something!" I pleaded, but he was already behind Gary pulling him away from the cascade.

"Come on, Gary, control yourself. You can do it!" he shouted.

The boy detached himself from the source, with his usual expression – wide, desperate, and blood-drenched red eyes.

The crimson liquid was everywhere. Destiny covered her mouth and stepped back; it was too much temptation even for her. Godric started asking the younger ones to go to the main hall. Emily pushed them with less kindness, and I just watched.

I watched every movement of the blood in the cascade; I could even hear the soft sound it made dripping from the table to the floor. My throat was dry again, without nausea, without disgust, just an uncontrollable craving.

I squeezed my eyelids tightly, trying to control myself, and then, I dashed out of the room to get as far away as possible and suppress the thirst.

CHAPTER 29

I literally drank a liter of water to try to quench my thirst. Gradually, I calmed down, but I knew it wasn't because of hydrating.

"What's going on with you?" Emily appeared in the kitchen and looked at me with crossed arms. "The guests are gone, and we've had all the blood from the cascade. You can come out."

"I don't know what's happening to me," I sighed. "When you turned into a vampire, how did you feel?"

"My gums hurt a lot because the fangs were growing. The sun initially gave me blisters, and I was sleepy even at night." She shrugged. "If you have doubts, you're not turning into a vampire. But it seems like you're a bit crazy."

"Yeah, thanks, Emily," I said, rolling my eyes.

She poured herself a glass of whiskey, raised it in a toast toward me, and drank it in one gulp.

"You did well today," she continued. "Gary is the only one I like besides Cedric, and I must say, you helped him."

"Yes, well... Until he saw the cascade and got a bit too excited..." I sighed, walking over to where she was and pouring myself a drink too.

"Let me ask you a question," she said suddenly, and I nodded silently. "What's going on between Cedric and you?"

"Nothing," I said quickly. "He's a vampire, and I'm human... or something like that."

"And does that matter?" She raised an eyebrow.

"Of course, it does..."

"Look, April, many years ago, I know I hurt him, and I know that after that, he was terrified. It's been over thirty years since our thing happened, and I haven't seen him with anyone since then." She bit her lip, thoughtful. "I was convinced he would never forget me and that we would have all eternity to be together later when he felt like it." That seemed extremely cruel to me. "But I notice how he looks at you, and I don't like it. If you're not interested in him, step aside."

"Do you think you deserve to be with him?" I said, frowning. "After what you did to him?" I almost spat out the words. She had used him to convert, ignored him for thirty years, and now she was concerned...

"He and I will be together, April, I just want you to know. If you step aside, you won't get hurt as much." She said with a fake smile.

"I'm not interested," I said, finishing the last sip of my drink and leaving before punching her in the face.

Gary was sitting in one of the armchairs, while the cat scratched his arm incessantly.

"What's wrong with you?" I exclaimed, running towards him.

He had bloody scratches. I pushed the cat away from the chair and looked at Gary with a furrowed brow.

"What happened?" I insisted.

"I'm tired of myself!" He shouted at me with a fury I didn't see coming. "I want blood! I want blood all day! I'm tired of controlling myself!"

"Well, you have to do it," I cut him off. "You have to learn to control yourself unless you want to be a murderer."

"I'm fed up!" His eyes were red, but not from thirst; he had started crying.

Oh, God... What was I supposed to do? I might have doubted it before, but seeing the thick tears rolling down his cheeks broke my heart. I hugged him tightly. He remained motionless, surprised, and finally returned the gesture.

"You'll be able to, Gary... I promise..." I stroked his dark hair, just like his brother's, with my fingers and felt him trembling with sobs.

"I don't want to be a monster," he said with a choked voice. "I want to learn to control myself like everyone else... But it's difficult."

"I know, Gary, we'll figure it out," I said, not letting him go.

"April," Cedric's voice resonated at the top of the stairs. "Come."

Gary stepped away and quickly wiped his eyes. It was obvious he didn't want to show that vulnerability in front of anyone else. I gave him an encouraging smile and ran upstairs.

I followed Cedric to the library, and he closed the door.

"There will be a blood moon in a month," he suddenly told me. "You have a month to convince your sister to come here and let us use some of her blood."

"How will I talk to her?" I said, playing with my fingers nervously.

"If you met her in the church, it would be full of vampire hunters trying to kill us, and I don't intend to cause a massacre," he said, shrugging. "You'll go alone, talk to her, and come back."

– You've certainly made progress in these weeks – I said with a sardonic smile.

– You said I had to earn your trust, and that's what I'm doing – he said, shrugging. – It would be very amusing to kill some of them, but I promised you, didn't I?

– Yes – I nodded – you did – he fixed his deep eyes on mine, and for a moment, I got lost in them. I think we both did.

– You can call her and tell her that you need to see her without hunters, during the day –

– What? – I said surprised – During the day?

– Call me stupid, but I'm also going to trust you – he said, rolling his eyes, as if he already knew that what he was doing was foolish – you'll go alone, talk to her, and come back –

– Are you aware that you're leaving everything in my hands? – I said, blinking, somewhat confused.

– Are you a girl of your word or not? – he asked, raising an eyebrow.

– Yes... – I swallowed saliva; I was too confused.

– You promised to help my brother, and you wanted to do it even before reaching an agreement with me. So I know you'll come back –

– Do you think your brother is reason enough for me to return to the place where they have me kidnapped... – I said, recapping.

– No – he finally dared to look me in the eyes and smiled maliciously – but you promised it to me, and I am reason enough for you –

– I'll do it – I nodded – but not for you...

Cedric smiled on the side and moved towards me slowly, still looking at me. I stepped back a few steps until my back leaned against the door.

– No? – he put one hand on each side of my body and got even closer – And why will you do it?

My heart started beating strongly. His eyes burned as he studied my face and looked at my lips.

– I'll do it because... – I really didn't know... Why would I want to go back? Why did it matter so much to me to keep a deal with him?

– Because you want me to trust you, right? – He smiled softly – Just like I want you to trust me –

My eyes reached his neck; I had to lift my gaze to see his face. At that moment, he felt so big, so tall, and so strong... And I felt small next to him, but capable of many things... With him.

– Why? – I asked, biting my lip while he didn't take his eyes off my mouth.

– Do you know?   Cedric brought his face close to mine.

My skin tingled just feeling his breath next to mine. He was so close that I could smell his perfume and feel the electricity running between us. How could I be so attracted to a vampire?

– Cedric... – I whispered his name without even knowing what to say.

Our noses brushed, my heart was about to jump out of my chest, but just when I thought he was going to kiss me... His face moved to the left, and he collapsed to the floor.

– Cedric? – I exclaimed, opening my eyes wide – What the hell!

I squatted down next to him, shaking his shoulders, but he was unconscious. I couldn't lift him, so I opened the library door and yelled for help. Cornelius was the first to arrive. I stepped aside, and he knelt beside his son.

He touched his forehead, his neck, opened his eyes, and then looked at me.

– It's vervain –

Those two words pierced my chest.

– Is he... Is he dead? – I asked, covering my mouth as my legs weakened.

– No, idiot. But something is poisoning him, and apparently the rest too – He took his son, hung his arm over his shoulder, and dragged him out of the library to his room.

I didn't want to think, under any circumstances, that it was my fault. Cedric had almost kissed me, and he hadn't done it because I had poisoned him. I was a horrible person, worse than any of them, and I knew it.

I couldn't continue with this. I couldn't keep hurting him, nor the others, even if they treated me like shit. I didn't want that; I didn't want to be like that. As soon as I could, I would get rid of the vervain. I just needed to wake up before the rest and throw it somewhere.

– It must be the donors – I heard Destiny's voice inside Cedric's room.

Everyone had gone to see him in a second, surrounding his bed while he remained unconscious.

– Those damn blood bags must be taking vervain. It was obvious we couldn't trust them – Godric said, almost spitting out the words.

– Maybe some hunter contacted them and asked them to do it – Emily seemed uneasy and kept biting her nails incessantly.

– You said you were going to investigate this, Destiny – Godric reminded her.

– Sure, because I don't do anything all day... – She replied, irritated.

– Enough of this, all of you – Cornelius ordered – the vervain could be in the donors or they might have left it somewhere in the house where we frequently are.

– What are we supposed to do then? – Emily asked.

– Search the entire house, every corner, and Emily, tell your father to come – he ordered, cold – maybe he has something to tell us –

She nodded and quickly left the room.

– I'll check the library – Godric reported.

– I'll check the kitchen – I offered quickly.

– No – Cornelius fixed his empty eyes on me – they'll do it, they are my trust.

– I am capable of searching... – I defended myself, pretending to feel offended.

– And also of lying – he said, raising his eyebrows.

Did he already know?

CHAPTER 30

There was no way I could calm down. My palms were sweating, and I felt cold sweat on my back.

What would they be capable of doing to me if they found out that I had been poisoning them?

My eyes stopped at Cedric, lying down, with his dark hair tousled, pale and without his usual playful smile.

What would he think of what I had done?

I sat on the edge of the bed. Everyone was looking for the vervain, and I had to stay there, with him, waiting for him to wake up.

Suddenly, his eyelids fluttered, and he slowly opened his eyes.

– What happened? – he asked in a raspy voice.

– You fainted...– I couldn't even look him in the eyes– it seems you got poisoned with vervain...–

– True– he put a hand on his forehead, furrowing his brow– with everything that happened, I forgot that something has been weakening us–

– Right...– I nodded looking at the floor– Do you feel okay? –

– No– he sat on the bed– I'm dizzy–

– Do you want me to get you something? – I asked, not knowing what to do.

– I should drink blood, but it's better not to until we find out where the vervain is–

I wanted to tell him that the blood bags in the fridge were not poisoned, but... How could I know without being suspicious?

Cornelius walked through the door, followed by Emily and Peter.

– Speak! – Cornelius grabbed him by the lapels of his coat and looked him straight in the eyes, hypnotizing him– Did you put vervain somewhere in the house? –

– No, sir! – Peter had wide-open eyes and looked at him frightened.

– Did you see anyone with vervain? – Cornelius asked again.

– I felt like I was going to faint.

– No! – he answered.

For a second, I didn't understand. Peter knew that I had put vervain in the food, once... If he was hypnotized, he should have said it, but...

– Do you know how we are getting weaker? –

– Because of vervain! – Peter replied.

Then I understood. They had asked him if he "had seen someone with vervain," and he hadn't seen me; he had felt it in the taste of the food. If they didn't ask the right questions, they wouldn't find out anything.

– Okay...– Cedric asked Cornelius to stop with a hand gesture– it's obvious he knows nothing, and it wasn't him–

– Damn it! – Cornelius let go of the butler, evidently annoyed.

– It's the donors, I'm sure– said Emily as her father straightened his wrinkled clothes– some new ones came lately... It must have been one of them–

– It wasn't one– Cedric cut her off– we are all affected, and we drink from different donors–

– Donors aspire to become vampires. They would never do anything against us– said Cornelius, rubbing his chin– it must have been someone else– he looked at me fixedly, studying my expression, but I made an effort not to show any emotion.

– I found it! – Destiny's voice echoed in the room, especially in my ears.

I felt the blood leave my face, and I began to tremble. I kept myself rigid so that it wouldn't show, and I just turned my head to look at her. There she was, holding the paper bag in her hands.

– It was in the kitchen–

– There were many cooks last weekend– Peter mentioned, knowing that she wanted to distract them so they wouldn't think of me.

If God exists, it was a good time for him to appear, kidnap me, and save me from them.

– That weekend we were already weak; it wasn't them. Vervain doesn't have an immediate effect– Cornelius ruled out– Mmm... Let's see– he took Peter by the neck and slammed him against the wall. He looked into his eyes again and spoke:

– You knew what you said didn't make sense, right? –

– Yes, sir! –

– So sincere...

– Whom are you trying to protect? – Cornelius asked again.

NO

NO

NO

– April–

That was the end. All eyes were on me. I could feel Cedric's gaze penetrating my brain, Cornelius's satisfied smile, and the surprise from Destiny and Emily.

I couldn't look at them, I couldn't move, I couldn't...

– You damn bitch! – that was the moment Destiny lost all her elegance.

She jumped on me and pushed me to the other end of the room. I was weak but not so much as to lose all her strength. As soon as my body hit the floor, she pounced on me again, took me by the neck, and lifted me.

I felt her firm fingers squeezing my trachea and lifting my feet off the ground. I was going to die; I knew it. They were going to kill me just as they had wanted to do from the very beginning.

– Destiny, let her go– Cedric's voice was colder than an iceberg.

She didn't even pretend to let go. She looked at me with furious eyes, full of hatred and contempt.

– You're going to die, you damn blood bag– she said through gritted teeth.

– Destiny– Cedric repeated.

She obeyed; with a swift motion, she threw me against the nightstand. I crashed into the wood on my ribs and fell to the floor, entangled with the ceramic lamp that shattered. I felt every piece digging into my hands and face. But that didn't hurt as much as the guilt I felt. I deserved all of it; I deserved to be killed. I had been weakening them, exposing them to the same fate; I had been the first to attack.

I got up as best as I could. My eyes burned; I had a lump in my throat that wouldn't let me breathe.

– Get out– I heard Cedric say.

– What? – Emily couldn't believe it.

– Get out! – he roared, facing away from everyone.

They complied. The silence became heavy around us. I couldn't lift my gaze; I couldn't look at him; I couldn't see him disappointed.

– Now you're going to look at me– he told me, dryly– you looked me in the eyes all this time, didn't you? –

I pressed my lips, trying not to cry.

– Look at me, you piece of shit! – he shouted at me angrily.

I looked up at him. I didn't know what expression I had, but seeing his was all I needed to break. He was furious, furious and disappointed. His eyes were dimmer than ever, fists clenched at the sides of his body.

– I'm sorry– I whispered, almost inaudibly.

– Sorry? Are you asking for forgiveness? – he let out a disgusted breath– this wasn't an accident, April; you thought about it, planned it, and you did it! – he reminded me– I offered you my damn help to find out what was happening to you. I was locked day and night in the library searching for something that could help you! –

– Cedric, I'm sorry... I... I regretted it...–

– I trusted you! You told me to earn your trust, and you weren't even honest with me! –

He began to walk around the room, furious, and punched the wardrobe, splintering the wood.

– You lied all the time...– he didn't look at me, and it was a relief because I couldn't avoid my eyes filling with tears.

– Cedric, I... Sorry, really, sorry–

– Go to hell, April! – he yelled at me– Go! Get out of my room! –

– No, wait...– I tried to approach him– I did it at first because I hated them... And then I... I started to...–

– I don't want to hear you! – he shouted, fixing his hurt eyes on mine– How can you even cry? –

I covered my mouth with my hand and stifled a sob. It was shit; I deserved every one of his words, and I knew it, but they hurt, and I felt like I was breaking every passing second.

– Go, April– Cedric turned his back, fists still clenched.

I ran out of the room; tears kept pouring out, like a damn waterfall. I locked myself in my room and slid down the door, sitting on the floor.

I hugged my legs and cried, cried like I hadn't in a long time. Why? Because I had felt close to Cedric an hour ago, because I was beginning to care for the vampire boy who needed my help. I was starting to think they weren't monsters just because they were different from humans, and I had thought about it many times before, but I had decided to let fear, what my parents had taught me about them, guide me instead of making an effort to draw my own conclusions.

I had played the role of the good girl, but I had been the monster. At least, they hadn't pretended to feel affection for me, nor interest... I had, lied to everyone, but what hurt the most was losing Cedric's trust, a trust I had just earned.

CHAPTER 31

It took me two days to gather enough courage to reappear. I had only left my room to go to the nearest bathroom, and I hadn't even eaten.

However, on the third day, my stomach was growling; I was hungry and thirsty. Besides, I had come to the conclusion that if I could explain myself, maybe Cedric could understand my reasons a bit more, even if they weren't a justification for poisoning them all.

I left my room almost without making a sound and went downstairs. I entered the kitchen; Peter wasn't there, so I grabbed a pack of noodles, cut some vegetables, and made a stir-fry substantial enough to make up for my days of fasting.

– What a pity, I thought you would starve to death, and I could drink the blood from your corpse– Gary said, appearing in the kitchen along with Cedric's cat.

I smiled at him, not knowing exactly what I was supposed to do. Should I kneel and beg for forgiveness or treat him as usual? I decided to go for the second option and just kept stirring the noodles to prevent them from sticking.

– I need you to eat quickly; we had agreed that you were going to help me– he continued – and you've dodged it for two days–

– Aren't you angry with me? – I asked, blinking like a fool.

– Let's see...– Gary took his chin as if he had to think about it– you poisoned my whole family, but... who doesn't want to kill from time to time? –

I didn't know what to say... Should I be glad that the psychopathic kid felt empathy for me?

– Besides– he continued– we kidnapped you. It's normal that you tried to do something; the strange thing would be if you had adapted perfectly, and we were all friends, right? –

I nodded, feeling my chest a little lighter. I drained the noodles, stir-fried them, and served them on a fairly large plate. I offered it to him, but he just took a bag of blood from the fridge and sat on a stool in front of me.

– What do you feel when you drink blood? – I asked him.

– Will talking help me become a good vampire? – he asked me while I swallowed a huge amount of noodles.

– Maybe yes– I nodded – so go ahead, talk to me– I encouraged him, waving a hand.

– Well, when I drink blood... I don't know, it's so good that I feel like I can't stop–

– Can't you or don't you want to? – I asked him.

– Both– he said after thinking for a few seconds– I don't know... When I'm drinking, I can only think about that, about the taste, the aroma... And I like everything–

– What else do you like? – I asked him while stabbing a piece of carrot.

– Nothing– he shrugged – well, yes: killing, torturing animals, people...–

– Okay, let's pretend you don't like anything else– I interrupted him– Did you enjoy playing soccer on your birthday? – I asked him, studying him with some discretion.

– Yes, I liked it... Although that girl was all the time stuck to me–

– Yes, well... She's a bit annoying– I smiled at him– you know, I think... You need to do more things you like, try new things... It's a good way to distract yourself–

– But the other vampires have the same education as me... Why don't they need to play soccer? Or I don't know... Have a birthday celebration? – he said, frowning and looking at me intensely.

– Because they're not as sad as you– I blurted out.

I knew it was a risky deduction; after all, I wasn't a psychologist. But I had seen the times when his eyes had lit up at something interesting or when he was engrossed in something.

– Sad? I'm not sad– he mocked me without looking at me.

– Well, I think you are– I limited myself to saying– you have to think about when you started feeling that blood was everything–

– Your talk is shit– he just said, getting off the stool– I'm going to look for the cat; it's more interesting than you–

I rolled my eyes and took care of finishing my plate. As soon as I had mentioned his sadness, Gary had become defensive and had left. It was clear that something was bothering him, and maybe understanding that or solving it could help him stop craving blood desperately.

However, I was sure he wouldn't let go of it so easily, so there was only one person who could help me, someone who didn't want to see me at all.

I knocked on Cedric's door with my knuckles. My heart was pounding a thousand times per hour. I hoped he wouldn't hear me from the inside because then I wouldn't even have the chance to talk to him before he kicked me out.

– Come in–

I opened the door almost trembling. It wasn't fear of him; it was anxiety about what he might tell me or how he would look at me.

Cedric was in front of the wardrobe, shirtless, exposing his muscular torso and the wings tattooed in black ink on his back. As soon as I closed the door, he turned and looked at me.

What are you doing here? – he asked me in a cold tone.

– We need to talk– I said, leaning my back against the door and forcing myself to look him in the face.

– We have nothing to talk about– he said, turning again towards the wardrobe, uninterested.

– It's okay if you don't want to talk to me, but I'm not here for myself; I'm here for Gary–

Yeah, sure... Well, I did want to help Gary, obviously, but the truth was that I wanted to see him, I wanted to talk to him again and try to fix things if there was anything to fix.

Cedric ran his hands through his hair, messing it up, and probably debating whether he felt like listening to me or not. Finally, he turned in my direction, leaning on the wardrobe and furrowing his brow.

– Speak–

– I need to know when Gary started losing control with blood...–

– I don't know, some years ago– he said thoughtfully.

– Do you have any idea why? – I asked, playing with my fingers– I think his addiction to blood is because only when he drinks does he feel good. That means the rest of the time, he's sad... There must be an underlying reason–

– Well, I have no idea– he shrugged, stepping away from the wardrobe and sitting on the bed–

– Cedric, I need you to think about it–

– You're not in a position to ask me for anything– he informed me as if I didn't already know that well enough.

– I'm asking for help for Gary, not for myself–

– And how do I know it's true? That you're not looking for another weakness to kill him?–

– I'm not going to kill Gary– I said, furrowing my brow.

– Well, I don't know, April– he shrugged, looking me in the eyes– I don't trust you anymore–

– I promised both of you that I would help. I just want to fulfill that promise–

Cedric advanced toward me with almost invisible speed. Suddenly, he was standing a few steps away. He took my chin with his index and thumb and stared into my eyes.

It didn't hurt physically, but it was a stab to the heart because I knew what he was about to do, and it was as if we had gone back to when we first met.

– Are you telling the truth? – he asked me seriously, hypnotizing me.

I hadn't taken vervain for two days, so his power took effect on me. But anyway, I had nothing to hide from him, not anymore.

– Yes– I said expressionlessly– I'm telling the truth–

Cedric let me go and stepped away from me.

– Maybe there's something– he said, sitting back on the bed– I think he started behaving like this three years ago. We thought it was normal because he was still young, and it might be hard for him to restrain himself–

– What happened three years ago? – I asked him, studying his face.

– Our mother died– he looked down; it was clear that it hurt him too.

– I think that's a good reason for him to feel this way– I nodded– Could he say goodbye? –

– No– Cedric raised his eyes again, tense; he seemed to want to run away without looking back– I mean, yes, he could, but he didn't want to. He was furious, didn't want to see her body in the coffin, and kept saying constantly that our mother would come back sooner or later– he swallowed with difficulty and continued– my father and I took out everything that belonged to her, trying to make him realize that she wouldn't come back, and over time, he stopped saying that she would return, but he lost control with blood–

– He's filling the void he feels for her...–

– But I don't think he can fill it–

– No, of course not... He won't forget his mother, and that's okay... But maybe what generates so much anxiety for him is the fact that no matter how much he knows his mother died, he didn't close the cycle with her. He didn't see her in the coffin, didn't say goodbye to her, didn't mourn her, and doesn't even have any related objects anymore– I scratched my forehead– I can't be sure, but we should try to do something with all that pain–

– Something like what? – he asked me, opening his eyes a little wider.

– I don't know... I have to think about it... Where did you keep your mother's things? –

– In the basement– he said, standing up and putting his hands in his pants pockets– Do you really think it can help him? –

– Yes– I said confidently.

– Then follow me; I'll show you.

CHAPTER 32

We went down to the basement in silence, where they had locked me up on the first day they brought me to the mansion. Cedric turned on the light, pulling the chain next to the door, and we descended the dusty steps.

– Here, we keep all her things– he said, burying his hands in his pockets.

I looked around; there was the painting of the woman I had already seen.

– It's her, isn't it? – I asked, squatting in front of the large portrait, and he nodded.

– You resemble her a lot; both of you resemble her– I said with a genuine smile.

– Yes, well, we have her eyes and... –

– Her nose– I said, looking at him, and he touched it reflexively.

– Yes– he nodded, looking away.

– What was she like? – I asked him, knowing that maybe I would only receive a hostile response from him.

– I don't think knowing will help you to help my brother– he said, approaching a small chest of drawers and running a finger over the surface to remove the dust.

– True. He doesn't need me to know, but he needs someone to talk about her as if her name weren't taboo– I said, standing back up and looking at him– Can you talk about her? –

– Of course, I can– he nodded, shrugging it off.

– Well, then I'll just look for something that... can make him feel good remembering her– I said as I scanned every object in the basement.

There weren't things that seemed especially important. Some paintings, antique furniture... And a fairly large bundle covered with a sheet.

– What's this? – I asked him as I took the edge of the fabric to uncover what was underneath.

– Wait! – he said, quickly stretching out his hand and taking mine to stop me– that's not... – his eyes met mine, and I didn't look away; I held his gaze while I felt his soft hand squeezing mine– okay, go ahead– he sighed.

He let go of my hand, and I pulled the sheet to discover that underneath it was a beautiful grand piano, glossy black.

– Wow! – I couldn't help but exclaim– It's huge and very elegant! -

– Yes, it was hers– he nodded.

When I looked back at him, he wasn't there. His body was in front of the piano, but his mind was immersed in thousands of memories that I didn't know. He calmly circled the piano, first caressing the smooth wood of the instrument and then sliding his fingers over each of the keys. He had a melancholic smile on his face, and his hair fell a little over his eyes. If I had had a camera, that would have been a good moment to immortalize.

Cedric sat down in front of it and closed his eyes. What could he be remembering?

– There was a song we used to play together... – he said, frowning a bit, probably trying to remember.

He positioned his fingers on the keys and, without further ado, began to play. It was a gentle and delicate melody, like rose petals falling slowly to the ground. The notes sounded like drizzling raindrops, tinkling on surfaces.

He slid his fingers slowly between the keys, with patience and a concentrated expression.

That melody was beautiful; it even gave me goosebumps as I listened to it. He kept playing, lost in his world and memories. It was beautiful to watch; suddenly, that irritating and cheeky vampire had become a boy, a creature as human as anyone, or even more so.

I studied his profile, his thick and sunken eyebrows, with a small wrinkle right in the middle, his lips slightly pressed due to concentration, his eyes suddenly bright, in those blue and violet tones that, honestly... I loved. His bare back was slightly hunched, and he looked so free with all of that, as if that were the real Cedric.

The one playing his mother's song on the piano and connecting the pieces of his heart with that so sad melody.

I didn't know why, I didn't know how I dared, I didn't know what he had that was special, but I did what I felt, the only thing that could repair the damage I had done.

While he continued to play, I walked slowly behind him and hugged him. I buried my face in his back and squeezed my eyelids shut, hoping he wouldn't tell me to go to hell, but he didn't.

He stopped playing, took my hands, which were resting on his chest, and held them there, firm, as if giving me permission to continue.

– How come I don't hate you? – he asked, almost more to himself than to me.

I didn't say anything and kept standing there, feeling the scent of his soft skin, perceiving the almost inaudible beat of his heart, which beat because he was undead.

– I'm sorry, Cedric– I finally said, letting go of him as he turned to look at me– tell me how I can regain your trust in me–

– I don't know– he shook his head, with a sad smile– but I want to regain it, and I don't know why–

– I want to, too... – I said, biting my lip– tell me about your mother... – I asked him.

– She taught me to play this song when I was a kid; she taught it to both of us, and every night we sat together to listen to it– he looked up at me– this house wasn't so silent before. My father was always cold, but she was so warm despite being like us... She was so human... Sometimes she got mad at me for being too cold and insensitive; she insisted that I should smile more, express myself more, be kinder... But well, it's evident that she didn't succeed– he continued with a grimace, and I smiled in turn.

– It's understandable that Gary and you miss a woman like her. She sounds fantastic– he nodded.

– She was... But, well– he stood up– What can we do for Gary? – he asked me while patting the piano wood, almost affectionately.

– I think we know the answer, don't we? –

About an hour later, Cornelius and Cedric had taken the piano and brought it back to the main hall. Cornelius didn't even bother to look at me, but to be honest, I cared quite little.

– What are you doing? – Emily appeared with a glass full of blood from the kitchen and watched them– Are you going to try playing again, Cedric? You know you're terrible at it...–

– Shut up, Emily– he replied very calmly, wiping the piano with a cloth to remove the little dust it had.

– He plays well– I told her, glaring at her.

– Oh... Wait... Who spoke? I think I heard a noise, like a very annoying mosquito, but I don't know what it was...– she said, holding her ear with her hand and making a puzzled face.

– I thought vampires were more mature than five-year-old kids– I replied, rolling my eyes.

– You're too participative for someone who tried to kill us–

Emily one, April zero. What a low blow...

– I don't know what they have in mind, but Cedric, be careful– Cornelius, for the first time, seemed concerned– Gary's mind is very... Unstable–

– This will be a moment between them; we should avoid being here. Gary needs to feel free to speak– I said, squeezing my hands nervously.

– Can someone explain to me why we keep hearing her? – Emily asked, looking at Cornelius and Cedric respectively.

– Because she's a manipulative bitch, but she knows what she's talking about– Cedric explained very calmly.

MANIPULATIVE BITCH?! WHAT?!

– Hey! – I exclaimed, looking at him with a furrowed brow.

– You still don't have the right to say anything– he reminded me, shrugging, and Emily seemed a bit more satisfied.

– Emily, tell Godric and Destiny that they can't come here– Cedric asked her, and she went upstairs, probably to find them.

– I'm leaving now– I said, following her steps.

Cedric stayed alone, standing in the middle of the room. The piano and him, facing each other. He took a deep breath, sat down again, and began to play the same song as an hour ago. I knew that was the song that could destabilize Gary, and that's what he had to achieve. A storm of feelings so that the sun could finally come out.

As soon as he heard the melody, Gary took very little time to come out of his room and go down the stairs. At first, he was petrified, looking at Cedric from above, seeing his mother's piano, with his heart stopped.

The melody slapped him with thousands of memories and feelings that he had been suppressing, that he had hidden so deep that he no longer remembered them.

Finally, he decided to move and keep going down to him.

– What are you doing? – he asked Cedric, stopping by his side.

– I don't want us to stay silent anymore– he replied, stopping playing– it hurts you to miss her in silence, and it hurts me too–

– I don't know what you're talking about...– Gary stared at the piano, avoiding his brother's gaze.

– You don't know? – Cedric smiled at him, as if he expected that answer– then come, play with me... Just to remember her– he moved to the side of the bench, and his brother sat down too.

Both of their hands trembled when they stretched them to start playing; both were nervous about what would happen next.

In silence, as if they had just practiced it, each began to play their notes on the piano. They did it with ease, like a poem you learn in school and never forget. They played for a long time, repeating the same song until they were tired, feeling more and more each time, letting themselves go further and further. The piano seemed to have a life of its own; their mother seemed to be with them, guiding them.

Suddenly the sound broke. Gary took his hands off the piano and closed his eyelids tightly.

– Gary– Cedric turned to him, trying to convey reassurance with his voice.

– I need...– Gary had his fists clenched so tightly that his knuckles had turned white.

– Do what you need to do– Cedric told him.

Then the boy stood up, planted his feet on the ground with clenched fists, his whole body rigid, and screamed. He let out the most heart-wrenching scream I had ever heard in my life, a desperate scream, a broken, sad, and loud scream. He released all the air he had in his lungs until there was nothing left, and then he fell to his knees on the marble floor, and Cedric was there to lift him up.

CHAPTER 33

– Come on, April, make the call– Cedric urged me, sitting on one of the armchairs.

I held his phone in my hands, staring at the screen as if it could explode at any moment, although what could happen if I called might be even worse.

– I don't have all night...– he said again, leaning back on the bed and crossing his arms behind his head.

– Fine– I sighed, finally giving in to dialing my sister's number.

– The phone rang three times before someone answered.

– Hello? – it was her voice.

– It's April– I said, smiling to myself.

– April! Where are you? Did you escape? – she exclaimed on the verge of hysteria.

I looked at Cedric, who rolled his eyes. Obviously, he could hear the conversation perfectly well.

– No... I didn't escape, but they... They want me to talk to you, in person–

– Is it a trap? You can tell me the word we agreed on...–

– No– I quickly denied – it's not–

– Are they with you? – Aixa asked me.

I looked at Cedric, who shook his head. I bit my lip and prepared to answer; I hated lying to her.

– No, they let me talk to you; they trust me–

– Well... When do we meet? Where? –

– Tomorrow? – I asked, suddenly getting nervous.

– Sure, yes...–

– There's a condition; the hunters can't go with you–

– Oh sure...– I felt a dry, indignant laugh escaping her– of course, it's a trap. They want me to go alone and unarmed, and they'll be there to kill both of us–

– No! Aixa, wait... You can choose the place... They won't go; I'll go alone–

– How can I know? How do I know they're not pressuring you? –

– Aixa, trust me, they won't hurt you– I swallowed hard– anything they might use to pressure me wouldn't work if the solution were to put you in danger–

– Fine– I felt that my words had managed to calm her a bit– tomorrow, when I'm at the location, I'll tell you where we meet, okay? –

– Sure– I nodded.

– I love you, April–

– I love you too– I sighed and then hung up.

– Whatever the time and place, I'll be there– Cedric informed me.

– Good– I said, throwing him the phone.

He caught it on the fly and looked at me with a furrowed brow.

– You can't act mad– he said, blocking my way– you were the one who lied–

– I know– I sighed, containing my anger– I'm angry with myself for messing it up; it's not with you–

I walked past him and left the room. The corridor was as dark as ever, and everything was too silent. I went into the library, picked a book, and took it to my room to start reading.

I opened the door, entered, and before I could close it, it slammed violently. I turned around. Godric's figure was standing behind me, with a hand against the door.

– So, you decided to get comfortable again? – he said, looking at me maliciously.

– I just took a book...– I said, lifting it so he could see it, in a peace offering.

– Look, blood bag, I was starting to like you a little because you were helping Gary, but now that you've shown your true colors, I have no intention of treating you as anything more than what you are. Food– his dark eyes were turning a reddish tint.

– Godric, I'm sorry for what I did, but get out of my room– I told him, holding his gaze with my chin up– you won't intimidate me–

– Well, you should feel pretty scared– he told me, taking the book I was holding and taking it from my hands.

He stepped away from the door and threw the book to the other side of the room.

– The time I tasted your blood, I was very impressed. It's really good...– he ran a finger over my neck while smiling lasciviously– I didn't do it again because Cedric didn't like it at all... But I think he's no longer interested in protecting you –

– Don't touch me– I said through gritted teeth.

– Oh, April...– he sighed dramatically– you shouldn't have used vervain with us... I'm very restrained, but...– with his hand, he wrapped my neck without barely applying pressure, but forcing me to stay still– I can't resist a good snack–

His eyes were completely red, and his fangs peeked out between his lips. I bent my knee and kicked him in the knee to make him let go of me. He leaned back, surprised, and I quickly grabbed the doorknob and pulled to open it.

As soon as I put one foot out of the room, I felt his hands grabbing my hair. He pulled me back and knocked me on my back against the floor.

– Let me go, you damn idiot! – I shouted, flailing my arms, trying to land a hit. He straddled me, preventing me from kicking further, and seized my wrists, pinning them to the ground.

– Let me go! – I yelled as I saw his diabolical smile approaching my face.

– You can scream all you want... Cedric's room is far; he won't hear you–

– I'm going to kill you! – I gathered saliva and spat in his face.

Godric furrowed his brow, let go of one of my hands, and wiped his face with the sleeve of his sweater.

– You shouldn't have done that– he said, wrinkling his forehead, leaned over me, and bit into my neck forcefully.

I clenched my teeth to avoid screaming in pain. I felt his lips eagerly sucking my blood, flowing out of my body like water pouring from a spilled glass. Godric pulled his lips away from my skin; I saw his contorted face and his chin stained and dripping.

He grabbed the collar of the T-shirt I was wearing with both hands and pulled it until I heard the fabric tearing. He made a cut long enough to expose more skin and bit me again on the shoulder.

I tried to punch him with the hand he had freed, but without stopping drinking my blood, he skillfully grabbed it and pinned it back to the ground.

There was something horrible about all of this, beyond the fact that he was biting me. He did it with fury and violence, demonstrating all his strength so that I would know I couldn't fight him.

I heard the sound of a door opening. I begged with all my being that it was Cedric. Footsteps echoed closer and closer, while I began to feel very weak and stopped struggling and thrashing.

– When you finish, leave her in her room– I heard Cornelius' voice, and then his steps moving away.

My vision was getting darker; I felt cold, with icy limbs, and his bites hurt a lot. I continued to hear the sound of each of his suctions until I lost consciousness.

I woke up with my face stuck to the floor. It was cold, and my body felt numb.

I slowly got up, with a headache that seemed to threaten to split my skull.

I was in my room, in the darkness. Around me was a small pool of blood, which had to be mine.

I took off the torn hoodie very slowly because I still felt the sting on my neck and shoulder. I turned on the bedside lamp and stood in front of the mirror. I had bites on both sides of my neck and several on my shoulders. They didn't look too bad, but more than usual, and I had bruised, purplish marks around each one.

I heard knocks on the door, and my heart skipped a beat. Would it be Godric again?

For a moment, I hesitated about throwing myself on the floor again and pretending to be dead so that he wouldn't bite me again, but I would know I was still alive; I could hear my heart.

– April! – again, a couple of knocks on the door, it was Cedric's voice.

I opened the wardrobe, put on the blue hoodie I had worn in cricket games, and pulled the hood up to cover my neck.

– Just a second! – with the torn shirt, I tried to clean the blood-stained floor and put everything away in the closet.

– Come on, April– just as I closed the cabinet, Cedric opened the door with a furrowed brow – What are you doing? –

– I was changing– I said, trying to keep an impassive face.

Cedric scanned my room, his eyebrows furrowed.

– Is everything okay? – he asked, turning his gaze back to me.

– Of course– I shrugged while my ears were buzzing.

I walked as best as I could to the bed and sat down, as if nothing were happening.

– Your sister sent a message; she says they can meet in a while...–

– So fast? Wasn't it supposed to be tomorrow? – I said, blinking.

– Yes... You called yesterday, April...– he looked at me as if I were an idiot, and I nodded.

Had a whole day passed while I was unconscious?

– You're acting strange– Cedric crossed his arms and looked at me intently– What's going on? –

Maybe it was stupid, but I didn't want to talk about it... I felt ashamed. Of what? Well, for not being able to defend myself as I hoped, for Godric tearing my hoodie off, leaving me half-naked, and for Cornelius passing by me, seeing all that, and not doing anything.

– Everything is perfectly fine– I said, wrinkling my forehead– Where is Aixa waiting for me? –

– That's the problem; she said she wants to meet you at your house–

Well, what's the problem? – I asked, quite distracted.

– It's your house; vampires can't enter–

My hands were still cold; I squeezed them together to warm them up. They tingled.

– Are you okay with that? – Cedric asked me. What? What had he asked me?

– Fine, yes– I said, biting the inside of my cheek.

– April, I asked you if you agreed to kill your sister...– he sighed, running his hand through his hair – let's pretend to get along for two seconds. What's wrong with you? – he walked over to me and squatted down, resting his hands on my knees.

– I'm still asleep... That's it– I lied.

Cedric looked me in the eyes, silently studying me until he sensed something.

– You smell...– he pressed his nose against the fabric of the pants covering my knees and then looked at me again with a strange expression– Were you with Godric? –

Well, was there anything you could hide from a vampire? I stood up like a spring and let out a fake laugh.

– No! What are you talking about? – I scoffed, downplaying it with a wave of my hand.

– Stay still– Cedric stood up and reached me– one second...–

Without much fuss, he approached and lowered my hood. He took one of the almost white strands of my hair and sniffed it..

– All of you... – he swallowed hard, looking at me as if he had seen a ghost – all of you... You smell like him–

– What? No... – I bit my lip, feeling my heartbeats quicken.

– You... Did you sleep together? –

Oh, Cedric, so sweet and so foolish...

– No, Cedric – I quickly said – Are you crazy? –

– Why do you smell like him? –

What was wrong with him? He seemed horrified, and he didn't even know what had really happened. Could it matter to him if I told him?

– Do you care? – I blurted out.

– Of course, I care! – he exclaimed, and I saw all his muscles tense under the thin fabric of his shirt.

– Why? – I retorted, lifting my chin – Why do you care about what I might do? –

– Because you're mine! – he exclaimed, and I opened my eyes in surprise – I mean... You are my hostage...–

I pressed my lips tightly. I'm his? What? I raised my head to the ceiling, thinking about how to respond to that.

– What's this? – Cedric's voice showed surprise.

I looked at him again; he was already in front of me and had taken me by the chin. He turned my face to the side, lifting it slightly.

– What the hell is this? – Cedric ran his fingertip over one of Godric's bites, and I babbled something nonsensical.

His eyes sparkled with anger.

– I'm going to kill this son of a bitch! – without a second thought, he turned, grabbed one of the wooden legs of my bed, and tore it off, getting a somewhat deformed stake.

– Cedric, wait! – I exclaimed, reaching out to him and gripping his arm.

– He won't touch you again! – he advanced, dragging me with him.

My feet slid on the floor as he walked into the hallway with the stake in one hand and me hanging from his other arm.

– Godric, show up now! – he shouted, speaking to no one in particular.

– What's going on, Ced? – the vampire appeared in front of us, finishing climbing the stairs.

– What the hell did you do to her? – Cedric grabbed him by the neck of his elegant jacket and punched him in the middle of the face.

I finally let go of him before being crushed by his fist.

– That bitch deserves that and more! – Godric exclaimed, swaying backward.

– That bitch is mine! And no one touches her! – Cedric grabbed him by the neck and threw him to the ground floor.

I just want to say... I'm no bitch...

CHAPTER 34

Godric fell backward to the ground, and Cedric lunged at him. He began to punch him one after the other, while I watched them with an imaginary bag of popcorn.

– What's happening? – Cornelius had just appeared by my side and was looking at both of them with wide eyes.

– I don't know – I shrugged – When Cedric finishes with Godric, should I tell him to leave him in his room? – I asked sarcastically, recalling what he had said when he saw me semi-conscious in the hallway.

Cornelius gave me a threatening look, which I ignored, and started to descend the stairs slowly.

Godric had managed to get Cedric off him, and both were observing each other, catching their breath and deciding who would be the first to attack.

– Drop that shit, Cedric! – Godric shouted, pointing to the improvised stake.

– No! I'm going to kill you! – Cedric lunged at him again with the stake raised.

I was sure that when the time came, he wouldn't do it. After all, they were friends, and I was the traitor.

– You always have to put up with the humans you like! – Godric exclaimed after receiving a punch to the jaw – I can't eat if you have them all marked! –

All of them? Interesting...

– Okay, stop fighting – I told them both.

Godric grabbed Cedric by the shirt and slammed him against the wall. However, the other vampire kneed him in the stomach, making him stagger backward. Cedric took advantage of that moment to grab him by the neck and throw him meters away. Godric fell onto one of the sofas, knocking it over with a crash, and then the other vampire approached again, raising the stake high.

– I'm going to kill you! – he said, almost spitting out the words.

Enough. I ran to where they were and took the stake from Cedric's hands.

– What are you doing? – he shouted, struggling with me.

– Let it go! It's over! – I exclaimed, pulling the stake with both hands.

Godric took advantage of that to punch Cedric in the face. Blood began to drip from his nose. His eyes were turning red from thirst and anger, and I realized they were going too far.

– April, let go of it, I'm going to kill this son of a bitch! –

– No! – I exclaimed, furrowing my brow – Stop acting like idiots! –

– I'm trying to defend you! – Cedric exclaimed while covering his nose with one hand, trying to stop the bleeding.

– I don't need you to defend me! And I'm not your bitch! –

Cedric let go of the stake, and with the little strength I had left, I bent my leg and used it to break the wood in two.

Both of them stared at me as if I had turned into someone completely new. What did they expect? I couldn't deal with the strength of a vampire, but I wasn't going to let Cedric defend me as if I were a damsel in distress.

I walked with a furrowed brow to Godric and looked at him with anger flashing in my eyes.

– You left me almost dead in my room – I said, pointing to his chest with my index finger – if you do something like that again, I'll carve a stake with my teeth and impale you with it – I gathered courage and, to the surprised looks of those present, I punched him in the cheek.

All my fingers cracked together, while his face didn't move even a centimeter.

– Damn vampires! – I shouted, holding my hand and trying not to show any more signs of pain.

I bit my lip hard and walked to the kitchen with quick strides. As soon as I disappeared from the scene and stopped being tense, I felt everything spinning around me. I clung to the counter not to fall and closed my eyelids for a moment, hoping it would pass.

– Are you okay? – Peter approached me and placed a hand on my back.

– I lost a lot of blood – I sighed, still with my eyes closed.

– Come, sit. I'll give you something to make you feel better – he said, holding my arm and helping me settle on a stool at the island.

I rested my face on the cold marble of the counter and watched him with half-closed eyes as he began to cook something skillfully.

– It seemed strange that it took them so long to want to kill you – he said with disgust – they're monsters, and they always end up proving it–

I wasn't sure if he was right; Cedric wasn't a monster, and Gary wasn't either. I had my doubts about the rest, but... If there were two exceptions, I couldn't generalize about them anymore.

– Here – he said, leaving a bowl of soup next to me – Can you? –

– Yes, thank you – I said, forcing a smile, and began to eat immediately.

It was tasty and somewhat salty, surely to try to raise my blood pressure. I drank it quickly, although it was still quite hot, and Peter handed me a freshly squeezed juice.

– April – Cedric peeked his head in first and then the rest of his body into the kitchen – Can you call your sister and tell her you'll see her another day? –

– Aixa! – I said, leaning my hand on my forehead – No! I'll see her today! –

– You're weak, and you have bite marks; I don't think it's a good idea – he reminded me.

– I think I can – I said, getting off the stool, but immediately I felt cold all over my body – or not... – I sighed, gripping the island.

– Here, talk to her and tell her that... In two days? –

– Okay – I nodded, taking the phone he offered me and dialing.

She answered quickly, and I apologized, saying that something had come up at the mansion and I had no way of getting there.

– Well, I'll stay home until we see each other – she replied – be careful, okay? –

– Of course – I smiled, even though she couldn't see me – you too –

We hung up, and I handed the phone back to Cedric.

– You know... You did well a while ago – he said, fiddling with the phone to avoid looking at me – You're a bit crazy, but... You have character – he said, smiling sideways.

– So... Since we're having this revealing conversation... Do you think you won't be mad at me anymore? – I said, taking another spoonful of soup into my mouth.

– Why did you do it? – he asked, finally, sitting in front of me – give me a good reason, and if you have one, I'll consider this matter closed – he requested, fixing his eyes on mine.

– When I was kidnapped, the only thing I had on me was vervain, so it was the only thing I had to defend myself – I began – as far as I knew, you wanted to kill Aixa, and if I could weaken you enough, she would have had a chance to survive –

– Is that the truth? – he asked, making his fingers drum on the counter.

– Yes –

I wasn't lying; I was just hiding that a hunter had entered the mansion and had strongly encouraged me to kill them and find my own weapons to do so.

– Let's start over – he sighed, reaching a hand toward me to shake mine.

I felt something in my chest, as if my ribcage stopped squeezing my heart. I shook his hand, and he smiled at me sideways... With his usual mischievous face.

– You know, it's a shame you said you're not mine... – he shrugged – you don't know everything I like to do to those who belong to me –

– Yes – I nodded – and from what Godric said, it seems like many humans belong to you, right? –

– Are you jealous? – he said, raising his eyebrows, with a sly smile.

– You wish – I replied and finished drinking the freshly squeezed juice while still looking at him..

CHAPTER 35

– What are we going to do? – Destiny asked, crossing her arms over the living room table – How will we get her to talk to Aixa and keep her under control? –

– I propose putting a leash on her like a dog. Once she's inside, she'll invite us in, and if she doesn't, we'll take her out again – Emily said, looking at me with narrowed eyes.

– I'm going to leave again, really – I sighed, sinking my cheek into the palm of my hand.

– Sure, and we're supposed to believe you? Why? – Destiny retorted, furrowing her forehead – you lied to all of us, remember? –

– I know – I rolled my eyes – really, tell me what to do to make you believe me –

– I believe her – Cedric suddenly said, with a cigarette between his lips.

– You're an idiot – Destiny replied with a sigh – we all have to agree on this. Especially me...

– Why? – I took advantage of the moment to find out.

– Because the vampire we're going to revive was my boyfriend –

– I didn't know anything... – I said, looking at her with raised eyebrows.

– Of course not, it's none of your business – she replied – Cedric, I understand all that about her helping your brother. But let's be realistic, if we leave her at her house, do you think she'll come out again? –

– Yes! – I exclaimed – I'll come out! I promise! –

– We could ask Declan to create a blood bond with one of us – Emily suggested, although I didn't know what she was talking about – she won't be able to disobey whoever has their blood bonded with hers –

– None of us is going to be bound to a human forever – Cornelius interrupted – we already have enough with a half-blood; we don't need to carry this blood bag too –

– Cedric, Gary, negotiate for me – I pleaded, pointing to everyone with a hand gesture.

– I believe her – Gary said, shrugging.

– I don't – Cedric pronounced – but if she wants to earn our trust, it's a good opportunity –

– Of course, we hand her back to her sister on a silver platter, and goodbye spell – Destiny mocked, looking at him as if he were an idiot.

– No, Destiny – Cedric gave her a condescending smile – both of them will be inside that house; either of the two will serve us, either for the spell or as an exchange... Eventually, one of them will have to come out, and then we'll have control again –

– Your threats are not necessary, Cedric – I told him, frowning – I'll leave my house and come back with you because that's the deal, and I keep my word –

– Yes, sure. For the deal – Emily mocked, making air quotes with her fingers – a deal called Cedric –

– If she doesn't come out, I'll stand day and night at her door until one of them shows their face – he said, looking at them all with serious eyes.

– No – Cornelius interrupted him – your pulse trembles too much. I'll take her there, and I'll wait for her until she comes out –

– I'm capable of doing that – Cedric said, frowning.

– I'm not interested. I want everything to go well, so I'll do it myself – his father concluded, with a firm voice – April, if you're ready, let's go –

– Of course – I said, standing up.

I ran to my room to grab the red coat that Cedric had given me the day I got drunk, wrapped myself in it, and stopped next to Cornelius at the door.

We left, and our feet sank into the layer of snow that was beginning to form on the ground. We advanced, hearing the crunch of our footsteps, and entered the limousine waiting for us on the other side of the gates.

– If you don't come back tonight, I'll come for you, and I'll kill both of them – Cornelius said when we were seated facing each other.

– Well, you'll be disappointed because I promised to come back, and I will –

The limousine started. Peter was driving calmly, while I couldn't stop biting my nails out of nervousness.

I had no idea what Aixa's reaction would be, but I knew she would be unwilling to help them. She had always been the toughest, most confident, and firm in her decisions, but this time, I had to manage to turn the tables and be the one who wouldn't budge from my decision.

It must have been about twenty minutes when the car stopped.

– Get out – Cornelius ordered me, while Peter opened the door for me.

I nodded and got out. The wind tousled my hair, and I looked around. It hadn't been that long since I was in the mansion, but it felt strange to be back on the street of my house. I walked to the door and rang the bell.

Aixa opened it in a fraction of a second.

– April! – she exclaimed, wrapping her arms around me and hugging me tightly – I missed you so much –

– And I missed you – I smiled, watching as she tried to hold back tears.

– Come in, quickly – she said, dragging me inside.

My house still had the same smell as always, that mixture of vervain with candle wax and old books. We closed the door, and both of us sat on the couch.

– I cooked something for both of us – she said without letting go of my hands – I'll bring it now –

She went to the kitchen and returned with a tray of baked macaroni. She served us both in two plates and sat next to me.

– You have to tell me everything. How are you? Did they hurt you? –

– Relax – I said, stopping her with a hand gesture – one question at a time – I smiled.

– Well, tell me everything! – she exclaimed as she took a bite of her food.

– Fine – I nodded, getting more nervous – they treat me well, no one has harmed me... They are like a family, there's a slightly strange child, but he's nice–

– Come on, April – she smiled, rolling her eyes – vampires are not nice–

– Aixa... Many things have changed in these weeks, and I... I think that's what's really important–

– What happened? – she asked while trying to calm down all the emotions of seeing me again.

– Well... Look, they... They're not as bad as we thought. They're not human, but they're not killers either... They have donors to drink blood... And when they hunt, they don't kill people–

– Where are you going with this? – she was completely serious now, chewing with a raised eyebrow.

– I want to get to the point that I'm here to negotiate for them and also for you – I blurted out – they told me they were looking for you because they needed your blood for a spell... A spell to resurrect someone very important to them, whom you killed–

– What? And how do they know it was me? – she inquired, pointing to her chest with a finger.

– I don't know, maybe the vampire you killed injured you, and they followed the trail of your blood or I don't know... But that's not the point; the point is that initially, they wanted to kill you because they needed all your blood for the spell, but... One of them sought another way to carry it out without having to kill you–

– And why would he do something like that? – she asked.

– We made a deal. The vampire child needs my help to control his thirst... So I agreed to help him in exchange for them finding another way to resurrect that vampire–

– Why should I believe any of this? That they will fulfill their part? You can't trust them, April, never–

– I saw it – I said, looking at her intensely, trying to convey my own certainty – I saw the spell written in a book, and I'm... very sure that Cedric is not lying–

– Who is Cedric? – she asked, furrowing her brow a bit.

– He... is one of them, but I'm sure I can trust him. Really–

– So, what does the new spell require? –

– They need a bit of your blood since you killed him. But it's just a small cut because the blood moon will take care of the rest of the blood–

– But no one knows when there will be a blood moon; they are very rare, and there was one recently... the day I left–

– I know – I nodded – but there will be another in three weeks. They just need you to go that day, and then... Both of us will be free to resume our lives without anyone looking for you–

– April, I don't want peace; I want to kill each and every one of the vampires on this earth – she cut me off – and you should want the same; you're one of us–

– I know, but I swear they're not like you think. I know it's hard to believe, but... I don't think it's fair to keep killing them–

– April, you took the hunter's oath! – she exclaimed, suddenly upset – you also killed some of them. The vampires killed our parents! You can't defend them now–

– I know! But I killed the murderer of our parents myself! Not all of them are like him– I took her hands to make her look at me – Aixa, I can't keep hunting them... And I want to help that child. Vampire or not... He's not a monster–

– You've been brainwashed! – my sister seemed horrified – Daniel warned me; he told me you were hesitating, but I ignored him. I thought you were more sensible! –

– Can you at least consider that maybe I'm not the one who's wrong? – I begged almost pleadingly – do it for me, Aixa... We've already avenged our parents... I want us to be at peace; I don't want to keep fearing that you'll be killed–

– But you will, until all of them are dead

– No – I cut her off, gathering all the courage I had inside – anyway, I'll go back with them and fulfill my part of the deal. But I need to know that they won't have to kill you afterward, that you'll cooperate, and then we can live in peace–

– You're wrong, April – Aixa told me, letting go of her hands from mine – you're turning your back on everything our parents taught us, everything we know... for a vampire? –

– It's not just for the child... It's for...–

My mind couldn't stop reminding me of Cedric's pained expression when he had caught me betraying him. All of this wasn't just to help Gary, and I knew it. I didn't want to disappoint Cedric again; that was the plain truth.

– It's for all of them – I lied, knowing that "them" encompassed only Cedric.

– You'll regret it, April; they're not what they seem. They won't do anything for you, not above their interests–

– I trust them – I told her.

– Don't lie to me; Daniel told me about one of them... One that seems to like you – she said, looking at me angrily – you're doing it for him, and you trust him–

– Yes – I nodded, biting my lip – I believe him, and you have to believe me. They won't harm you–

– Well, I'll do it – she said, pushing the plate aside and standing up – but I want it to be clear that you're selling your own sister by trusting a monster –

– I'm not selling you! – I exclaimed, feeling it like a stab.

I wasn't stupid. I had seen the spell with my own eyes. Cedric had celebrated it, and we had both placed our trust in each other. She was the one who was mistaken.

– We'll see about that – she replied, serious, turning her back..

CHAPTER 36

The words of my sister weighed on me throughout the entire journey back. I hated that she believed I was selling her, putting her in danger when I would have given my own life for her.

The limousine parked at the entrance of the mansion. I got out, with Cornelius behind me. The front door was illuminated, and there was a silhouette, standing, leaning against the frame outlined against it.

"So predictable," Cornelius muttered under his breath, letting out a sigh.

I ignored him and advanced a little more until I finally realized it was Cedric. He had a small smile on his lips, seemed somewhat subdued, even though I didn't know why.

However, as soon as our eyes met, he raised his eyebrows and looked at me with his usual insolent face.

"Couldn't you live without me?" he said when I stopped in front of him.

"Alright... Step aside," Cornelius interrupted us, rolling his eyes and pushing us to let him pass.

Peter closed the door behind him and went to the kitchen.

"You came back."

"That's what I said all along," I said, squinting at him.

"How did it go?" he asked, scratching his neck.

"Mmm... Let's say he'll come in three weeks, that's all you need to know."

"And the rest?" he continued insisting.

"The rest is that she doesn't believe you, thinks everyone wants to kill her, and that I'm a traitor idiot," I said, frowning, feeling a knot in my stomach.

"I'm sorry," Cedric bit his lip, and I shrugged.

"Yes, sure," I mocked and began to walk towards the stairs, but he quickly took hold of my arm and pulled me towards him.

"No, April. I really am sorry," he said, locking his gaze with mine. "If there was anything I could do..."

"But it's not like that," I said, unable to take my eyes off his. "She'll believe me when they fulfill their part."

"Look who's back!" Emily said, coming down the stairs. "What a pity," she sighed. "Cedric, come with me, I need to talk to you."

Cedric let go of my arm, and it took a couple more seconds for him to look away from me. But he finally did and followed her into the kitchen.

I swear it wasn't my intention to listen to that... Either they were shouting, and I could hear their conversation from the sofas by the stairs, or my hearing was developing a new skill because I could hear everything perfectly.

"What do you want, Emily?" he asked her with a rather irritated tone.

"I've been thinking a lot since I came back... And... I want to apologize for everything I did to you..."

"Interesting... You remembered to apologize for something from forty-five years ago..." he mocked her. "What happened that made you decide it was the right time?"

"Well, what happened... is that I never wanted to use you... I mean... Well, I did want you to turn me, but I did have feelings for you... Before you did it and even after."

"Haha! Yeah, right," I thought internally, but I couldn't just come out of nowhere and insert myself into that conversation.

"Emily, don't be ridiculous, you disappeared after that. Of course, you didn't feel anything for me, and that's okay because I'm not interested anymore."

"I know you still care!" Emily exclaimed. "You have to tell me I still have a chance... I... I left because I knew we had all eternity to try. I was too confident that you loved me, and I thought we could be together at any time..."

"Well, you were wrong," Cedric laughed. "I stopped waiting for you a long time ago."

"That's not true... I asked Godric; he told me you haven't been with anyone since I left..."

"Of course I have... With many donors, in fact..."

"Oh well, the one missing! Fuck boy in sight."

"But I haven't loved anyone as much as I loved you," she cut him off, very sure. "I saw that you still have my clothes in your closet."

"That's because I forgot to burn them," he replied, sounding tired. "I know perfectly well what's going on with you. You were very sure I would be your lapdog for eternity, and now you're starting to have doubts... Or you're jealous, or whatever's going on with you..."

"And am I right?" she asked. "Should I be jealous or worried?"

"It doesn't make sense because even if you feel that way, you'll never interest me again. You're despicable, Emily, and nobody told me; I saw it with my own eyes."

"I know you still love me deep down. It's just that now you're entertained with that blood bag."

"Oh, Cedric... You and your weakness for humans... Like me."

"I'm not going to turn her!" he exclaimed, annoyed.

"Of course not... You were willing to live an eternity with me, but you don't even think about turning her," she seemed to be smiling, finally satisfied. "That means I don't have to worry... You don't feel anything real for her; you don't want her by your side forever."

"Really, Emily, that's none of your business," he replied cryptically.

"Sure," she smiled again, "of course not."

I wanted to sink into the couch and disappear. Well... Lucky for me, Cedric had no intention of turning me. I didn't want to be a stupid blood-sucking vampire.

Why did it bother me so much that he had said he didn't want to do it? As soon as he denied it, I felt a stab in the heart. What had I been expecting him to say?

"You are really unbearable," I heard Destiny's voice close to my ear. "But I swear I prefer him to be with you than to go back to that idiot."

"What?" I asked, looking at her with confusion. "Were you listening?"

"We all heard... There are no private conversations in this house," she smiled as she circled the couch and sat next to me. "So, does that mean they can hear us now?" I asked, pointing at both of us, and she smiled at me.

"Yes, April," Cedric's voice echoed from the kitchen until he finally came out and walked toward us. "Did you hear us?"

"No! Of course not!" I said, looking away.

"Yes, she did. Her ears were about to grow twenty centimeters to capture every word," Destiny laughed, rolling her eyes.

"Anyway, I couldn't care less about what they were talking about," I shrugged it off, and he smiled maliciously at me.

"Sure," he coughed, "this is weird... A human shouldn't be able to hear something like that."

"I'm starting to suspect that Thomas Dumont was right about me not being human," Destiny said, looking at me with her perfect, shiny coffee-colored eyes. "Maybe I'm a troll or something."

"Yeah, right, Destiny," I smiled tightly. "Maybe we should run some tests on her... See what abilities she has, what she can do... Compare them to those of a human," she continued calmly.

"I'm not a guinea pig," I reminded her, but Cedric pointed his finger at her and nodded.

"Destiny is right; it's a good idea," he said.

"Call Lucy," Godric was coming down the stairs and joined the conversation. "I'm hungry, and since she's here, I'm sure she'll help us with whatever."

"Is it just me, or do you love having Lucy always around?" Destiny asked, frowning.

"I don't see why I shouldn't like it. She has rich blood and does everything. She's very versatile," he chuckled.

"Okay, Godric," his sister sighed, making a disgusted face. "Call her already."

The vampire quickly dialed on his phone and spoke like a buffoon for a few minutes until he finally hung up.

"She's on her way," he smiled. "I told you; she's very willing."

"Oh, April..." Cedric looked at me absentmindedly. "Come with me for a second."

"If you're going to talk, why not do it here? Anyway, we'll hear you," Destiny said, looking at both of us with amusement.

"No, you won't. Because my room is soundproof, remember?" he said, looking at her with an unfriendly expression.

"How boring."

I followed Cedric to his room. He let me in and closed the door.

"What's going on?" I asked, crossing my arms.

"When I brought you here on the first day, my father told me to give you the clothes I had in the closet. I didn't want to give them to you, and you had to ask Destiny for them. I think if you need clothes, you should have them," he explained.

"Do you want to give me Emily's clothes?" I asked, furrowing my brow.

"I see you didn't miss a word of the conversation downstairs, did you?" he smiled, approaching me with crossed arms.

"Yeah, well," I sighed, rolling my eyes.

"I remembered that I had them, and I really don't want anything of hers, neither in my closet nor anywhere else."

"Neither do I," I said, shrugging. "Besides... You might regret it, I mean... You wanted to spend eternity with her... It's too intense to forget overnight."

"No, if there's someone better—"

My heart skipped a beat, and it rose to my throat. Cedric was standing in front of me, studying my face with that smile of his, so characteristic and so... enticing. I swallowed, and he moved a little closer to me, looking down at me, while I had to lift my head a bit to observe him. We were silent, but it wasn't an uncomfortable silence.

Cedric placed his palm on my face, and I felt a shiver. I pulled away, and I knew why. He wasn't really interested in me, I was sure. Hadn't he said so while talking to Emily? I wasn't going to be his momentary distraction, and then he would move far away from me, not even remembering me. There's a characteristic that is common to every human being, and it is that we all want to leave a mark. I wanted to leave one, and I wouldn't be just another human he amused himself with. I aspired to something much better for myself.

"I have an idea of what you can do with the clothes," I said, looking at him with a devilish smile. "You gave me the idea yourself."

He looked at me strangely but played along, with a hint of doubt on his face. We bundled up all of Emily's clothes and went downstairs.

"What are you doing?" Godric asked, looking at us strangely from the couch.

"Come, I'm sure you're going to love the idea," Cedric said, not stopping as he walked to the door.

Godric, Cedric, Destiny, and I surrounded the house to the backyard. We piled up all of Emily's clothes, including her high-heeled shoes and lace panties. Cedric exchanged a playful look with me, and we smiled.

"I don't understand," Destiny looked at us alternately with a furrowed brow until her eyes lit up as soon as she saw Cedric.

He had taken a lighter out of his pocket. He knelt beside the stack of clothes, lighting it, and the fire began to spread from one garment to another. We all watched as the fire began to grow before our eyes. I looked up at the mansion and saw Emily watching us from one of the upper windows, her eyes burning with fury. Our eyes met for a moment, and I smiled triumphantly... Because if she was a bitch, I would be a worse one.

CHAPTER 37

!

Lucy arrived at the mansion half an hour after we started burning everything.

We opened the door for her and settled into the sofas, thinking about the best way to test ourselves. "The abilities that differentiate a vampire from a human are speed, strength, reflexes, and hearing," Destiny began, pacing back and forth as if giving us a class. "Let's start with hearing."

"Okay," Lucy nodded, tucking a strand of her long brown hair behind her ear. "I'll take care of it," Gary said as he headed to the front door.

We all fell silent, trying to listen. I could hear his somber voice on the other side of the door, but it was almost inaudible. A few minutes later, he came back in and looked at me, crossing his arms. "What did I say?" "I have no idea," I said, scratching my forehead. "I heard you talking, but I didn't understand what you were saying."

"What about you, Lucy?" Godric asked, sitting next to her. "I didn't hear anything at all," she said, almost embarrassed. "Alright... you hear more than her, but not as much as we do," Destiny concluded, nodding.

"Let's measure their strength," Cedric proposed with gleaming eyes. "Let's see if they can break or lift something..." "What's the limit for a vampire?" I asked curiously. "Hmm... a car could be... we can lift or stop them a bit, but no more than that," he explained. "You should start with something lighter."

"We should grab them, and they try to break free," Godric suggested. "I know! Let's measure their strength and speed at the same time. We chase them to catch them, and then they try to break free." "I like it," Cedric nodded. "I'll catch April," he winked at me, and I sighed.

"It will be fun!" Lucy seemed like a child at Disney.

Godric, Destiny, Lucy, Gary, Cedric, and I headed to the backyard. It was large enough for us to run freely, so we got ready. "We'll give you an advantage so it's not boring," Cedric said, putting his hands in his pockets. "Ready?" I said to the donor as I stood by her. "Of course," she smiled confidently. "On your marks..." Destiny began. "Get set... Go!"

I ran as if my life depended on it, and Lucy did the same. Both of us headed in different directions. The winter air was so cold that I thought it would cut my face.

I heard Cedric start to move behind me and pushed myself even further forward. I took long, violent strides, while I strained to hear how far away he was from me.

"You're too slow!" I shouted as a snowflake got into my mouth. He didn't respond. How many meters away was he? I heard Godric catch Lucy. I gritted my teeth and veered through the rose bushes to make it harder for him to catch me. I ran harder until I felt like I was barely touching the ground with my shoes on the snow. I felt his hands grabbing my waist. His weight made me fall to the ground, and he ended up on top of me.

"You're fast!" he said, looking into my eyes, with no intention of moving. We both breathed heavily. "And you," I said, trying to catch more air. His face was inches from mine, and despite the snow cooling my back, there was a part of me that wanted to stay still in that position for a long time. "Why are you looking at me like that?"

he said, smiling slightly. "I don't know what you're talking about," I said, unable to look away from his lips. "What's wrong with you?" he asked, squinting his eyes slightly. "What's wrong with me, April?" I didn't know what to say. My heart started pounding, and I knew he could hear it. "I understand you," he smiled at me, "I feel the same way."

"Come on, Cedric," I said, looking away.

I couldn't bear to look at him without wanting to kiss him. He had a magnetism impossible to describe. He was on top of me, and I felt like I wanted to have him even closer. "You have to try to break free," he smiled, maliciously.

His fingers slid down my arms, took my hands, and held them against the ground to prevent me from moving. Did he really want me to break free? No, but I had to, right?

I tried to get him off me, shaking my feet like a madwoman, but it didn't work. I tried to free my hands, but he held me too tightly. He kept looking at me while I struggled futilely, and when I stopped to catch my breath, he smiled smugly. "Is that all you've got?" he asked, pressing me with his body. "No!" I said, biting my lip. With all my strength, I managed to free one hand and used it to push myself up and push him hard. Cedric fell beside me, onto the snow, smiling, and he took me by the waist to drag me with him. I placed my hands on his shoulders with sparkling eyes of pride.

"And you?" I asked him with a mischievous smile. "Is that all you've got?" "No," he sat up abruptly; his icy hands took my face... and he kissed me.

As soon as his lips touched mine, I felt electricity throughout my body, and something fluttered in my stomach. It wasn't a gentle kiss; it was one filled with hunger. My slightly open mouth received his.

He caught my lower lip with his. It was a wet kiss, full of eagerness to devour each other. My hands clung to his hoodie to pull him closer, while our tongues tangled. He caressed my hair, wet with snow, until his hand reached my nape, and he pressed me even harder against him, fiercely.

He bit my lower lip and pulled back a bit to roam my face with his violet and seductive eyes. Then, I wished time would stand still. "I've wanted to do this for a long time," he whispered with a husky voice.

"You should have done it earlier," I said, unable to hide a small smile.

"The ones from the rose garden!" Destiny's voice brought us back to reality. "Come out from there and come here!"

"I think they're calling us," I whispered while he looked at my mouth and bit his lip. "Well, but I have more," he smiled sideways, "we're not done."

We stood up, and I followed him through the garden to join the others. I had no idea what my expression was at that moment, but Destiny was looking at me with curiosity, and I felt like I was floating on a cloud, outside of space and time.

"What's going on with you?" Godric asked, amused. "Nothing," I said, clearing my throat, "nothing at all." "That's right," Cedric was by my side, and without the others seeing, he slipped his hand inside my coat and caressed my back with the tips of his fingers.

I tried to suppress a shiver without success, as my whole skin tingled under his touch. "Lucy couldn't break free, and I caught her as soon as I started running," Godric informed us, oblivious to the heat that was beginning to spread throughout my body. "April is fast, undoubtedly faster than a human, and she managed to break free," Cedric informed them as I looked at him from the corner of my eye.

"In summary... April has vampire abilities. Some more developed than others, but she has them," Destiny reflected, rubbing her chin.

"And what does that make me?" I asked, wrinkling my forehead. "I don't know," she answered as if not knowing what kind of creature I was wasn't relevant at all. "Here," she handed me a bottle of energy drink.

I opened it and took a long sip. Unlike them, I did get tired from running. The taste of that drink flooded my mouth. It was so sweet that I felt a tingling on my lips.

"Wow, it's delicious," I said, wiping the corners with the back of my hand. "I know," she nodded, looking at me strangely, "it's blood."

CHAPTER 38

As soon as I understood what Destiny had just told me, I ran to the bathroom. The urge to vomit surged in my stomach, and I began to feel saliva in my mouth, ready to make me retch into my intestines. I burst into the bathroom and emptied everything I had just drunk into the toilet. Everything was stained with red and thick drops, blood coming out of my mouth, human blood...

I was hit by a wave of nausea, and then another... How could I have even thought that it tasted good? How could I have drunk human blood when I was human myself?

I retched at least ten more times, and finally, I rinsed my mouth, feeling nauseous. Suddenly, I was sweating cold, and the taste of that dense liquid filled my mind.

"April, open the door," Cedric knocked with his knuckles on the other side. I was embarrassed. I had just done something horrible, and I had enjoyed it. I couldn't understand how I hadn't realized that it could be blood.

"April..."

"No, leave me alone," I said, trying to hold back the urge to cry. What would my sister think of that? Who was I? Or rather, what was I?

Cedric didn't wait any longer and opened the door. He silently watched me as I hugged myself in front of the sink and looked at myself in the mirror, not recognizing myself.

"Calm down, April," he said, approaching a bit, but I stopped him with a hand gesture.

"What did I do, Cedric?" I said, still looking at my reflection. "What am I?"

"You're a dhampir, April."

"A what?" I said, opening my eyes wide and turning to look at him.

"Half human, half vampire," he sighed. "I don't know anything about it... There's one in a million."

"I can't be a hybrid... My parents are human," Cedric didn't say anything, just waited in silence, looking me in the eyes. "They are my parents," I said, frowning. "I am the same as my mother and the same as Aixa."

"I don't know, April... Maybe she is the human, and she was with a vampire."

"But they hated vampires! They were hunters..."

"I don't know what to tell you," he ran a hand through his hair, messing it up, and lowered his gaze.

I was so confused that I thought my brain would explode. A dhampir? I had never heard of anything like that, and I was one... And my parents? They were hunters... It was impossible that my mother had been with one... And that my father wasn't my father... Where did that leave me?

"You have an immense library," I said, trying to make my voice sound calm. "Tell me you have a book that talks about this."

"Listen, this changes nothing," Cedric wanted the ground to swallow him, and I could perfectly understand. "You are still you... No matter what you are."

"What does it not matter?" I exclaimed, taking my forehead like a crazy person. "I don't know who I am, I don't know what I am, or what I'm supposed to do. I know nothing about my family, not even if it's my family... I understand nothing."

"Well, listen... I'm going to look for everything I can... Just... Calm down," he took my hand and forced me to drag myself out of the bathroom. "I'm sorry for that, April," Destiny sighed as soon as she saw me appear in the living room. "It was the missing test to know if you were a vampire."

"You should have warned me!" I exclaimed, clenching my fists.

"Calm down, April, you're not going to hit anyone," Cedric told me with an unfriendly face. "Destiny was trying to help you."

"But she gave me human blood! Without asking me!" I exclaimed, looking at both of them with a frown.

"Listen... Now that we know what it is, we need to look for everything about dhampirs," Cedric continued, ignoring my comment. "Does anyone come with us to the library?"

"I'll go," Godric said, standing up from one of the armchairs. "What are we looking for exactly?"

"Whatever," I said, squeezing my hands nervously. "We know nothing about this, so whatever... Will be fine."

"I'm going too," Gary said, biting his lips. "I owe it to her," he looked at me and made a face.

"Thank you," I smiled at him as a lump formed in my throat.

The four of us went up and locked ourselves in the library. We rummaged through books that exclusively talked about vampires, their types of abilities, and the importance of pure blood. I armed myself with a good number of them and settled on a small sofa next to the window covered by a curtain. Cedric and Godric scanned dusty volumes on the table, without even sitting, and Gary went back and forth, handing them all the books they asked for.

"Here's something!" Godric exclaimed, sticking his index finger on one of the pages. We all pounced on him, expectant. "It says: 'From the union of a human and a vampire, hybrids called dhampirs are born. These creatures have the same abilities as vampires, but not the same weaknesses. Dhampirs develop a very difficult-to-handle thirst from birth.'"

"What else?" I asked, biting the inside of my cheek.

"That's all it says," he shrugged.

I took the book from between his hands to corroborate it myself, but it was true. After that little paragraph, it continued to talk in broad strokes about other crosses with vampires.

"What the hell..." I sighed, handing it back to him.

"Anyway, that information must be wrong," Gary said, taking his chin. "Do you have a blood thirst?"

As far as I remember, I have never had it," I said, scratching my forehead, "except recently... But it generates a lot of rejection in me; I couldn't drink it."

Actually, it generates rejection only psychologically," Cedric interrupted me. "You drank it with pleasure until Destiny told you what it was."

Well, it's blood... Of course, it's disgusting," I said, furrowing my brow.

Yes, but you're very susceptible to that," he reminded me. "You even vomited when you saw Gary drink it... And also today. There must be something more."

I don't choose to vomit...

That's why I say it's psychological... I don't know, maybe something happened to you with blood once, or... Did you see something?"

No," I denied, furrowing my brow. "Not that I remember."

Well, for now, the only thing that occurs to me is that we keep looking," Gary walked back to the shelves, focusing on reading each spine.

I nodded and immersed myself back into the sofa to keep flipping through pages and more pages. If that paragraph was true, there were many things that still didn't fit. The thirst for blood was one, but there was also the fact that dhampires were born from a human and a vampire... I was more than sure that I was just like my mother; I had her eyes and the same white hair. My father, on the other hand, had always had curly brown hair, a slightly round nose, and a square jaw. Aixa had the same nose and the somewhat small shape of her eyes... But what did I have of him? Was I his daughter, or was I a bastard without even knowing it?

I yawned as my eyes closed, but I kept searching through the books beside me until I fell asleep.

I didn't know how long I had been there, but at some point, I smelled Cedric's delicious perfume close to me and felt him covering my body with a thick, soft blanket.

Do you like this girl, right? - Godric's voice sounded somewhat distant as I snuggled in to fall asleep again.

Too much," Cedric responded as his footsteps moved away from where I was.

Does that mean you're going to tell her the truth?" the other vampire asked.

You know I can't," Cedric sighed, getting farther away. "She would hate me."

CHAPTER 39

!

I woke up with a terrible neck pain and stiff neck muscles. I pushed aside the quilt that Cedric had covered me with and stretched, trying to feel less stiff.

Finally, you wake up," Cedric said, looking at me with a smug smile and arms crossed.

Seeing him, I felt something strange, as if I were forgetting something but didn't know what it was.

I'm sorry... I don't know when I fell asleep.

It doesn't matter; we were searching all night until Godric and Gary got tired.

Did they find anything?" I asked as I walked to the table and looked at the books they had left open.

Nothing," he said. "Vampires usually don't have knowledge about this... It's very rare, and generally, no one tries to relate to dhampires... After all, pure blood is very important, and even if they are not hybrids, they still have a human part.

Am I not enough for you?" I said, stopping in front of him, eyebrows raised.

Yes, you are," Cedric quickly took me by the waist and pressed me to his body, leaving our faces a hand's breadth apart. - For me."

He leaned in and kissed me gently, making me want more. He ran his tongue over my lower lip and smiled over my lips as his hands descended slowly.

Easy, soldier," I said, placing a hand on his chest and removing his hands from my backside.

I have a better idea than continuing to search here," he suddenly said. "Why don't we see if there's anything at your house?"

What could be there?" I asked, furrowing my brow.

I don't know... Some clue about your parents, for example," he coughed.

Well... Let's go," I said, starting to walk to the door, but he took my arm and turned me toward him.

It's still evening... We have some free time...

I bit my lip as I looked into his eyes. He had my arm clutched, and he looked at me with a pair of devilish eyes. Slowly, a small smile began to appear at the corners of my lips. Without hesitating for a second, Cedric pulled my arm, bringing my body close to his. He kissed me eagerly, craving more of my lips, and I of his. Our tongues tangled fiercely, asking for more.

His hands slipped under my sweater, caressing my skin, which tingled with his touch. His lips began to slide down my neck as I entwined my fingers in his tousled hair. I felt his wet kisses on my skin, and I shivered. It was so magnetic...

Cedric breathed in my scent with a deep inhale. He took me by the waist again, making me turn, and sat me on the table with determination. His hips were between my legs. We kissed again desperately. I grabbed a part of his shirt and tore it off forcefully. We heard the fabric rip, and in a second, his chest and abdomen were exposed.

Damn, April..." he whispered over my lips. "You're going to drive me crazy." His fingers tangled in my hair, and he pulled gently, making me tilt my head back.

He slid his tongue down my neck to the lobe of my ear. He gave it a soft bite, and his breath in my ear made me let out a little moan. I wrapped my legs around his waist as he took off my sweater. He kissed my collarbones, and I bit my lip. I felt the heat and desire running through my entire body as he did whatever he pleased with me. Slowly, with half-closed eyes, I slid my hand from his chest to the waistband of his pants. His firm and sculpted abdomen excited me even more. From the denim fabric of his jeans, I could feel the hardness of his bulge... For a second, our eyes met, and he smiled maliciously.

Do whatever you want to me," he whispered in a hoarse voice. "I'm yours."

And then... The library door opened.

Oh, no, it can't be!" Destiny exclaimed, covering her eyes with one hand.

What are you doing awake?" Cedric asked her, helping me get off the table quickly.

Me? What are you two doing?" she exclaimed, determined not to leave us alone.

With cheeks burning with embarrassment, I ran to her side, where Cedric had thrown my sweater. I put it on in a millisecond and stood very still, waiting to blend in with the walls, but it didn't happen.

Put on a shirt, Cedric!" she continued, frowning.

It's torn... I'm sorry," he said, taking what was left of his shirt and showing it with a playful smile. "April is a bit wild..."

I just came because I woke up and wanted to help, but I think you don't need me... - she looked at both of us, hands on hips. - Continue...

There's nothing to continue," I said, swallowing saliva, red as a tomato. "I... I have to go home to find something useful to clarify my thoughts."

I'll go with you," said Cedric, following me.

We should take Gary, so he keeps distracting himself," I told him, shifting my weight nervously from one foot to the other.

Are you afraid to be alone with me in an empty house?" he said with his irritating smile, looking down at me.

God, use one of the rooms!" Destiny exclaimed, covering her ears with her hands.

You can come too," I said to her as I left the library, and Cedric followed me.

Twenty minutes later, Gary and Destiny had joined us, and we were getting into the limousine driven by Peter.

When we arrived, we stopped in front of the door. It was locked, and there didn't seem to be anyone inside.

We can break the lock," Gary said with a wicked smile.

And then how do we lock it again?" I responded, raising an eyebrow.

Maybe through a window, then," Cedric shrugged. "I can break one on the second floor; no one can get in from up there."

You underestimate the skills of thieves," I said with a grimace. "But I don't think we have more options; go ahead."

Cedric started looking at the ground in all directions until he found a rounded stone, the size of a brick. He threw his arm back and violently launched it at the window of what used to be my room. The glass shattered as if a bomb had just exploded. He moved forward and jumped, hanging from the window frame. He removed the remaining glass from the edges and looked down at me from above.

I need you to invite me in," he asked with a look of annoyance.

Fine... Come in, Cedric..."

He slid inside. A few seconds later, he opened the front door for us. I entered and let Destiny and Gary follow suit.

Aixa was no longer there. Everything was dark and silent.

Your house is full of vervain," Gary said, looking at me angrily.

I'm sorry; I come from a family of hunters... What did you expect?" I said uncomfortably.

Maybe we could start with... I don't know, family photos or something like that?" Cedric suggested, putting his hands in his pockets.

Cedric, I'm not adopted," I said with a stern look.

I'm sorry, but at least one of them wasn't your father... Or they were always vampires, and you didn't notice," Destiny reminded me, without a drop of sensitivity.

I'll go to their room... Maybe there's something there," I continued, staring at the floor. "Could someone check the study? It's the door under the stairs."

I'll do it," said Cedric, pushing his brother to walk with him.

Destiny had no other choice but to follow me upstairs. Opening the door to my parents' room was painful, even though a year had passed since they died. I turned the doorknob slowly and entered. A wave of familiar scents slapped me in the face. I could sense the faint hint of my father's masculine cologne, mixed with the myriad creams on the dresser, belonging to my mother.

Destiny moved forward, paying no attention to anything, and began to look around. In the center was my father's double bed, adorned with a green quilt that had a bit of dust. To the right was a huge dark oak wardrobe. To the left, the dresser, with Christmas lights hanging from the edges of the mirror, their batteries depleted.

I approached the dresser, sliding my fingers over the dark wood. I couldn't understand how my parents, so warm and reliable, could have hidden something as important as my own origin. I didn't understand how behind all that simplicity, those familiar objects could be hiding something more.

I heard the creaking of the wardrobe doors the moment Destiny opened them. My father's suits and my mother's dresses were neatly hung on hangers. She squatted and checked the wardrobe floor; there wasn't much: shoes and old boxes with photos of me and my sister.

Indeed, it's your mother," Destiny said, taking a photo and handing it to me.

I approached her and took it. It was quite old, but there she was: my mother in a hospital bed after giving birth to me. I was wrapped in a pink blanket, still with my eyes closed.

So... the question would be, who is my father, right?" I said, biting my lip, while a lump tightened my throat.

I wasn't going to cry, not there, and not in front of Destiny. I handed her back the photo, and she put it back into one of the boxes. Finally, she stood up and moved the clothes aside to check the bottom of the wardrobe. It didn't sound hollow. It was embedded against the wall and didn't hide anything.

We observed the dresser, began opening my mother's jewelry boxes, my father's cream jars, and perfumes. Destiny took the mirror frame and moved it a few centimeters to see if there was anything behind it.

Be careful; it's broken on the edge and could break even more," I asked, pointing to the small gap at the top.

Of course, I imagine that at some point in your life, you'll want to use the mirror of your deceased parents," she said as she put it back in place.

I rolled my eyes, but she didn't pay attention; her eyes focused on the mirror, precisely on the broken part. She reached out carefully and touched it.

It has a lot of relief," she said, hooking it with one of her long nails painted with black lacquer.

You're going to peel it off!" I pointed out, furrowing my brow, as if it weren't obvious what she was trying to do.

She pulled, with her nail, and the piece of glass fell onto the dressing table, revealing the gap left in the mirror.

Wow... But look how clever," Destiny smiled pleased.

In the gap was a small silver key, taped against the plastic back of the mirror. I peeled it off and turned it in front of my eyes.

Any idea what it opens?" she asked me, also contemplating it.

No..."

Right then, we heard Gary shout from downstairs.

Hey! You have to see this!" We exchanged a quick glance, and finally, with the key still in our hands, we ran downstairs..

CHAPTER 40

Gary and Cedric were inside the study my father used when he needed silence to work. This place consisted only of an antique desk, a black leather swivel chair, and a floor-to-ceiling bookshelf that covered the entire wall behind the desk.

However, when Destiny and I entered, that room had something different. To the side of the table where my father worked, there was a square hole big enough for at least two people.

I exchanged glances with both, somewhat confused, and approached the hole or rather the door, because underneath, you could see an improvised cement staircase.

Where did this come from?" I asked them, unable to take my eyes off the stairs.

You didn't know it?" Gary asked. "I told you it was important," he said, looking at his older brother, satisfied.

We were checking the library," Cedric explained. "Gary started moving the books, and when we took this one," he showed me the volume he had in his hands, "a part of the floor lifted like a sewer cover..."

I never saw it," I said, pressing my lips. "Did you go down already?"

Yes, there's a closed metal door, and we can't open it," Cedric explained. "In fact, trying to, we pushed it in a bit."

I turned to look at Destiny, and she smiled at me sideways.

We have the key," I said, showing it to both.

This is what I call teamwork," Destiny smiled. "Shall we enter?"

Just like that?" I asked as my heart skipped a beat in my chest.

I don't know... Do you want to perform a ritual first?" she replied, looking at me as if I were an idiot.

Come on, go down," Cedric rolled his eyes at my hesitation.

He placed his large hands on my shoulders and began to guide me to the foot of the stairs.

No, wait..." I swallowed saliva, pressing the key against my chest for him to take it. "First, you two..."

Cedric looked at me with a furrowed forehead and a smirk, but finally, he took the key and started down the steps, followed by Destiny, Gary, and me.

He inserted the key into the lock, and as expected, it fit perfectly. My heart started beating even faster as he pulled the doorknob... I was too nervous to know what would be behind that door; I wasn't sure, but I felt that there was something there, something very important.

What the hell?" I heard Cedric say as he entered first.

I almost pushed Gary to let me in at once, but as soon as I got through the door, I regretted it.

It was a small gray cement room. It was cold, and there was a smell of dampness. The walls were filled with crucifixes of all sizes, and there was a wooden chair with armrests. Thick and somewhat rusty chains hung from it.

April is full of crucifixes," Cedric said, holding onto one of the walls with a face even paler than usual. "We need to go up."

Sure, wait for me upstairs," I said with a forced smile.

I heard the footsteps of the three as they went back up, and I focused on the room. Next to one of the walls, there was a fairly large trunk. I approached and opened it effortlessly. Inside, it was filled with bottles of holy water, vervain solutions, wooden stakes, and even a leather whip. My heart seemed to stop for a moment when I saw all that... I felt something in my stomach, a knot that tightened more and more, and my body tingled with nerves. Unconsciously, I began to tremble.

I took a few steps away from the trunk and approached the chair. I had never been there, I was sure... But then why did everything seem so familiar? I hesitated a bit but decided to sit. Touching the wood of that seat felt strange, and I began to feel somewhat dizzy. I closed my eyes, waiting for everything to return to normal, but as soon as my eyelids closed, an image appeared in my mind: a child's hands, fingers tightly gripping the armrests, with wrists chained.

I opened my eyes frightened... That simple image had been too vivid. Whose were those small hands? Still in the chair, with my breathing somewhat agitated, I ran my fingers over the chains, making them creak. That sound felt so loud in my ears, as if they were inside my head.

I clenched my teeth and continued touching them. They were cold and somewhat slippery due to dampness. They were... Too... Wet. I looked at them startled, and another image crossed my mind: those same chains, between small fingers, soaked in dark and slippery blood. I jumped from the chair, determined to stand up, but it was as if my arms were tied to it and wouldn't let me move. I let out a stifled groan as I looked at my free wrists but stuck to the chair. I felt cold sweat on my back, and a shiver ran through me, as if someone had breathed on my neck.

I opened my mouth to scream, but the voice didn't come out; it was like a nightmare, but I was sure all of this was real. I squeezed my eyelids shut, terrified, dizzy, nervous, and confused, and then everything came to my mind in an instant.

"Let's see how you do today..." my father's unmistakable voice echoed around me while I, at seven years old, was sitting in the wooden chair, chained, in that dark place where they used to lock me up.

My father rummaged through something in the trunk, and I watched him with my eyes wide open, filled with tears of terror. He turned toward me with a serious face, wielding a dagger.

He held a hand in front of my face and inflicted a deep cut. The blood, shiny and abundant, began to flow from his wound, and I breathed in the delicious aroma it had. My throat burned with the thirst it provoked. I lunged abruptly toward him, but the chains kept me immobile in the seat.

"No, April..." he sighed, "you still have a long way to go... Your eyes have turned red," my father wiped the blood on the fabric of his shirt, and I shook, trying to free myself.

He returned to the trunk and took a leather whip, shaking his head as if he genuinely felt sorrow for what was happening.

"We haven't managed to suppress your vampire side yet," he swallowed saliva and stopped in front of me, looking into my eyes. "I'm sorry."

He swung his arm back as much as he could, and then with a quick motion, he whipped my legs with devastating violence.

I screamed like I had never heard myself scream.

"Enough, Dad! Please!" I pleaded with tears streaming down my face, watching as the blood began to flow.

But he showed no mercy. He whipped me again forcefully while muttering more to himself than to me.

"We can only suppress it with pain," another lash on my legs.

They were so red, bloody, and sore that I didn't even feel the fourth blow. I couldn't stop crying; I was drowning in my own tears.

"She can't take it anymore," I heard my mother's voice coming down the stairs, joining him. "Stop that," she asked my father, looking at me with pity.

"It's the only way, my love," he explained, leaving the whip on the floor and looking at her sadly. "There will come a time when she'll loathe anything that brings her close to a vampire, and she'll effortlessly suppress that part of herself."

"But she's so small," my mother held her forehead. "What if she can't bear it?"

"She'll bear it, my love. Your daughter will be human," he said while pressing the wound he had made, causing it to bleed again.

He brought his palm to my face once more and stared into my eyes. My legs throbbed; they stung so much that I wanted to remove them just to stop feeling that pain, but the blood from his hand slid gently down his arm, and I wanted it... I wanted to drink it as much as I wanted to breathe.

"You have to make it, April," he sighed again and took a bottle of holy water from the trunk.

"No, Dad, no!" I started screaming and kicking with all the strength I had. "Not that!"

He grabbed my face roughly, squeezing my cheeks with force, forcing me to open my mouth.

"I can't!" My mother ran upstairs, leaving me down there with him.

He uncorked the bottle of holy water with his free hand and poured the contents into my mouth.

That liquid burned as if I had been swallowing tongues of fire. I shook violently, trying to break free, but he was much stronger than I was.

"Drink it!" he exclaimed as some of the water spilled from my mouth, blistering the corners of my lips. "Stop wanting blood, and all this will end!" he shouted at me while I let out muffled cries.

"April! Open your eyes!" Cedric held me by the shoulders and shook me a bit.

I opened my eyelids abruptly, and my eyes locked onto him.

"What's happening?" he exclaimed with a worried look.

I couldn't speak; I couldn't articulate a word. My face was soaked with tears, and I felt cold and rigid.

"What's wrong with her?" Destiny appeared next to him and looked at both of us with horror.

"I don't know! April, talk to me!" I couldn't even open my mouth; I could only keep crying. I could still feel the throbbing pain in my legs, my body stained with blood... The holy water choking and burning my throat inch by inch.

"I'll get you out of here." Cedric picked me up and ran upstairs.

"What happened? What's going on?" Gary ran behind him, toward the door.

Cedric didn't hesitate for a second; with a kick, he broke the entrance door and pulled me out of there at full speed. The cold air hit me in the face, but I was already cold; I felt dead... I didn't even know if I was breathing. My vision began to darken, probably as the only defense mechanism to endure that string of traumatic memories. Because that's what my parents had done, traumatize me to such an extent that I suppressed everything: those memories, their eyes looking at me like a real monster, each of the tortures they had subjected me to, and above all, my vampire side.

CHAPTER 41

I didn't cry all night, as if my eyes were an infinite cascade of tears. We had returned to the mansion in silence, and I had rushed to my room without saying a word.

"Can I come in?" Cedric knocked on the door of my room with his knuckles as dawn was beginning.

I didn't want to respond; I didn't want to move my lips or even breathe. Cedric knocked again, and I waited for him to leave, but the creak of the doorknob indicated that he was coming in.

"April... Tell me what's happening," he asked with his back against the door, looking at me with furrowed brows and sad eyes. "I don't want you to be like this."

I shook my head. My eyes were swollen, and they burned like never before. Cedric bit his lip, seeing my expression, and walked to my bed.

"I don't know what to do," he said with a sigh, sitting next to me.

I knew that all of this cost him a lot, but I wasn't in a condition to help him; I didn't even know what he needed.

"I brought whiskey," he said, showing me the bottle, and began to unscrew the cap.

He took a long sip and then handed it to me. I sat up on the quilt, kneeling, and wiped my eyes with the back of my hand. I took the bottle he shared with me and started to drink one sip after another, while my mouth and throat burned.

"I think you needed it," Cedric said, scratching his neck and giving a small smile.

I parted my lips from the bottle and tried to smile at him, but tears filled my eyes again.

"Don't cry, April, please." Cedric wrapped his muscular, bare arms around me.

I pressed my face to his chest, trying to suppress the painful knot in my throat, and breathed in his scent, in small inhalations to try to calm myself.

"I can't talk about what happened," I finally said, my voice muffled by his shirt.

"You don't have to; just tell me what you need," he said, burying his face in my hair.

"I don't know."

"I'll sleep with you," he said, sliding his hands to my face and pulling me away to look into my eyes.

I didn't oppose at all. Like a little girl, I moved aside for him to open the sheets, and I lay down, letting him cover me up to my chest. He got in with me, and our feet, clad in thick socks, got tangled. I rested my head on his chest, and he kept me hugged, tightly. It wasn't enough to hurt me, but enough to remind me that he was there and that he wasn't going to let go.

"Everything will be fine," he said, slowly stroking my hair.

I didn't respond; I stayed silent, feeling his fingers in my hair until I fell asleep.

When I woke up again, I wasn't in the same position. My cheek was pressed against the pillow, one arm up, and the other down, as if I had fallen from the seventh floor and ended up just as sprawled. I groaned a bit when I felt something walking on my arm... Wait a second... What was crawling on my arm?

I opened my eyes in fright and found Cedric's eyes sparkling as he slid his finger over my arm, caressing me gently.

"I thought you were an insect," I said with a sigh of relief.

"Well... I'm much better than that," he said, smiling slightly. "But anyway... It seems like you slept well. I can't say the same for myself; you kick like a damned."

"I'm sorry." I buried my head in the pillow and didn't move from there. "I forgot to mention it."

"It's already dark... What do you want to do?" he asked, taking me by the waist and turning me over on the bed to look at him.

"Nothing," I told him.

"Do you want to eat?"

"No." I shook my head, starting to feel the knot in my stomach again.

"You're not going to stay here, wallowing in your pain, April."

"Well, there's nothing I want more," I replied, trying to turn around again.

However, Cedric sighed, wrapped me in his arms, and lifted me on his shoulder as if he were kidnapping me again.

"Put me down! Put me down, Cedric!" I shouted, starting to kick, but he held me very calmly and began to walk towards the door.

"What do you think you're doing?" I exclaimed as I felt him starting to turn on the shower. "Don't even think about it, Cedric!"

"It's time for a shower," he said, lowering me right under the water.

"I'm going to kill you!" I shouted, clinging to his shirt and also shoving him under the warm water.

In a millisecond, my whole self was soaked, and my clothes stuck to my body. Cedric looked at me triumphantly despite being just as wet as I was.

"You have no idea how much these boots cost me," he said, feigning annoyance.

"You should have thought about it before." A stream of water got into my mouth, and I choked while starting to laugh.

"What are you doing?" Godric poked his head in because the door had been left open.

!

– Close it, thanks– Cedric said to him with a sly smile.

Godric closed the door and left us there, as if it were the most normal thing in the world.

– We should be getting out now– I said, sliding out of the shower, but he stretched an arm and blocked my way, placing his hand on the wall.

I looked at him, while my heart skipped a beat... Or rather, what was left of my very broken heart skipped a beat.

– Here– with the hand that was free, he squeezed the shampoo bottle onto my head–

– Now you'll see! – I tried to take it from his hand, but he was taller than me. I stood on tiptoe, letting my head be just under the water, and tried to reach it, but he was faster.

He let go of the bottle, which fell to the floor, and wrapped his arms around my waist. He studied my face for a few seconds, with a mischievous smile on his lips, and leaned in to kiss me. His mouth caught my lower lip gently, playing with me until his tongue sought its place inside my mouth. The water continued to wet us, sticking the fabric against our bodies.

I didn't think it was possible, but the moment his hands descended from my waist, down to the edges of my shirt, I forgot everything. I forgot the pain I felt, the pressure in my chest, the tears from the whole night. I only focused on how he quickly removed my shirt.

With his own body, he pushed me against the cold wall tiles, and I also took off his shirt. I wrapped my arms around his neck, but he took my wrists gently, lifted them above my head, and turned me, making me face away. My chest, still with the bra on, rested against the wall as he kissed my neck, sending shivers down my skin. He gave small bites on my shoulders and placed the open palm of his hand on my stomach, slowly making it descend.

Slowly his hand began to slide down the waistband of my jeans, still clinging to my legs. I knew what he wanted to do, but at that moment, I preferred something else.

I released one of my hands and stopped his.

– Don't you want to? – he purred in my ear.

I turned to him and looked at him maliciously.

– I want something else– I said, biting my lip, not taking my eyes off his.

He noticed my provocation and returned the smile.

– I'll give you anything you want– I stood on tiptoe to kiss him and then whispered, not pulling away from his lips.

I want you to bite me.\

CHAPTER 42

– What? – Cedric suddenly let me go and tilted his head back to look at me better.

– I want you to bite me– I repeated as the shower rain continued to fall on us and began to cool down.

Cedric stared at me for an eternal minute, with an expression I couldn't comprehend. He seemed surprised but conflicted with himself.

– Hey...– I said finally, turning to close the tap– What's wrong?–

– I can't...– Cedric frowned, ran his hand over his soaked face, and stepped out of the shower without saying more.

– What are you doing? – I said, looking at him perplexed... Wasn't someone asking to be bitten the dream of every vampire?

– I won't do it like this– was all he said before leaving.

I was left alone in the bathroom, soaked to the bones, feeling like a complete idiot. But the stupid one wasn't me... It was him, obviously. I didn't even bother to follow him. I took off the clothes I still had on and took a shower.

Suddenly, under the water and surrounded by foam, the pain I felt overwhelmed me again. The memories of my parents torturing me kept appearing in my mind, one after another. I clenched my fists and started banging on the wall tiles, holding back the tears, screaming in silence.

When my fingers began to wrinkle, I decided to get out. I wrapped myself in a fluffy white towel and tiptoed to my room to get dressed. I entered my room and stood still.

Emily was sitting on my bed, with her legs crossed, waiting for me.

– What are you doing here? – I asked her.

If there was something I didn't need, it was for her to come bother me at that moment.

– I come to revel in your foolishness–

– Excuse me? – I said, raising an eyebrow and holding the towel against my chest.

– –Cedric is too much of a gentleman for you...– she shrugged– Didn't he want to bite you? –

– You should inform yourself a bit about the right to privacy– I said, looking at her fiercely.

– I know that in this house, it doesn't exist– she smiled falsely– I remember that when I slept with Cedric, everyone could hear it–

– Are you going to give me a jealous ex-girlfriend scene? – I asked her squinting my eyes– I'm not in the mood for that–

– Oh no, don't misunderstand me– she said without stopping smiling– in fact, I came to advise you–

– And I don't want to hear you–

– Well, you will– Emily stood up and approached me, looking at me very closely–

– Do you know why Cedric didn't bite you? Because it's too intimate for vampires... And it's obvious that he doesn't feel that much for you yet–

– I guess I have to believe you...– I said, raising my eyebrows– you must be a very reliable source–

– I generally am not– she shrugged– but this time I have decided to be, for a little solidarity among women–

– Fine... Speak– I said rolling my eyes.

– Cedric doesn't love you enough, and that's why he hides things from you– she shrugged– as he's such a gentleman, he doesn't plan to do something as important as biting you before you know the truth. But you don't matter enough to him to tell you everything–

– What is he hiding according to you? – I said, wrinkling my forehead.

– My solidarity has a limit, dear– she let out an annoying laugh– whatever he's hiding from you, he'll have to tell you. Although if you ask him, he'll probably deny it–

– And how do I know you're not lying? – I knew she wasn't, I could see it in her expression, she was too happy about it all for it to be a lie.

– Do you want to test it? –

– No– I shook my head frowning– leave me alone–

– As you wish... You'll come crawling to ask me for help soon–

Emily left my room and slammed the door. Stupid bitch, I hated her so much that I felt capable of driving a stake into her right at that moment.

I got dressed quickly and went downstairs. My stomach was tight, but I was aware that I needed to eat something if I didn't want to pass out. I entered the kitchen and saw him.

Cedric, shirtless, with his smooth back covered in black ink. He poured himself a glass of whiskey and didn't even bother to look at me.

– You started the whole sexual play– I said to him without more– so tell me what your problem is now– I sat on a stool and took an apple from the fruit bowl on the island.

– I don't want to bite you, that's all– he replied, turning to look at me.

– Emily says you're hiding something from me, and I suspect it's true– I said as I chewed a piece of apple.

– Emily is an idiot, she should know that– he replied, placing his hands on the countertop near me.

– She also said you would deny it–

– And you believed her? –

– Of course, because at least she gave me an explanation... You're not doing that– I lifted my chin to look at him– I don't like being taken for a fool, Cedric, not by you or anyone else–

– April, let it go... You don't even know what you're talking about. I'm fine with you...– he reached out to caress my cheek, but I took him by the wrist and quickly pulled it away.

– Forget it– I locked my celestial eyes with his, sparking anger– you're not going to touch me until you explain yourself– I got off the stool and walked past him, bumping him with my shoulder.

– April...– he tried to say, but I had already left.

– You! – Destiny pointed at me with an accusing finger as soon as I left the kitchen– put on a jacket, we're going out–

I looked behind me, hoping she was referring to someone else, but it was just me.

– Are you talking to me? – I asked, pointing to my chest and furrowing my brow.

– No, I like telling walls to go out with me– she looked at me as if I were an idiot.

– Where are we going? – I said, ignoring her sarcastic joke.

– We have to accompany Godric to do one of his chores as Cornelius's assistant. That's all I'll say–

I ran to my room, wrapped myself in my red coat, and came back down. Both of them were waiting for me at the bottom of the stairs.

– I don't understand why you invited her– Godric sighed when he saw me.

– It's none of your business, let's go– his sister responded, walking towards the door.

The three of us got into the limousine, and Peter drove for about half an hour before stopping.

– Does anyone want to tell me where we're going? – I asked with intrigue, looking at both of them.

– The Leblanc family hosts a masquerade every year as a Christmas party. Since I'm training to be Cornelius's right hand, he asked me to go get masks for everyone–

– But isn't Christmas coming up soon? – I asked, scratching my head.

– No, April... It's in two days. Where the hell is your head? – Destiny said, holding the bridge of her nose with her fingers.

– Well... In many other things– I muttered.

– Didn't you notice the snow or the cold? – Godric laughed, shaking his head negatively.

– Why do vampires celebrate Christmas? – I asked, changing the subject so they would stop treating me like a fool.

– It's a tradition... Many humans celebrate it without even remembering why... We take advantage of the day to gather with the vampire society– Destiny explained to me.

– Does the vampire community refer to all the vampires who went to the mansion last time? –

– No, only the friends of the Leblanc family... And obviously the Council–

– Great...– I muttered under my breath, but they both heard me–

As soon as Peter parked, the three of us got out and stopped in front of a small store. It was very late for that place to still be open, but as soon as the vendor opened the door and exclaimed that he had been waiting for them all day, I understood that they must have notified him in advance that they would come.

– Come in, come in– the man gestured with his hand.

The place was small and warm. It had so many things everywhere that it was difficult to concentrate on just one. Masks of all sizes, mannequins with majestic dresses, harlequin costumes... It seemed like we were submerged in medieval times, although with more elaborate garments and accessories.

– Let's see the dresses...– Destiny hooked her arm with mine and dragged me towards the mannequins at the back of the store.

– Are you feeling okay? – I asked her as I began to look at them disinterestedly.

– Of course, pick one–

– Am I going? – I asked, raising an eyebrow.

– You're not just human, so I don't see why not– she shrugged.

– So are you being kind to me now because I'm not just a blood bag anymore? –

– No– she said, looking away and stroking the fabric of one of the dresses, a blood-red one – I'm kind to you because I saw your face when you came out of that basement. I don't know what you saw or remembered... But you're very broken, and that's all I can do to help you–

– But you do have a heart– I said, forcing a smile– thank you–

My eyes stopped at a golden dress. It was simply stunning. It had a square neckline with straps. It was tight to the waist and then flowed down to the floor, soft as a cloud. The top was covered with small handmade white lace flowers, falling down like a spring vine, in a cascade.

– We'll take this one– Destiny said with a satisfied smile – and I want this red color–

– Excellent choice! – Godric said, sticking his head in between both of them– And what color will Emily's be? –

– Black... Like her charred clothes– she replied

CHAPTER 43

We returned to the mansion loaded with bags to the brim, but the only ones carrying them were Peter and me. Destiny wanted to be kind to me, but the limit was holding her own bag for more than half a meter.

– What is all this? – Gary asked, approaching as soon as we entered.

– Things for the Christmas party– Godric replied, asking us to leave the bags on the sofas.

– How do you celebrate? – I asked.

– It's a very elegant dance, with masks, donors everywhere, and traditional dances– Destiny explained with sparkling eyes.

– Traditional dances? – I inquired, raising my eyebrows.

– They're easy...– Gary shrugged.

– Don't you decorate Christmas trees? – I suddenly blurted out.

– Decorate what? – he asked, looking at all of us for explanations.

– They're human nonsense– Godric replied, shaking his head.

– People buy pine trees or assemble plastic ones, and decorate them with lights, colorful balls, and garlands– I explained enthusiastically– it's very nice–

– Yeah, well... It doesn't make sense, really– Godric refuted.

– And does a masquerade party make more sense? – I asked, raising an eyebrow.

– I'd like to see that...– Gary said, looking down and putting his hands in his pockets.

– Destiny– I turned to look at her– you said you wanted to lift my spirits–

– Don't push it– she said with an unfriendly face– Christmas trees have nothing to do with vampires, and they're not stylish–

– You can choose the decorations you want... That way, it would have style...– I smiled, raising my eyebrows.

– Godric? – she asked, giving him an inquisitive look– you're in charge of decoration...–

– Let's vote– I heard Cedric's voice coming down the stairs– I like the idea... And not just because it's April's–

– Yeah... Whatever– Godric sighed, rolling his eyes– I'm against it–

– In favor...– Gary said.

– I'm also in favor– I joined, although I think my opinion didn't count in the vote– New friend? – I said, addressing Destiny.

She looked at the ceiling with a sigh.

– In favor– she finally responded.

– Perfect, we'll set up the tree tomorrow– Cedric smiled– don't worry, Godric, I'll talk to my father–

– Well, it's better– the vampire muttered Where will we put it? –

– Leave it to me, I'll look for images or something...– his sister responded with a satisfied smile.

– April, can we talk? – Cedric approached me, taking my arm gently.

– Are you going to tell me what you're hiding from me? – I lifted my chin, ready to confront him.

– I'm not hiding anything from you– Cedric lowered his gaze.

– Look me in the eyes and tell me you're not hiding anything– I requested.

Cedric pressed his lips together and slowly lifted his face towards mine. He locked his deep gaze with mine.

– I'm not hiding anything–

– Then what's the problem in biting me? – I insisted, with everyone paying close attention to what we were talking about.

– You only asked me because you need me to ease the pain you feel... And I don't want it to be like that–

– I'm not easing anything...– I lied, feeling a lump in my throat– I just wanted you to do it–

– If I start, I won't be able to stop...– he cleared his throat.

– Don't you think there are too many excuses? – I retorted.

– Oh, don't fight because of me– Emily poked her head between both with an annoying smile.

– Are you going to let what she says affect you? – he asked me, completely ignoring her.

– Yes, if it's the truth– I moved away from him and walked over to where Destiny was, listening to the entire conversation– Can I help you with the decoration? –

– Of course– the doorbell rang at that moment – I think it's the food I ordered– she smiled as Peter appeared to open the door.

Four familiar faces made their way through the living room. They were the donors, two of whom I didn't know the names of, Lucy, and Daniel.

– Hi! – I greeted him, walking towards him.

– Hello... April, right? – he said, pretending confusion.

– Yes...– I nodded– I was with you when they broke your shoulder. Are you better? –

– Well, the donors could do their job, right? – Cedric interrupted us with a sour face. If you want, talk on another occasion–

– Excellent idea– I replied sarcastically– how attentive, Cedric–

I saw the hateful look they exchanged. Cedric waited for Daniel to leave with Destiny to leave me alone. He sat on one of the armchairs next to some bags, and his stupid donor sat on his lap to allow him to bite her neck. Because, of course... Not me, but her, he bit.

Even more annoyed, I went up to my room and locked myself in there, covering my ears with the pillow because in all the adjacent rooms, someone moaned and screamed.

I didn't know exactly how much time had passed, but suddenly someone knocked on my door. I assumed it would be Cedric, but I was surprised when Daniel poked his head in to see me.

– What's happening? – I asked, jumping up.

He had his ash-blonde hair tousled, tight jeans, and the white shirt half unbuttoned.

– We need to talk– he whispered as low as possible so no one could hear.

He closed the door behind him and approached me quickly.

– Listen... I had promised your sister that we would get you out of here without any harm, and both would come out unscathed, but she told me what you asked–

– She agreed...– I said, furrowing my brow– What happens now? –

– Well, April, she's scared! – he scolded me as if I were an idiot– She wants me to convince you to change your mind–

– I promised to help them, Daniel–

– I know, listen...– he nodded– from what they said. They only need a bit of your sister's blood, right? – I nodded– Aixa will give me a good amount of blood, and we'll leave it for them. But listen... will they have the Christmas masquerade? –

– How do you know? – I asked, widening my eyes.

– I'm the best vampire hunter... If I didn't study my enemies, I'd be a bit stupid, wouldn't I? – he smiled at me– Will they have the dance? –

– Yes, that's right–

– Well, we'll leave your sister's blood, and in the midst of the confusion, I'll get you out of the mansion. On the day of the blood moon, when they need it, they'll have the blood, and you won't have betrayed them–

– But you expect me to leave silently... Secretly–

– That's not what I intend, April. I trust you, and I know you're smart... But they are vampires, they've known each other for over a hundred years... Do you think they could have the same loyalty to you in a month as they have among themselves? –

Daniel was right... What was I to them or to Cedric? I was even aware that something was being kept from me... and everyone knew except me. That left me at ground zero; he didn't trust me as much as the others did. And it was fair; we had only known each other for a short time.

– I trust them, Daniel–

– But your sister's life is at stake... Aixa would do anything for you... Wouldn't you do the same? –

Was it true? Would Aixa do anything for me? She hated vampires as much as our parents; who guaranteed that she wasn't aware of everything they had done to me? What if she knew from the beginning? If she knew about that basement and, hearing me scream and cry, didn't come for me?

– Yes, she would... But I need to see her eyes and talk to her– I said, stepping back from him.

– See her? You'd put her in danger! –

– I'll get an invitation for her, okay? – I said, biting my lip– they'll come masked, and no one will notice who they are... But truly, I need to talk to her. I'm not going to disappear, nor help her until I ask her a question–

– Fine– Daniel seemed upset, but I cared least about his reaction.

He rummaged in his pocket and handed me a card.

– There's my address and phone number. Get that invitation, April, because I want to save you, you have no idea, but I also want to save her–

– I promise – I nodded.

– And convince them to let me be a donor that night. Somehow–

Right at that moment, the door to my room swung open wide. Cedric stood in the doorway, staring at both of us. Daniel was holding me by the arms, and we weren't too far away; it was a somewhat confusing scene.

– What is he doing here? – he asked me with lifeless eyes, looking like the devil himself.

– We were just talking– I shrugged with disinterest– not that it concerns you anyway–

– Get lost, blood bag– he ordered Daniel, looking at him with clenched jaws and white knuckles.

Daniel gave me a final warning look and left my room at the speed of light, before Cedric could throw him to the other end of the mansion.

– What's going on between you two? – he said, crossing his arms.

– I don't know– I shrugged with indifference– you have your secrets, and I have mine.

CHAPTER 44

The next day, when I woke up, the house was in complete chaos. Destiny kept giving instructions to a group of men who were moving a massive pine tree back and forth in the main hall.

– I said in the middle, not on the left– she grumbled with an irritated expression– April, finally! As soon as they finish, I want you to help me decorate it–

– I don't know how you expect me to reach the top of that tree; it's so tall– I reminded her, unable to stop looking at it.

– Let Godric take care of it…– she shrugged– There! Leave it there! – she shouted again.

I continued downstairs. Cornelius was sitting with Gary, talking about something. I approached them and waited for them to finish talking.

– Standing there like a post is no more polite than interrupting the conversation– Cornelius told me, turning to look at me.

– I'm sorry…– I said with a grimace– I wanted to test Gary… To see how he's doing with his anxiety–

– I'm fine– he said, showing me a thumbs-up.

– I think it's a good idea– Cornelius nodded– go to the backyard, there are too many humans here– he pointed.

I nodded, and Gary stood up.

– What do you want me to do? – he asked, scratching his neck.

– You're going to bite me– I closed the door behind us, and we started circling the mansion to reach the yard.

– And Cedric? – I asked, looking around as if his brother could be anywhere.

– This time, it'll just be the two of us, Gary– I said, stopping in the middle of the lawn– no one will hear us here, so it all depends on you, we'll see if you can control yourself or not–

– I could kill you, April...– he said, taking a step back– I like killing, but not you– I smiled at him, trying to control the fear I felt.

– I trust that you'll be able to control yourself then– I said, pressing my lips.

– No, I won't bite you–

I was as terrified as he was, but I had made a promise. I had said I would help him if they didn't hurt my sister, and if I was going to leave the next day, I needed to know that I had fulfilled that promise... And that Gary wouldn't turn into a monster.

From the pocket of my kangaroo, I took a knife I had grabbed from the kitchen. I slid the blade across the palm of my hand, and blood began to well up from my wound, dripping onto the grass.

– No! Get away! – he exclaimed, stepping back even more, but I advanced toward him with my hand outstretched.

His eyes turned red in less than a second.

– April...– he covered his nose and mouth with his hands to avoid smelling my blood.

– Drink– I said– show that you have self-control–

He couldn't take it anymore. Suddenly, he was in front of me, took my hand, and began to drink the thick liquid coming from my wound.

He kept his eyes closed tightly, and his teeth sank into my palm.

– Drinking blood isn't the only thing that will do you good...– I started to speak– you felt good on your birthday... You liked that everyone was there to celebrate with you...– Gary continued to grip my hand tightly and didn't stop drinking– you were happy playing the piano with your brother, sharing your feelings...–

His eyes opened, and without detaching his lips from my hand, he looked at me sideways. I nodded and smiled at him as best I could.

– You'll feel good when we decorate the Christmas tree... And when you dance at the party with that unbearable girl– I swallowed hard– Can you let go of me? –

Gary looked at my hand again, and then at me. Gradually, I felt the pressure of his teeth decrease until he separated from me and wiped his blood-soaked lips.

– You did it! – I exclaimed, unable to help but smile broadly.

– I did it! – Gary opened his eyes wide and looked at me happily– I didn't kill you! I missed a great opportunity! – he laughed.

– Better shut your mouth– I laughed with him, rolling my eyes– come on, we have to set up the tree–

We went back inside, still smiling.

– Did you manage? – Cornelius stood up and looked at his son with wide eyes.

– If his idea was to let me kill myself, he failed– I told him, furrowing my brow.

– It would have been a tragic incident– Cornelius shrugged, placing his hands on his son's shoulders– well done, Gary– they both exchanged a satisfied look.

The dress looked marvelous on me. I looked at myself several times in the mirror, twirling around until I felt satisfied.

– Just for today, I'll lend you my makeup– Destiny said, sitting on my bed while rummaging through her case– use these–

I took the eyeliner she offered and lined the upper line of my eyes, forming a small tail at the end; I coated my lashes with black mascara and dusted blush on my cheeks.

– You'll look much better than Emily the bitch– she smiled while touching up her lipstick.

Her blood-red dress looked beautiful. It had bare shoulders, and below the waist, the fabric billowed as if it were a princess's dress. Everything fit her tremendously perfectly.

– It's a shame we're using these masks; I won't be able to show off my beautiful face– she sighed as she took hers and approached me for me to tie it behind her head.

– The guests are arriving; we don't have all night! – we heard Godric's voice on the other side of the door, knocking on it with his knuckles.

– Finish the makeup and come down– Destiny told me as she left my room.

I tied the golden mask that matched my dress, painted my lips a deep red, and gathered my courage. My sister would be there; I had managed to change the address on one of the invitations and redirected it to Daniel's house. I was nervous. I wanted him to tell me he knew nothing about what our parents had done, but I also wanted an excuse to stay there, close to Cedric, Gary... and maybe even Destiny.

I descended the stairs carefully, making sure not to trip on the fabric. In the hall, there were already some masked vampires, dressed even more elegantly than on the day of the dance. As I continued down, a sung waltz began to play, and my eyes met Cedric's. He was dressed in a black suit, and his mask gave him a certain air of mystery, along with his dark, well-groomed hair. He stopped at the foot of the stairs, never taking his eyes off me, piercing me with his gaze.

I tried to look away from him, but then I found another pair of eyes. Daniel was at the other end of the stairs, observing with slightly parted lips and his green eyes shining in a way I didn't understand. He was dressed entirely in white, with a black shirt and well-polished shoes.

He smiled at me and extended his arm to receive me, at the same time Cedric did.

I swallowed hard as I reached almost the last step and then... I took Daniel's hand.

It almost hurt not to take Cedric's, but he still wouldn't tell me the truth, and if he wasn't going to, there was nothing more to do together.

– You look incredible– Daniel smiled at me.

– And you– I returned the gesture– Is she here? – I asked while we started dancing. It wasn't the typical waltz dance. We only brought our hands close to each other, without actually touching, moving at the same time as the other couples present.

– Not yet– he whispered softly– try to enjoy this– he said, looking at me so intensely that I began to feel nervous.

We all moved around the immense Christmas tree, decorated in red and gold.

– This dance is very typical for vampires– he told me without losing his smile– it's as old as they are–

– How do you know everything? –

– I'm prepared for whatever comes. It's just that– he said calmly.

At that moment, all the women turned clockwise, changing partners.

I found myself face to face with Cedric, who was looking at me very seriously.

– If he keeps looking at you like that, I'm going to rip his eyes out– he whispered, referring to Daniel.

– Are you jealous? – I flashed a mischievous smile and locked eyes with his.

– Very much–

– But you don't want me enough to tell me your secret...– I reminded him.

– No, April– he said as we moved to the rhythm of the music– I like you so much that I'm afraid to tell you–

His hand wrapped around my waist, and we continued spinning along with the others, under the lights of the tree and surrounded by the music.

– I've never felt the same way as I do with you– he whispered, pressing his lips to my ear– if it were up to me, I'd bite you and take you so hard that you'd forget what it's like not to have me inside you–

My heart raced so much that I thought it would burst out of my chest.

– And why don't you? – I replied, also in a whisper.

– Because maybe you were right when you met me... And I'm a monster... who doesn't deserve you–

– Just that you forget something...– I said, looking at him again– I decide who deserves me.

CHAPTER 45

!

Cedric slammed my back against the door of his room after closing it with a kick. I took a small leap and wrapped my legs around his waist as he held me firmly by the hips. He pressed his lips to mine with ferocity, devouring my mouth in a passionate kiss. Our tongues entwined, and he slid one of his hands to the nape of my neck to add even more force.

Without stopping the kiss, he retreated toward the bed but collided with the wardrobe. I unhooked myself from his waist and pulled his shirt with both hands until all the buttons jumped to the floor.

– Do you like breaking my clothes? – he whispered with a playful smile, looking at me devilishly.

With a swift motion, he took my waist and positioned me with my back to him, then pushed me somewhat roughly onto the bed. I placed my hands on the mattress, and Cedric slid his fingers down the zipper of my dress to remove it gently. His fingers brushing against my warm skin ignited me. The dress fell to the floor, and he tangled his fingers in my hair to help me stand again.

– Can I do whatever I want to you? – he asked, pressing his lips to my ear, sending a shiver through my entire body.

– Anything – I said, feeling his bare chest against my back.

His tongue traced the curve of my neck without releasing my hair, tilting my head back. His free hand slid down my abdomen, causing my skin to tingle, and his fingers caressed my inner thigh, over the fabric of my panties. In a second, I was already soaking wet, and everything seemed to pulse, asking for more of him.

– Damn it, Cedric... – I said, biting my lip.

He sighed, similar to a smile, and then turned me toward him to look into his eyes. His entire face expressed desire, and his eyes blazed. I smiled lasciviously and slid my hands over his firm, sculpted abdomen until I reached his belt. I unbuttoned it in one pull and pulled it down, kneeling in front of him and never breaking eye contact. He kicked off his pants with one swift motion, leaned toward me, grabbed my neck firmly but without causing harm, and threw me backward onto the bed. He pounced on me like an animal ready to attack its prey. All the muscles in his body tensed when, without bothering to unhook my bra, he pulled it off forcefully. He brought his mouth to one of my breasts, enveloping the nipple with his lips, giving it a nip with his teeth while holding the other.

I let out a moan and wrapped my legs around his hips forcefully, making his erection press against the fabric of my panties.

– Do you want me to take you, April? – he asked, moving his hips up and down, making me want him more and more.

– Destroy me, for God's sake – I moaned, covering my mouth with a hand to avoid releasing too loud moans.

Cedric leaned in to kiss me once again with ferocity.

– Turn around – he whispered over my lips.

I turned quickly as he removed his boxers. He took the edge of my panties and swiftly took them off. I placed the palms of my hands on the cushions and spread my legs a little. Cedric grabbed me by the nape of the neck, and in a second, he penetrated me forcefully. I let out a moan of pleasure, an pleasure that intensified with each of his movements inside me.

– You drive me crazy, April – he said, also groaning, urgently.

– Harder – I pleaded, biting my lip.

He intensified his thrusts while sliding his free hand over my skin, circling to touch me again. I couldn't take it; he was driving me mad. I felt electricity running through my body, and I exploded into a furious orgasm at the same time as he quickly withdrew, soaking the sheets.

– Damn – he exclaimed with a playful smile, looking at the sheets – we need to use a condom next time.

I rolled on the bed to give him space to collapse, and he lay down for a few seconds, sliding an arm over me to pull me against him.

– You're amazing – he said, kissing me on the lips – Shall we go for round two in five minutes? – he smiled.

– You're amazing too – I smiled back, returning the smile – but there's a party we should be at... – I reminded him.

– Damn... – he sighed, kissing me again and again, while smiling, and I felt something fluttering in my stomach.

We stayed embraced for a few minutes until finally, we got up. Cedric found another shirt, and then he helped me put on the dress again, although the bra had died forever. We walked to the door of his room, and he took my arm for a second so that I would look at him.

– I want to do this for the rest of my life – he said with no trace of joking.

And what about me? Of course, I wanted to, but outside that room, there was a decision to make... A decision that completely separated me from Cedric.

– Me too – I said, swallowing hard.

And then, we returned to reality. Downstairs, everyone continued dancing, completely unaware of our presence. We went down the stairs, and Destiny approached Cedric with her arms crossed.

– I've been looking for you for an hour so that we can dance – she said, pressing her lips – Can I borrow April? –

– Of course – I smiled.

She took him by the arm, and they joined the rest of the couples dancing cheerfully.

– She's here – Daniel's voice echoed behind me.

I turned to look at him, and he signaled with a nod for me to follow him. We slipped through the crowd of vampires until we headed to the backyard. In the midst of the darkness of the garden, there was a woman's silhouette. She had white hair, like mine, tied up in a bun, an elegant dark blue dress that highlighted her eyes, and a silver mask. She turned to look at me and smiled; it was my sister.

– You came – I said, forcing a smile.

– Of course – she nodded – but we must hurry... Or they might realize you're not there – in her hands, she held a glass jar filled with a dark red liquid – here's the blood they need... What do you want to ask me?

– I need you to tell me the truth... – I said, swallowing hard and forcing myself to look her in the eyes despite the fear of her response

– I need you to tell me if you knew that our parents were torturing me in a basement.

– What? – she asked, completely surprised – Where do you get something like that?

– I remembered... I'm sure of what I'm saying – I assured her, clenching my fists tightly to try to keep myself together despite the pain I felt at the thought.

– No, April... No... I never thought they were doing something like that to you... Never – she studied me as if I were going to tell her it was a tasteless joke – When did it happen?

She knew nothing; I could see in her eyes that she wasn't lying, that she was completely surprised by what I had just told her. And where did that leave me? It left me far from the Leblanc mansion, silently running away in the middle of the night, without saying goodbye, after what I had just done with Cedric, and after desperately wanting it never to end.

– I'll leave the jar inside the mansion – I said, with a knot tightening in my throat.

She handed me the jar, and when I turned toward the mansion, my body froze.

– April? What are you doing here? – Cedric was a few steps away from us, looking at me with bewilderment.

Part of me felt terribly relieved, even though behind him, Godric, Gary, and Emily were approaching.

– She's his sister! – Godric exclaimed, pointing at Aixa.

– Listen. Everything's fine – I said with the jar in my hands – here's the blood you need for the spell... She just wants me to go back home – I clarified, looking only at Cedric with a half-smile.

His face, however, suddenly darkened.

– I can come back here whenever you want – I said, walking toward him and offering him the jar. He lowered his gaze, I didn't know why, but he couldn't look at me – Cedric... This changes nothing...

– This changes everything... – he said in a deep voice, refusing to take the jar I was offering.

– What are you talking about? – I asked, blinking without understanding and also looking at the rest.

– That I lied to you, April... The only way to perform the spell is by killing your sister.

EPILOGUE

I didn't have time to react. None of us did. Godric appeared as fast as lightning behind Aixa and wrapped his arm around her neck.

– What the hell are you doing? – I shouted, still in shock.

– Don't move, or I'll break her neck – he threatened, squeezing her tighter.

Daniel pulled a small glass ball from inside his jacket and threw it at them, but he missed, and the holy water vial shattered on my sister's forehead.

Godric started walking, dragging her in front of him.

– Cedric! – I shouted at him with wide eyes, but he didn't move from his spot; he lowered his gaze to the ground and let her be taken away.

Without hesitation, I ran towards Godric with all the speed I could muster. I jumped on his back and clung to him like a leech.

– Let her go, idiot! – I demanded.

Godric fell to the ground, crushing my sister, but then Emily grabbed me by the hair and pulled me away from him, dragging me across the floor.

– Stay still! – she roared as I struggled to break free.

Before I could realize it, she punched me in the middle of the face, and blood started flowing from my nose like a cascade.

– Don't touch her! – Cedric roared, addressing his ex, while helping me to my feet – take care of the other one – he ordered, referring to Daniel.

– Let me go, Cedric! Damn it! – I spat the words furiously, shaking myself in his arms and punching his chest, but he wouldn't let go – You're a piece of shit! The worst shit I've ever known! – I kept shouting.

Finally, I managed to push him away, and I ran after Godric, who was taking my sister again.

I knew Cedric was behind me, but I stretched every muscle in my legs to run as fast as possible, away from him and closer to Aixa.

Godric burst into the room, with everyone still dancing. He pushed everyone aside and kept moving forward with her.

I ran behind them, and everyone stood still, embarrassed by the spectacle.

Godric started climbing the stairs, and I stopped. I stood in front of the immense Christmas tree and tore off a branch, ready to use it as a stake.

– April, stop, please – Cedric took me by the waist, and I stabbed him in the foot with my heel with all my strength.

Still, he didn't let go, trying to stop me, but no one would.

– Give it to me – Cornelius stopped in front of us, with his blue eyes, cold as snow.

– No – Cedric denied, making me stay still.

– You're going to give it to me, or I'll kill you both – his father ordered, extending a hand.

Cedric pushed me behind him.

– You won't kill me, and you won't kill her either. You already have who you wanted; leave her alone –

– I'll repeat it one more time – he said with a lugubrious tone – I am the head of the Leblanc house; you will do as I command –

– April, go – Cedric suddenly let go of me.

For a moment, I stood still, terrified by Cornelius's furious eyes, but I remembered that my sister was heading straight to death, and I wouldn't let it happen.

I ran away under everyone's gaze. Cornelius lunged at me, but Cedric intercepted him, violently pushing him against the Christmas tree. The pine collapsed to the ground with a loud noise, and one of the branches came out bloodied from Cornelius's chest.

The vampire stood still, with wide-open eyes. Was he dead?

I couldn't verify it; I kept running down the left corridor, opening every door, searching for where Godric could be.

– Come with me – Gary's voice echoed in the corridor.

I turned, and I met his lugubrious eyes fixed on mine.

– I know where they are – he said as he approached me.

– Are you planning to help me? – I frowned.

– I owe you, don't I? – he said, looking at me as if I were an idiot – Are you coming or not? –

I nodded, and he led me through the maze of corridors in that wing of the mansion. There were thousands of doors, but at the end of all of them was a different one.

– April! – Daniel caught up with both of us, sweaty, with torn and bloodied clothes.

Gary opened the door, and the three of us went through it. On the other side was a spacious and empty room with two stone tables.

– Get out! – Destiny yelled, standing between us and the tables.

On one of them, my sister lay, tied up and unconscious, with a syringe stuck in her arm, extracting blood. On the other, there was someone else, although I couldn't see well, I assumed it was the vampire they wanted to resurrect.

– They won't kill my sister! – I yelled, jumping over her, but she dodged me, and I hit my forehead on one of the tables.

Daniel wielded a stake, advancing toward her with narrowed eyes, studying her, but Destiny, quicker, violently struck his arm, and the stake flew through the air, landing on the ground with a dry noise. I got up with blurred vision and ran towards the stake, but Godric beat me to it, picked it up from the ground, and stared at me.

– Do you want it? – he said, raising his arm above his head. I punched him in the stomach as hard as I could, and it must have hurt because he doubled over, hugging himself. Gary took the stake from his hands and threw it at me. I drew my arm back, gathering strength to plunge it, and then Destiny's hands grabbed my arm and twisted it at a strange angle, making me hear the crunching of my bones.

– Enough! – Cedric's voice echoed in the room, and we all froze – his shirt was soaked in blood, but that didn't seem to stop him. His eyes were full of rage, his jaw clenched, and all his muscles tense. – Destiny, let her go right now – he said, almost spitting out the words. She let me go; I stumbled and clung to the edge of one of the tables. The vampire's table. My eyes focused on his face; he had closed eyes, pale skin, and familiar hazel curls. My heart began to race, while I kept staring at him... That vampire... He was the murderer of my parents.

– I killed him! – I exclaimed suddenly, lifting my eyes to Cedric.

– What? – he asked, confused.

– I killed this vampire, not her! – without hesitation and taking advantage of everyone's surprise, I unhooked the needle from Aixa's arm – you'll have to kill me –

Daniel, lying on the floor, began to rise slowly, with his temple full of blood from a deep gash. Cedric looked at Destiny and Godric, and they did the same. Godric was the first to lunge at me, but Cedric jumped on him and slammed him forcefully against the wall. Destiny ran in my direction, and Daniel stood between us, wielding another stake. He stabbed her in the stomach with force, and she collapsed to the ground.

– Go! – Cedric shouted at us while squeezing Godric's neck to keep him away from me. Daniel took Aixa in his arms, ready to take her away. Cedric turned to look at me, and our eyes met. I had no doubts about him; he was a traitor and a liar.

All that time, he had only used me to save Gary, while he didn't even bother telling me that there was no way to save my sister. We had kissed passionately, he had comforted me in my worst moment, we had slept together, and I had been thrilled with each of his words and gestures... But all that had lost its meaning the moment he admitted lying to me.

I averted my eyes from his and turned to run after Daniel, who was already starting to walk away down the hallway with my sister in tow. As soon as I looked ahead, however, I found someone else.

Emily smiled at me with satisfaction, and before I could realize it, she plunged a dagger into my stomach. She watched me in silence as I fell to my knees, and I heard a desperate scream from Cedric as soon as he saw us.

Blood began to gush out of the wound, and my body collapsed to the ground as my vision darkened more and more. There was a moment when I perceived something, a moment when my heart stopped, and I felt a part of me moving away from my body. For a moment, I saw my life like a movie; I felt again the blows of my childhood, the caresses of my mother before bedtime; I saw the games in the park with Aixa, my boring school days, Cedric the day we were drunk, Gary shouting next to the piano, and finally, I remembered a sunset. The last one I had seen.

The warmth of that sun flooded my whole body and pressed against my heart. I didn't know what I felt until a soft sound began to gallop in my chest, almost inaudible, but faster and faster.

I opened my eyes and took a huge breath of air. I was lying on the stone table, where my humanity had fallen asleep.

But I was a hybrid, and my vampire side had just awakened..

TO BE CONTINUED...

Don't miss out!

Visit the website below and you can sign up to receive emails whenever Rose Knight publishes a new book. There's no charge and no obligation.

https://books2read.com/r/B-A-DBTZ-ZPBCF

Connecting independent readers to independent writers.

Did you love *Blood Moon: Dark Vampire Romance*? Then you should read *Blood Lust: Dark Vampire Romance*[1] by Rose Knight!

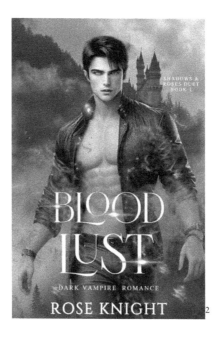[2]

In the heart of New Orleans, Scarlett's once-ordinary life takes a thrilling twist with the arrival of Tristan, a powerful and enigmatic vampire who's as ancient as he is irresistible. Suddenly, her world isn't just quiet—**it's electrifyingly supernatural.**

Tristan insists Scarlett is his eternal soulmate and destined bride. Sounds romantic, right? Not for Scarlett. She's not buying into the whole dark and mysterious vampire thing. She's determined to keep her life normal, and Tristan is not part of the plan.

Yet fate has other ideas. The unbreakable bond between them is more than just intense—it's downright excruciating when they're apart. As Scarlett is pulled into the hidden world of vampires, she

---

1. https://books2read.com/u/m2KGw6

2. https://books2read.com/u/m2KGw6

discovers Tristan's chilling role as the formidable vampire governor. Their connection is a rollercoaster ride of hurt and betrayal. A wild mix of desire and pain, and a dark, addictive lust that keeps pulling them together **They're drawn to each other like magnets, even though they know it's gonna hurt.**

Things take a darker turn when Tristan's shady past comes back to haunt them. The mystery behind Scarlett's parents' death surfaces, and when Tristan keeps it from her, trust crumbles. And just when she's desperate to break free from Tristan's magnetic pull, along comes his twisted brother, Roman. **Enter plot twist: Scarlett's life gets thrown into a dangerous showdown between the two brothers, hanging on the edge of danger.**

As Scarlett's humanity starts to slip away and her world becomes infused with the supernatural, she's left wondering if her feelings for Tristan might change.

Can a vampire governor, known for his icydemeanor, ever allow love to melt his cold heart?

It's a wild ride of supernatural passion, ancient mysteries, and the quest for a future that's anything but ordinary.

"Every step I took was watched by a vampire, hidden among the shadows, waiting for me. What I knew ceased to make sense; what I used to be no longer mattered. It was and would be his will always.

Or at least, that's what he thought."